4/18

Hayner PLD/Large Print
Overdues .10/day. Max fine cost of
item. Lost or damaged item: additional
$5 service charge.

DEATH IN
THE STACKS

Center Point
Large Print

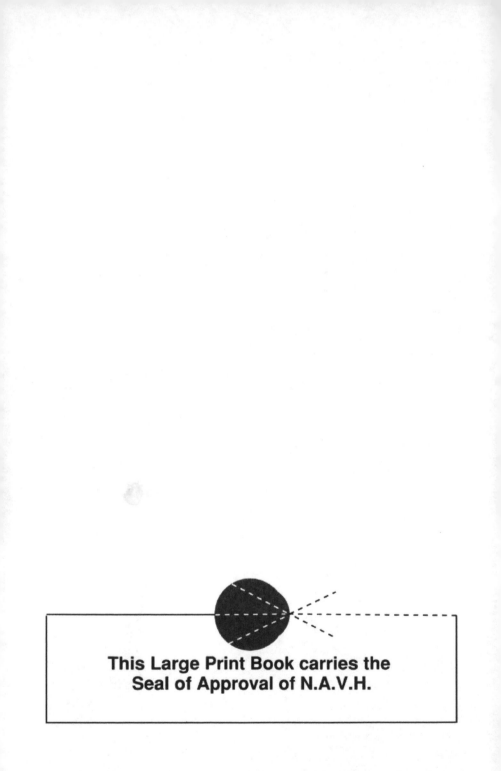

**This Large Print Book carries the
Seal of Approval of N.A.V.H.**

DEATH IN THE STACKS

A Library Lover's Mystery

Jenn McKinlay

CENTER POINT LARGE PRINT
THORNDIKE, MAINE

This Center Point Large Print edition
is published in the year 2018 by arrangement with
The Berkley Group, an imprint of Penguin Publishing
Group, a division of Penguin Random House LLC.

The text of this Large Print edition is unabridged.
In other aspects, this book may vary
from the original edition.
Printed in the United States of America
on permanent paper.
Set in 16-point Times New Roman type.

ISBN: 978-1-68324-756-2

Library of Congress Cataloging-in-Publication Data

Names: McKinlay, Jenn, author.
Title: Death in the stacks / Jenn McKinlay.
Description: Center Point Large Print edition. | Thorndike, Maine :
    Center Point Large Print, 2017. | Series: A library lover's mystery
Identifiers: LCCN 2017061676 | ISBN 9781683247562
    (hardcover : alk. paper)
Subjects: LCSH: Large type books. | BISAC: FICTION /
    Mystery & Detective / Women Sleuths. | GSAFD: Mystery fiction.
Classification: LCC PS3612.A948 D44 2017b | DDC 813/.6—dc23
LC record available at https://lccn.loc.gov/2017061676

To my amazing editor, Kate Seaver, who has been with me for thirty-plus books in multiple series and new genres. Your patience, positivity, and sense of humor never let me down. Thank you for always being the gentle red pen in my life. I like to think we're just getting started.

Acknowledgments

Deep thanks to all of the library lovers out there who have enjoyed reading this series as much as I've enjoyed writing it. I couldn't do this without you. Special thanks to the Phoenix Public Library for inspiring the setting of this story with their annual Dinner in the Stacks fund-raiser. And, as always, I am ever grateful to my family and friends, who put up with canceled plans, fend for yourself dinners, and unreturned texts and phone calls and still consider me family or call me a friend. Someday, I will actually catch up to my deadlines, I swear! Lastly, to my two teams—the many industrious folks at the Jane Rotrosen Agency, especially Christina Hogrebe, and the many talented people at Berkley Prime Crime, especially Kate Seaver—there is never enough thanks for all of you, working your incredible magic to help me do what I love: write! Thank you from the bottom of my ink-stained heart.

1

September in New England was about as perfect a season as there was on earth. The days became cooler, pumpkins ripened and colorful leaves decorated the trees like they were getting ready for a party, the last colorful gala before winter.

Lindsey Norris, director of the Briar Creek Public Library, rode her bike into work, enjoying the crisp snap to the air and the fresh smell of the briny sea as it rolled in for high tide. She felt a happy burst of optimism fill her up as everything in her world seemed to be all right, especially at work. She'd been in charge of the small library for a couple of years now, and she had come to love the seaside community in which she resided.

Today was Thursday, her favorite day of the week, as it was the day that the crafternoon group met at lunchtime to share a meal, a craft and a discussion about the book they were reading, which currently was *The Talented Mr. Ripley* by Patricia Highsmith.

She stopped in front of the building and parked her bike in the rack. She wrapped the thick cable and lock around the wheel and the frame and grabbed her purse and book bag out of the basket.

The book bag was just as heavy as it had been the night before when she brought it home. As she hefted it over her shoulder, she decided she needed to reevaluate this compulsion that caused her to bring what amounted to luggage, but was actually books she was reading, planned to read or had just finished reading, to and from work every day. She told herself it was because she was never sure what she wanted to read and she liked to have choices, but she suspected it was more like a security blanket type of thing.

Her life only felt centered and well-balanced if she had a stack of books to read with her wherever she went. Granted she had an e-reader and even read books on her smartphone, but she was a book addict, and only the comforting feel of paper beneath her fingertips could truly soothe her.

As the ache in her shoulder testified, however, she had to face the fact that there was no way she could plow through this many books in one night, and bringing them back and forth was an exercise in futility. Then again, at least it was exercise. She strode to the front doors and stepped on the rubber mat that triggered the automatic doors. They whooshed open, and she stepped inside and took a deep breath, inhaling the wonderful scent of books.

"Good morning," she said to Ms. Cole and Paula Turner, the library's two employees in charge of circulation.

Ms. Cole, also known as the lemon for her rather puckered disposition, pursed her lips and gave Lindsey a nod of acknowledgment, which coming from her was practically a hug. Known as a monochromatic dresser, Ms. Cole's color du jour was orange, fitting with the season for sure, but her palette ran from the pumpkin orange of her sweater to the safety cone orange of her slacks, which, when Lindsey stared too long, started to make her eyes water.

Paula on the other hand perked right up and gave Lindsey a cheery wave and a wide, warm smile while she continued assisting a customer. Her long, thick braid was dyed a fantastic shade of deep purple, which stood out against her bright red sweater. Looking at the two women, Lindsey was reminded of the brilliant leaves outside and felt more than a little drab in her gray sweater. Tomorrow she vowed to dress more in season.

She rounded the circulation desk and was halfway to her office when a cow crossed her path. Yes, a cow, black and white with ears, a tail and udders, the whole bovine package.

"Stomp your feet! Clap your hands! Everybody ready for a barnyard dance!" sang the cow, also known as Beth Stanley, the children's librarian.

"Moo," Lindsey said.

Beth pushed back her white hoodie with the big black spots and cow ears sewn onto it and grinned at her.

"You're supposed to bow to the cow," Beth said.

"I thought you bow to the horse first," Lindsey said.

"You're right!" Beth opened the burlap sack she carried over her shoulder and pulled out a stuffed horse. "But the horse says, *'Neigh.'*"

"Cute," Lindsey said as she peeked into the burlap sack to see the rest of the farm animals.

"Miss Beth," a little voice cried, and they both turned to see a two-year-old boy, pedaling his legs as fast as he could in Beth's direction. Beth dropped the bag and crouched just in time as the boy launched himself at her when he was within a yard of her.

"Good morning, Sawyer," she said as she scooped him up. "Are you ready for a barnyard dance?" The boy nodded his head, almost clocking Beth in the nose, but she was a pro and shifted him to her hip before he connected.

"I take it today is Sandra Boynton day?" Lindsey asked.

"Oh yeah," Beth said. "We're doing all the faves: *Barnyard Dance*, *But Not the Hippopotamus*, *Pajama Time* and *Moo, Baa, La La La.*"

"Remember those, Sam?" Sawyer's mom, Tara, asked her older son as they joined them.

"I'm too old for those," Sam said with the dignity only a five-year-old could muster.

"I know, but since you don't have school today, you get to come to the library with your little brother," Tara said. Sam did not look thrilled, and

12

Tara exchanged an amused look with Beth as she held out her arms to take Sawyer.

"You're right, Sam," Beth said, handing over the younger boy. "You are too old for Toddler Time. How about if you're my assistant librarian today?"

Sam gave her a considering look as if he suspected this was code for having to clean up the room or some other undesirable chore. *Smart boy.*

"You get to hand out the instruments for music time, and . . ." Beth paused for dramatic effect before she said, "*You* can give out the hand stamp at the end of class."

Sam's eyes went wide. He grabbed his mother's free hand and tugged her toward the story time room. "Come on, Mom, let's go. I have work to do."

Tara gave them a delighted laugh as she carried one boy and was dragged by the other to the back room. Lindsey felt her heart swell. There was nothing she loved better than laughter in the library.

"Everybody's doing the barnyard dance," Beth said as she took back her horse and picked up her bag and followed her people into the children's area.

"See you at crafternoon," Lindsey called after her.

Lindsey shouldered her own bag, thinking it

weighed enough to have a barnyard of animals in it, and continued toward her office. When she strode into the workroom, she noted that the door to her office was open, which was weird because she usually kept it shut when she wasn't here. Not locked, but definitely closed.

She pushed the door open wide as she stepped inside and then drew up short. There was a woman sitting at her desk, talking on her phone. The woman had her back to the door, giving Lindsey a moment to try and figure out how to demand, *What the hell are you doing in my office?* without the *hell* part or the yelling. She couldn't manage it.

Instead, she dropped her book bag on the floor with a thump, causing the woman to jump and swivel her chair toward the door. Lindsey wasn't normally a very turfy person, but still, this was *her* office.

"Hello, Olive," she said.

Olive Boyle, the new president of the library board, stared back at her. Lindsey should have known it would be her. Olive had beaten out Milton Duffy, Lindsey's longtime friend, for the position of president in an election over the summer, and since she'd taken the post, she had gone out of her way to be a thorn in Lindsey's backside.

Olive held up her finger, indicating that she just needed a minute. Lindsey took a deep breath and debated the repercussion of pressing the disconnect button on the phone. Knowing Olive and her dramatic streak, it would be unpleasant, but the daydream kept Lindsey from gnashing her teeth, mostly.

"I do not care what your previous arrangement with the library board was," Olive was saying. "I want you to donate all of the food to the Dinner in the Stacks event for free."

Lindsey felt her eyes go wide. Olive was speaking to either Mary or Ian Murphy, the owners of Briar Creek's only restaurant, the Blue Anchor, and she was demanding that they provide the food for the library's biggest fund-raiser of the year for free. A dinner that charged fifty bucks a plate to well over two hundred people. Lindsey felt her finger twitch with the need to end the call.

"What? What did you say to me? You're going to put me in a sack and throw me off the pier?" Olive cried into the phone. "How dare you!"

Lindsey could hear a male voice, so it was Ian, then, letting loose a stream of unhappy that she had never heard come out of the affable restaurateur before. Then it was suddenly silent, and Lindsey had the feeling someone on the other end of the line, his wife, Mary, most likely, had ended the call.

"Hello? Hello?" Olive called. When there was

no answer, she huffed out an annoyed breath and slammed the phone into the receiver. She glanced up at Lindsey and said, "We'll need to find a new restaurant for the dinner. The Blue Anchor is too pedestrian for what I'm trying to achieve anyway."

Lindsey sucked in a deep breath. She could feel her temples contracting, and the urge to bodily toss Olive from her office was almost more than she could resist.

Middle-aged, skeletally thin, with hair dyed a perfect shade of copper and styled in delicate waves that framed her oval face, Olive had that spoiled-ice-queen thing going that Lindsey found incredibly off-putting, and she wasn't the only one.

Olive had lived in town for over ten years and yet didn't know anyone's name, except for her select group of friends, because she considered most residents beneath her. No one was sure why she'd run for the library board, but given that she had also gotten on the school board and the zoning board, there were rumors that she was planning a run for mayor.

Olive lived in a stretch of colossal McMansions that ran along the shore on the north side of town. The houses were reviled by the locals, as they'd been put in right after several historic homes had been washed away by a hurricane. The monster houses blocked the view of the ocean from the neighborhood behind them, and the residents of the new houses had put in a tall wooden fence to keep the locals out of their beach area.

It was a bone of contention that had been going on for several years, and every now and then it boiled to the surface and oozed out all over a zoning board meeting. These meetings had become grand entertainment for the town, and most everyone attended them, bringing their own popcorn and jujubes.

"The dinner is just a week away," Lindsey said. "I'm pretty sure it's going to be a challenge, if not impossible, to get a new caterer in such a short amount of time."

Olive stared at her for a moment and then tipped her head to the side as if Lindsey was some sort of unknown insect that she had found in her garden. The scrutiny made Lindsey overly self-conscious about her lack of makeup—she was a mascara-and-coffee-and-go sort of gal— her windswept long blond curls and her casual denim skirt, brown boots and gray pullover sweater.

"Don't you think that as the director of the library, you should perhaps dress the part?" Olive asked her. "I mean, this washed-out, middle-management, career-woman look you've got going really doesn't do your position justice, does it?"

Lindsey closed one eye and took a deep breath,

trying to ward off the pounding in her right temple. No such luck. She opened her eye and focused on Olive.

"Given that my job requires me to do a wide variety of things, not the least of which is unclogging the occasional stopped-up toilet, I think my wardrobe is more than adequate," she said.

She stared at Olive with an air of expectancy, trying to get her to vacate her chair. Olive was not taking the hint.

"Close the door and sit down," Olive said.

Lindsey stared at her. Surely, she didn't think that Lindsey was going to sit on the visitor's side of her own desk, did she?

Olive gestured to the vacant seats that faced Lindsey's desk. Okay, then, she did.

Lindsey was unclear on how to handle this. Did she insist on being directorial and sit in her own seat? Did she play pleasant hostess and let Olive have her desk chair? She was uncertain. This was the first time anyone had ever put her in this position before. She didn't like it.

Deciding the best course of action was to let Olive say her piece and leave as soon as possible, Lindsey decided to play pleasant hostess. She shut the door and took a seat.

"I hope you weren't offended by my observations about your wardrobe," Olive said. "I'm just being helpful."

"Of course not," Lindsey said, still playing nice.

"Good, because I have drafted a proposal for a dress code for all of the library staff that I'll be introducing at the next board meeting," Olive said.

"I'm sorry, a what?" Lindsey asked.

"Dress code," Olive said. "I just can't abide coming in here and seeing the staff dressed as they are with purple hair and clashing colors—why, I saw one of your people dressed as a cow this morning."

"That's the children's librarian," Lindsey said, fighting to keep her tone even. "She was in costume for story time."

"Well, I think that's excessive," Olive said. "She'll have to wear the uniform just like everyone else."

"Uniform?" Lindsey choked.

"Yes, I think we'll go with black pants and white dress shirts," Olive said.

"For everyone?" Lindsey asked. She could not even imagine telling her staff about the latest Olive Boyle brain spasm. Nor could she envision dressing like that herself.

"I think it will make the staff look very smart," Olive said.

"Or, you know, like waiters in a restaurant," Lindsey said.

Olive snapped her fingers at Lindsey as if

she was finally catching on, clearly missing the sarcasm in Lindsey's tone. "Exactly. After all, you do serve the public, but with books instead of burgers."

A sharp metallic taste alerted Lindsey to the fact that she had bitten her lip so hard, she'd drawn blood. Another first.

2

Breathe," Nancy Peyton said as she pushed Lindsey's head down between her knees. Nancy was Lindsey's landlord as well as one of her crafternoon buddies. "Stay down until your blood pressure evens out."

"She's right," Violet La Rue agreed. "You're so red in the face I'm worried you'll stroke out on the spot."

Lindsey did as she was told, knowing it would do no good to argue with the two women. Nancy had thick, short-cropped gray hair and merry blue eyes and favored dressing in sweatshirts and jeans, while Violet preferred long, flowing caftans and wore her gray hair scraped back into a bun on the back of her head, giving her high cheekbones and dark complexion a dramatic air.

While Nancy was a native Creeker, Violet had come to Briar Creek later in life, after retiring from a long career on the Broadway stage. Despite their different life journeys, the ladies were the best of friends and shared an indomitable will that Lindsey knew she could not go up against and win.

She drew a deep breath in through her nose, held it for a few seconds and then released it through her mouth. After three such breaths, she slowly rose to a seated position.

"Do I look better?" she asked.

Both Nancy and Violet scrutinized her face and then nodded. Nancy resumed her knitting. She was teaching the crafternooners to knit slouchy beanies for the upcoming winter. So far Lindsey's striped endeavor looked like it was meant to fit the head of a giant, but still she persevered.

"You need to talk to someone about that woman," Nancy said. "She's just . . . She's so . . . I don't know how to say it."

"I do. Mean," Violet supplied. "She is downright mean. In my career I met straight-up divas who were warmer and fuzzier than Olive Boyle."

"She was sitting in my chair," Lindsey said.

"So you've mentioned," Nancy said.

"Several times," Violet added.

"I'm not sure what to do," Lindsey said. "I mean, she's not my boss, but she and the rest of the board members are supposed to work with me in an advisory capacity. She seems to think I'm her employee."

"Well, if she can't fire you, then I say to heck with her," Nancy said.

"To heck with who?" Beth asked as she entered the room with Paula wheeling a book truck right behind her.

"Olive Boyle," Lindsey said.

Both Paula and Beth made a *bleck* face, and Lindsey knew she wasn't alone in her dislike of the new library board president.

"What's her deal anyway?" Paula asked. It was her turn to bring the food, and she had opted to go completely vegetarian with a cheese and spinach strata, a salad and decadent brownies for dessert.

Despite her upset with Olive, Lindsey felt her stomach rumble with hunger. Nice to see that even a mild altercation with Olive hadn't put her off her food. She rose from her seat and crossed the room to help Paula set up the spread.

While they were working, Paula gave Lindsey the side-eye and said, "It's my purple hair, isn't it?"

Lindsey blinked at her. "Um . . ."

"It's okay," Paula said. "It's been known to get some mixed reactions. I got the feeling Ms. Boyle did not approve when she asked me if I felt it was appropriate in the workplace."

"She did, did she?"

"Yes."

"What did you say?"

"That until my boss, Ms. Norris, told me otherwise, I felt that it was just fine," she said. "Was that wrong? She really got under my skin."

"No, that was perfect," Lindsey said. "Let me know if she approaches you again. That really isn't her place, and I have no problem letting her know that."

"Will do," Paula said.

Lindsey didn't think she was imagining the way Paula's shoulders relaxed, as if Olive's words had been weighing upon her. Lindsey felt her temper spike—again.

She huffed out a breath and glanced around the room. They were missing a few members today. Charlene La Rue, Violet's daughter, was working on a story for her nightly newscast in New Haven. Hannah Carson, the local high school librarian, had a meeting today and couldn't duck out of school to join them. And the one male contributor that they'd had over the summer, Matthew Mercer, had taken a job as a professor at Southern Connecticut State University and no longer had weekdays free. Lindsey felt a small wave of panic that their little group might dwindle to nothing, but just then the door flew open and in strode a very pregnant and very cranky-looking Mary Murphy.

"The nerve of that woman," Mary began.

"Uh-oh, we've got another one," Nancy said to Violet.

"Here, Mary, come sit." Violet waved Mary into the seat Lindsey had just vacated. "You don't want to get the baby riled up, so just relax and we'll get you something cold to drink."

"Lemonade? Iced tea?" Nancy offered.

Mary slumped back onto the couch, looking even bigger than Beth did in her cow costume.

As if sensing that this might be noticed by Mary, Beth scuttled back behind the door where she unzipped her cow hoodie and hung it up on a rack by the door.

Lindsey nodded at her, and Beth gave her a look that said, *That was a close one.*

"I bet I know who you're irked with," Lindsey said. "Olive Boyle."

"Nailed it," Mary said. "Can you believe she actually wants us to pay for all of the food for Dinner in the Stacks? Is she insane? Does she not comprehend how much that would cost us?"

"Yes, she is, and no, she doesn't," Lindsey said. "Listen, I'm sorry she tried to call off your involvement with the dinner. I was hoping when I saw you here that I could talk you into forgetting about her and doing it anyway. You know the library will pay for the food just like we always do, and I can even arrange to have you and Ian paid for your time."

Mary rubbed the sides of her belly as if trying to ease the hard knot of baby just inside. "No, just the food is enough. We're happy to donate our time. It's our one big red-carpet night of the year. We'd hate to miss it. Plus, it's sold out. What was she about, thinking that another restaurant would just pick up the tab for food and personnel time with a week's notice? She's demented."

"Agreed," Lindsey said. She started to feel her

anger do a slow boil as she thought about Olive's idea to have the staff in uniforms, her words to Paula and her interference with the dinner. Lindsey huffed out a breath.

"Then it's settled," Mary said. She grinned. "The Blue Anchor is on food detail, and to heck with Olive Boyle."

"It's going to be terrific. My nephew Charlie is providing the music," Nancy said.

"And Robbie has agreed to act as the master of ceremonies for the auction," Violet informed them. "You know, I really thought he'd go back to England once his son left for college, but he's still here."

"That's because his girlfriend, Emma, lives here," Beth said.

All of the heads in the room swiveled to Lindsey to see how she felt about Robbie and Emma.

"What?" she asked. "You know Robbie and I are just friends."

"I know," Violet said. "I was just checking to make sure you hadn't had a change of heart."

"She hasn't," Nancy said. "She and Sully are going strong. Right, Lindsey?"

Months before when Lindsey and her boyfriend, Captain Mike Sullivan, the local tour boat guide and water taxi driver known to all as Sully, had temporarily broken up, Robbie Vine, an old acting friend of Violet's, had expressed an interest in Lindsey. Despite her breakup with Sully, Lindsey never got over him, and eventually they found their way back together, much to Robbie's chagrin.

Since he was her friend and she wanted him to stay in town, Violet had been staunchly Team Robbie, while Nancy, having been married to a sea captain herself, had been Team Sully all the way. It had never caused a rift between the women, but they had both made their preferences known, repeatedly.

Before the conversation delved any deeper into her love life, Lindsey grabbed her copy of *The Talented Mr. Ripley* and asked, "What did you all think of Mr. Ripley?"

"And there she goes, ducking any talk of relationships," Beth said with a laugh.

"It's my gift," Lindsey said.

"Ripley was a psychopath," Nancy said. "And yet, I found myself rooting for him. That's weird, right?"

"I did, too," Violet said. "Ms. Highsmith managed to make him charming and accessible, and when things went bad, very bad, I found I was still hoping for him to win. Quite the moral dilemma."

"Well, I watched the movie," Mary said.

Everyone turned to look at her, and she hugged her belly. "Too tired to read, plus Matt Damon and Jude Law, duh."

Beth laughed and said, "I watched the movie, too!"

The two women exchanged a high five, and Lindsey shook her head at them.

"Mary gets a pass," she said and then pointed at Beth. "But you don't."

"Aw, is that fair?" Beth asked. "I'm busy planning a spring wedding. I don't have the mental juice to read a dark and twisty tale of psychological suspense. I'm really all about puppies and kittens and rainbows right now."

Lindsey rolled her eyes. Beth had recently gotten engaged to her boyfriend, Aidan, a children's librarian in a neighboring town, and she had been in giddy bridal mode ever since. It was pretty adorable.

"Well, I think the genius behind Highsmith's Ripley is that she shines a light on the complexity of character that resides in us all. Maybe that's why we root for Tom Ripley," Paula said. "You know, because he is the conflicted bad guy in all of us."

"Speaking from your own personal experience, Ms. Turner?"

As one, the crafternoon group turned toward the door. Standing there was Olive Boyle, and she was staring at Paula with singular dislike.

"I'm s-sorry," Paula stammered. "What did you say?"

"Oh, you heard me," Olive said. "You may

have everyone else fooled, but I am onto you with your tattoos and wild hair. There are going to be changes, young lady, mark my words."

Paula's eyes went round and her face paled. She looked like she might keel over into her strata. Nancy put down her knitting and hopped up from her seat. Turning her back on Olive, she moved to stand beside Paula, wrapping her in a one-armed hug that comforted as much as it supported her.

"That's enough, Olive," Lindsey snapped. "I don't know what you think you're doing—"

"Your job, apparently," Olive retorted.

Lindsey blinked as she heard Beth whisper, "Oh no she didn't."

"Outside, Olive. Now," Lindsey said. She rose from her seat and marched toward the door as if heading into battle. She turned and stared at Olive until the woman had no choice but to follow her.

Yanking on the sleeves of her fitted navy blazer, Olive gave them a haughty look and a toss of her copper hair before she spun on her heel and strode into the hallway as if going out there had been her idea all along.

"Go ahead without me," Lindsey said to the group. "I'll be right back."

She saw Nancy and Violet start to dish the food, while Paula looked at her with an expression that was pure misery. Lindsey met her gaze and forced a smile. She had no idea what Olive thought she was doing, but Lindsey was going to shut her down even if she had to get her removed from the board to do it.

She gently closed the door behind her and then turned to face Olive. She thought about doing some controlled breathing exercises to calm her temper, but then she decided no. If Olive was going to go after Lindsey's staff, she was going to feel her wrath.

3

Walk and talk, Lindsey. I have a meeting at the mayor's office in ten minutes," Olive said. She turned on her heel and began striding down the hallway into the main library.

On sheer principle, Lindsey debated ignoring her order and going back to her lunch hour in the crafternoon room, but she didn't want to leave Olive's harsh words to Paula unaddressed, so she followed Olive into the main part of the library.

While Olive paused to check her reflection in the glass wall of a conference room, Lindsey decided to get right to the point.

"Perhaps we haven't discussed the actual purpose of the library board," Lindsey said. "Our board here in Briar Creek works in an advisory capacity. Governing library boards who set policy are generally found in private libraries, but we're public and are governed by the town. So while you have input into the workings of the library, you do not have any say in the staffing of the library. That is done by myself and the town's human resources department."

Olive touched up her lipstick, blatantly ignoring Lindsey. It was a passive-aggressive tactic, but Lindsey was not intimidated. She crossed her arms over her chest and glared at Olive's profile.

"I would appreciate it if you would refrain from addressing my staff in such an aggressive manner," Lindsey said. She was pleased that her voice was even, because inside she felt like a firecracker about to pop.

"And what manner would that be?" Olive capped her lipstick and turned to face her. "A manner where they are actually held accountable for their actions. Yes, I can see how that would go against your seat-of-the-pants lackadaisical managerial style."

Lindsey closed her eyes for a moment. When she opened them, she tipped her head to the side and studied Olive. It was becoming apparent that the woman was a bully. Lindsey knew the only way to handle her was to have no reaction, but that didn't mean she wasn't going to call her on it.

"Are you trying to provoke me?" she asked. She kept her voice light. "Because I don't see how that's conducive to an open dialogue."

"Provoke you? Is that how you see it?" Olive asked. "Are you always this sensitive? I'm merely offering you some constructive criticism, and you accuse me of provoking you. Honestly, Lindsey, you need to have a much thicker skin if you're going to continue on as library director."

"Continue on?"

"That's right," Olive said. "I'm going to be

making a motion at the next board meeting to review your position. I think it's time for some changes, don't you?"

With that, Olive turned and strode out of the library. Lindsey stood staring after her, feeling as if the other woman had just kicked her legs out from under her, except she was still standing. She glanced down at her boots just to be sure. Yep, still standing. With a sinking feeling, she wondered for how long.

"How much money does this fund-raiser make?" Sully asked from his perch atop the stepladder. Lindsey handed him a large multicolored paper lantern, one of many that they had strung through the main room of the library as decorations for Dinner in the Stacks.

"At fifty bucks a plate for over two hundred people . . ." Lindsey said. "Hmm, let me do the math—a lot."

Sully grinned down at her, and Lindsey felt her insides go all aflutter. With his sailor's broad-shouldered build, his thick mahogany curls and his bright blue eyes, Sully was impossibly handsome. The fact that he was unfailingly kind, book smart, brave and funny didn't hurt him on the attractive scale either.

They'd been dating for the second time around for several months now, and Lindsey was feeling pretty confident that this time it was going to last.

Thank goodness. She really didn't know what she'd do without Sully in her life.

"Don't forget the silent auction," Robbie Vine said as he strode past them, pushing a stack of chairs on a rolling cart. "My donation alone should bring in some bank for you."

"That signed eight-by-ten glossy of you?" Sully asked. "Yeah, that should bring in at least a nickel."

"I'll have you know, I've had fans pay fifty dollars for a signed photo and a selfie with me," Robbie said. "Besides, as master of ceremonies, I am sure I can drive the price up."

"You're giving him a mic to talk into?" Sully looked at Lindsey in horror. "We'll be held hostage by the bloviating Brit and his love of his own voice."

"Bugger off, water boy!" Robbie said.

Lindsey shook her head at Sully, who did not look repentant in the least. "Who knows? Maybe you'll get overly attached to him, like a Stockholm syndrome situation, and become his biggest fan."

Sully gave a mock shudder and Lindsey laughed.

Sully and Robbie, while not exactly friends, did seem to enjoy their verbal sparring. When Lindsey had chosen to give her relationship with Sully another chance, Robbie had taken the news well enough, but the two men continued to razz each other, and she suspected it had little to do with her and everything to do with the fact that they both enjoyed it. Men.

Since Dinner in the Stacks was happening in just over two hours, the library was abuzz with activity. The library staff, the crafternoon ladies, as well as a crew from the town's facilities department were cleaning, arranging furniture and showcasing the highlights of the library, while trying to fit enough large circular tables to accommodate the number of tickets they had sold to tonight's event.

A dais was set up in front of the fireplace in the magazine area with a podium from where Robbie would host the evening's entertainment. Lindsey was charged with giving the opening greeting, which she did every year, and she was fine with that. Really, she was.

She glanced at the dais and felt her hands get sweaty. Okay, she was a big fat liar. She hated public speaking. Hated it. It made her feel self-conscious, and she became overly aware of everything she didn't like about herself. The sound of her voice, too nasal; the size of her nose, too big; the way she used her hands to talk, too distracting. Honestly, she looked like she was guiding planes down runways. She really hated public speaking. It was straight-up torture.

Sully finished fastening the last lamp and

climbed down the ladder to stand beside her. "You all right, darling?"

"Dreading the public speaking portion, actually," she said.

He nodded. If anyone could understand her reluctance, it was Sully. Despite being friendly and kind, he was not a big talker except when he was out on his boat, giving a tour of the archipelago called the Thumb Islands that dotted the bay off of Briar Creek.

"I hear that," he said. He squeezed her shoulder under his calloused palm. It was a gesture of reassurance that she truly appreciated. "I've discovered if you talk about what you love, it's not so difficult. If you talk about the library, the way you talk to me about it, you'll be just fine."

She blinked at him. Now that was a solid idea. If she found him in the crowd and spoke directly to him, she would be fine. He was her rock, and she could pretend it was just the two of them. Suddenly, being onstage in front of everyone didn't seem scary in the least. Lindsey melted into his side and gave him a half hug.

"You're pretty smart," she said.

He kissed the top of her head. "Only when it comes to you. Then I'm smart enough to hang on and never let go."

"I'm gagging, positively gagging," Robbie said as he strode past them again.

Lindsey laughed and Sully smiled. He kissed her quick and then straightened.

"Next on the to-do list?" he asked.

Lindsey picked up her clipboard and checked off the lanterns. One detail down, two hundred to go, and the clock was ticking. It would be fine. Really.

"Do you hear me? You are to leave the premises at once. Blink if you can comprehend my meaning."

The voice was loud and outraged. It made the hair on the back of Lindsey's neck prickle. She glanced around the room to see who was speaking but noticed that everyone else who had been working had stopped to listen as well.

She exchanged a baffled look with Sully and then moved toward the front of the library to see who was making a commotion.

Paula and Ms. Cole had been tasked with clearing off the large circular checkout desk. The beverage service would be set up there, and Ms. Cole usually had fits about anything happening to her precious circulation area. Lindsey couldn't believe that she'd get so overwrought that she'd yell at anyone, however.

When she came around the desk, it was not Ms. Cole she found but Olive Boyle. Olive had her hands spread wide, bracing herself against the counter as she leaned over it into Paula's personal space.

"Did I stutter? Leave," she said.

Paula's eyes were wide. She looked small and diminished and afraid. Lindsey felt a spike of rage light up inside of her like a signal flare. No one talked to her people like this.

"Back away from the desk, Olive," she ordered. "Right now!"

Lindsey's command brought everyone's attention to the front of the library. Out of the corner of her eye, she saw Ms. Cole come charging out of the workroom to see what the ruckus was about. When she took in the sight of Lindsey confronting Olive, she looked wary, as if Lindsey were taking on a snake about to strike.

"Excuse me?" Olive said.

"You heard me." Lindsey frowned. "As we discussed the other day, the staff of this library is my concern, not yours."

"She is not to attend tonight," Olive said. She pointed a bony finger at Paula. "I have it on good authority that she is a crimin—"

"Enough!" Lindsey interrupted. "Say one more word and I will have you removed from your position as president of the library board for violating the privacy of a staff member."

Olive's eyes narrowed as if she hadn't expected Lindsey to put up a fight and she didn't like it.

"And I am telling you that she is not welcome to attend tonight's event. It would be best for all if she would turn in her notice at the earliest opportunity—like now. If I can't guarantee the safety of everyone in attendance, I will cancel the event."

"Safety? What are you even talking about? And you are in no position to cancel this event," Lindsey said. She stalked forward, looming over Olive. "You. Have. No. Authority. Here."

She could feel Sully at her back, and she appreciated the support even as she feared he might hold her back if she took a swing at the vile woman in front of her. Lindsey had never thrown a punch in her life, but she'd never been more tempted.

"I am the president of the library board. That gives me the authority," Olive sniffed. She jutted her chin in Paula's direction. "Ask her about her past." She turned to give Paula a contemptuous glance. "You never should have been hired to work here, should you?" She turned back to Lindsey. "Hiring that convict is going to cost you your job."

Paula's eyes went wide and she glanced away. Convict? What was Olive talking about? Lindsey refused to believe it. She had seen Paula work with their teens, getting kids who professed to hate books reading. She'd seen her work with the elderly, assisting them to gain proficiency with the digital age.

When Old Man MacGower bragged about wooing a hot widow in his assisted-living facility with a social media app Paula had taught him, Lindsey was sure Paula was going to bust. Whether it was from laughter or pride was still unclear, but it didn't matter. Paula was an invaluable member of their team, and Lindsey would not stand to have her threatened.

"It's time for you to go, Olive," she said. "You are crossing the line, again, and we'll be discussing this episode at our next meeting."

"Episode?" Olive asked. Her lips compressed into a furious white line. "I am merely trying to maintain the integrity of the place that the taxpayers support out of their own pockets. Do you think they'd be okay knowing their hard-earned money is going to fund the life of a criminal? I think not."

Lindsey was seething. "One more word, Olive, one more, and I swear I'll choke you out."

"Is that a threat?" Olive looked delighted. Then she cast an evil smile at Lindsey. "Enjoy this gala, Ms. Norris, since it will be your last."

4

With that, Olive spun on her heel and stalked out of the building. When the doors whooshed shut behind her, Lindsey let out a breath while Paula sagged against the counter.

"You all right?" Sully asked.

"Yeah, I'm okay," Lindsey said.

She glanced at Paula. "How are you?"

"Fine," Paula said. "Really."

"You don't look fine," Ms. Cole said. She frowned. "In fact, you look like something the tide spit out onto the beach to die."

"Um . . . thanks?" Paula said. She gave Ms. Cole a wobbly smile. The lemon shrugged, having managed to diffuse the situation with her own particular brand of blunt speak.

Paula glanced back at Lindsey with concern. "She can't really do all of the things she says, can she? She won't cost you your job, will she?"

"No. I might be in trouble for snapping at her, but that's it," Lindsey said with a lot more confidence than she felt.

Olive's library board position was appointed by the mayor. With no salary or benefits, it was really more of an honorary position. The fact that Olive was taking it to the next level and looking into the backgrounds of Lindsey's staff made Lindsey acutely uncomfortable. It was an invasion of privacy, clearly a scare tactic, but for what purpose? Lindsey could determine no good reason why Olive would want to start firing people or causing distrust and discord amongst the library staff. It boggled.

"If it's all the same with you," Paula said, "once we're done setting up for the party, I think I'll go home."

"No!" Lindsey and Ms. Cole said together. They exchanged a look, and the lemon lifted her eyebrows at Lindsey before she continued speaking, "You most certainly will not go home. This is the biggest night of the year for the library of which you are a part. You can't miss it."

As if that was the end of it, Ms. Cole turned on her heel and went back into the workroom.

Lindsey looked at Paula with a small smile. "Listen, I understand why you'd want to avoid seeing that woman ever, but I can assure you I am going to do everything I can to make sure she never bothers you again. In fact, I think attending tonight will show her that you can't be intimidated."

"I don't know," Paula said. "There are some things in my past, my youth, that I'd rather keep private."

"I understand," Lindsey said. "But remember, it's not just you she's coming after. She came after me, too, and I'll be here. We could show her a united front."

Paula thought about it for a moment before she nodded. "All right, I'll come to the dinner, but I'm giving her a wide berth, and I'm only coming because I doubt she'd want to make a scene in front of the whole town, right?"

"Absolutely," Lindsey said. "And as an added precaution, we'll get everyone to run interference if she comes near you. We won't let Olive Boyle ruin your first Dinner in the Stacks."

"Thanks," Paula said. It was a genuine smile, and it warmed Lindsey's heart. It felt good to have her staff's trust, and she was determined to keep it.

"So help me, I am going to stab that woman right in the heart with my pruning shears!" Kelsey Kincaid, owner of the local flower shop, barreled into the library pushing a cart that was loaded down with big, beautiful flowery centerpieces for the evening's event.

Kelsey was a petite thing, and the cart was almost as big as she was, but she looked to have her temper fueling her strength as she maneuvered the cart as if she were driving a tank.

"Who's got you so mad?" Charlie Peyton asked as he left his bandmates to set up onstage and hurried across the room to help Kelsey with the cart.

"Olive Boyle," Kelsey spat. She tossed her

thick brunette braid over her shoulder. "She said she wasn't going to pay me for my flowers because they weren't to her taste. She's made me change them three times—how could they not be? I swear if I am left alone in a room with that woman, there will be bloodshed."

"She's like Typhoid Olive," Lindsey whispered to Sully. "Everyone she comes into contact with is poisoned."

"She does seem highly toxic," he agreed.

"Yeah, she tried to fire my band," Charlie said to Kelsey. "She told us she wasn't impressed with our lack of musical ability. Oh, and we play too loud."

Lindsey felt Sully stiffen beside her. Charlie was invaluable helping Sully run his boat tours and water taxi around the Thumb Islands during the peak summer season. Although Charlie only worked for him part of the year, Sully was very protective of his employee and encouraged his musical ambitions.

"What happened?" Kelsey asked.

"I told her she wasn't the boss of me," he said. "That I worked for Lindsey, not her. Man, was she ever steamed about that. It was the best."

"Nice." Kelsey nodded and slugged him on the shoulder. "I wish I'd thought of that."

Lindsey and Sully approached them and Lindsey looked over the cart in awe.

"Kelsey, the centerpieces are stunning," she

said. She wasn't even trying to make Kelsey feel better. The flowers were truly works of art.

Kelsey had taken old wooden card catalog drawers and lined them with thick plastic to protect the wood. Then she had filled them with small pots of flowers, miniature roses, violets, pansies, filling in the spaces around the potted flowers with ivy and ferns. They were delicate and lovely, and she'd even drawn the table numbers in gold calligraphy on antique paper and put them in the metal frames on the front of the drawers. They were simply fantastic.

"Thank you," Kelsey said. "I was really pleased with them until I ran into *her* outside. She's a horror."

"Yes, well, I'm going to see what I can do about that situation," Lindsey said. "And don't worry, you are absolutely going to get paid for the flowers."

"See?" Charlie said. "Lindsey won't let you down."

"Thanks," Kelsey said. She turned to Charlie and batted her eyelashes at him. "Do you have a minute to help me get them set up?"

"Sure," he said, looking utterly smitten. He waved at Sully and Lindsey and pushed the cart for Kelsey into the thick of the dining area.

Looking back at her clipboard, Lindsey scratched off flowers and scanned the list trying to figure out which items would take the longest and would need to be done first. She glanced at the hustle and bustle happening around her. The library was immaculate, the displays all dazzled, the decorations for the party were subdued but still magical—it really was coming together.

"I don't want to be overly optimistic," she said, "but despite Olive, I think this might be our best Dinner in the Stacks yet."

"I'll bet you're right," Sully said. "Even my parents are coming ashore for it."

Lindsey's eyes went wide. She adored Sully's parents. They were lovely people, and while they seemed to have taken to her, too, she was pretty sure they expected her to have at least showered before the big gala.

"Oh my God, your parents cannot see me like this!" she cried.

Sully glanced at his watch. "You've got over an hour to get ready."

Lindsey glanced at her reflection in a nearby window. She had on a wide headband, no makeup, ripped-up jeans, a flannel shirt, and she was pretty sure she smelled like cleaning fluid.

She looked at the list in dismay. She still needed to decorate the entryway. Panic made her heart pound in her chest.

Sully pulled the keys to his truck out of his pocket and handed them to her.

"I've got this," he said. "You go."

"Really?"

"Of course," he said. "I'm a dude. It takes me like five minutes to change clothes and be ready."

Thank heaven for manly men. Lindsey hugged him hard and kissed him firmly on the mouth. "I love you."

His grin was almost blinding. "I never get tired of hearing that. I love you, too. Now go before I add 'find a dark corner and make out with my favorite librarian' to the to-do list."

Lindsey laughed and hopped out of his arms. She grabbed her purse and her coat and hurried for the door, calling, "I'll be back as fast as I can."

"I'll be here," he said.

As Lindsey hurried to the truck, she knew no words had ever been truer. Sully would be there, always. He was dependable like that, and it was one of the things she valued most about him.

As she climbed into the truck and put the key in the ignition, she spotted Olive Boyle across the parking lot. She was standing beside an ancient dark blue Volvo, talking to the person inside. Lindsey didn't recognize the car and couldn't see the driver, but she could tell by the tense set to Olive's shoulders and the way she was wagging her finger in the open window that Olive was giving them what for.

Lindsey had a flash of sympathy for the recipient of Olive's ire. She could only imagine what minor traffic transgression the poor person had perpetrated to tick Olive off. With any luck, Olive would be so mad she'd rant at them for a few hours and miss the gala entirely. Yeah, it was wishful thinking, but Lindsey still held out hope.

The entryway was incredible. Not because of the amazing job Sully had done, although he had, but because the man himself was standing in the doorway, waiting for her and looking so unbelievably handsome in his black suit and blue tie that Lindsey forgot to breathe for a second or two.

Although they hadn't coordinated their clothing, they were a perfect match, as Lindsey's tea-length cocktail dress was the same shade of heather blue as his tie. Her dress was simple, but it had beading on the bodice and on the hem of the flouncy skirt, which made her feel ridiculously girly. She wore her hair in loose curls about her shoulders, and she'd kicked up her makeup to include eyeliner and a cherry red lipstick.

When Sully saw her walking toward him, he did a double take and then let out a low whistle, like a kettle letting off steam.

"Darling, you are beautiful," he said.

Lindsey felt her face grow warm, but she refused to be embarrassed. "You clean up pretty good yourself."

"Thanks," he said. He gently kissed her lips

as if trying not to smudge her lipstick. Ever the gentleman.

"And this," she said, gesturing to the entryway, "looks spectacular."

It really did. At the entrance, he had placed a long red carpet leading into the building. Just inside the doors were two balloon pillars made up of blue and silver balloons that twisted in stripes like a barber's pole with a big silver star balloon perched on the top.

A small table just inside the doors was staffed by the president of the Friends of the Library, Carrie Rushton, and her boyfriend, Dale Wilcox. They were in charge of telling people what their table assignment was. Carrie looked very chic in a red sheath dress, while Dale kept his look simple with a black leather blazer over a dress shirt and jeans. The dress shirt covered half of the jailhouse tattoo on his neck, but the gold incisor that shone when he smiled made it clear that Dale still had a pirate's soul.

"Lindsey, you look amazing," Carrie gushed.

"I was just going to say the same about you."

The two women hugged, and when Carrie stepped back, she said, "I think this is going to be our best fund-raiser to date. We sold more tickets than ever before."

"Happy to help," Robbie Vine said as he joined them with his girlfriend, Emma Plewicki, who was also the chief of police, on his arm.

Robbie was looking very James Bond in a white tuxedo jacket over a white shirt with a black bow tie and black slacks. Emma was in a curve-hugging black satin number that made her the perfect arm candy for Robbie.

"You two are perfect," Lindsey said. "Very Ian Fleming."

"Thanks," Emma said. "I was going for a *Casino Royale* sort of look."

"Not *Live and Let Die*?" Sully asked as he kissed her cheek. He glanced at Robbie. "Pity."

"Very funny, Captain Hook," Robbie said. He turned to Emma with a small smile and said, "I was thinking we were more *The Spy Who Loved Me*."

Emma's eyes went wide and her cheeks turned pink. Lindsey had never seen the police chief flustered before. Ever. It was delightful.

"All right, that's enough of that," Emma said, shaking her head as if to get her senses back. "I'm off duty tonight, so our first stop—"

"—is the bar," Robbie finished for her. "Right this way, my beautiful black swan."

"Incorrigible," Emma said with a shake of her head, but she was grinning.

"He's too much. I don't know what she sees in him," Sully said.

"Oh, I do," Carrie said. She was fanning her face with one hand. Both Dale and Sully looked at her, and she shrugged.

"I just meant his accent, right, Lindsey? No woman can withstand a good British accent," Carrie said. "They're irresistible. Come on, back me up here."

"You're on your own—" Lindsey began, but a group of guests arrived, cutting off her words.

"Oy, did you hear that, mates? Our accents are going to make us irresistible tonight."

Lindsey blinked at the man who spoke. He was wearing a purple velvet suit over a lime green dress shirt, and if his suit wasn't eye-wateringly painful enough, the group with him included four women, all of whom were wearing the most incredible hats Lindsey had ever seen. Hats? In Briar Creek? Weird.

5

"Good evening," Carrie said. Her gaze flitted over the group as she was clearly trying not to stare at his outfit or the hats on the ladies. "Are you here for Dinner in the Stacks?"

"Hello, Carrie. Yes, we are. We're a party of nine." Mrs. Parker, a fairly new resident to Briar Creek, waved to her from the back. She pointed at the redhead beside her. "My daughter Scarlett is visiting from London with her friends, and we thought it would be such fun for them to attend the fund-raiser for our local library."

"Mrs. Parker." Lindsey stepped forward to greet the older woman. "So nice of you to come and to fill a whole table. I'll be sure your name is at the top of the list for the next Hannah Dennison mystery."

"The series set in Devon?" Mrs. Parker's blues eyes sparkled, and her British accent thickened as she said, "You know the way to my heart."

"Oh, I like this place." A tall, willowy woman with dark eyes and skin joined them. She was dressed in a sunshine yellow cocktail dress that matched the yellow streaks in her curly bob.

She held her hand out to Lindsey. "Hi, I'm Fiona Felton, but everyone calls me Fee. I'm a milliner. We're supposed to lead with our occupation when introduced in the States, yeah?"

"Yes, very American of you, Fee," Mr. Parker said. "Good to see you, Lindsey."

"You, too, Mr. Parker."

"And it's nice to meet you," Lindsey said to Fee and shook her hand. "I'm Lindsey Norris, the library director, and I can honestly say I've never met a professional hat maker before."

Fiona patted the brown silk cap that was circled with bright yellow sunflowers on her head. "Well, I'm happy to be your first." She turned to Sully and smiled. "And yours as well."

Sully looked at Carrie and said, "You're right about the accent." Lindsey frowned at him, and he laughed and looped one arm about her as he offered his hand to Fee.

"I'm Mike Sullivan, but everyone calls me Sully," he said.

"Librarian?" she asked.

"Boat captain," he said.

"Oh, very nice," she said. "Here, I'll introduce you properly to the woman responsible for our visit. Lindsey, library director, and Sully, boat captain, this is Scarlett Parker. Her parents invited *all* of us to visit. Daft, yeah?"

Lindsey shook hands with a pretty redhead who was wearing a cocktail dress and a darling pillbox hat both in a shade of violent pink, which clashed spectacularly with her red hair, and yet she managed to carry it off.

"Nice to meet you," Scarlett said. At Lindsey's surprised look, Scarlett grinned. "Yes, my dad and I are the lone Americans in our group. This is my boyfriend, Harrison Wentworth."

A tall man with wavy brown hair and bright green eyes in a charcoal gray suit that fit his broad shoulders to perfection shook Lindsey's hand.

"Delighted," he said.

Carrie was right. The accent was a killer.

And so it went as Lindsey was introduced to the man in the vivid velvet suit, Nick Carroll, and his partner, Andre Eisel, who was wearing all black and was as subdued as Nick was flamboyant. He was also a photographer and had brought his camera with him.

"Is it all right if I take pictures?" he asked.

"Absolutely," Lindsey said.

She met Scarlett's cousin Vivian Tremont, also a milliner, in a daring purple ensemble with a heavily plumed hat to match, and her date, Alistair Turner. They were a loud and boisterous group, and as she escorted them to their table, Lindsey listened to them trying to out-pun one another.

"Mrs. P., I'm so glad you booked us for this event," Nick said.

"Yes, we were overdue for a night out," Vivian quipped.

"En-titled, even," Harrison added.

"More than read-y," Fee agreed.

"Clearly, we're all on the same page," Andre said.

The group laughed, and then Alistair threw his arm around Vivian's waist and pulled her close and asked, "Love, do I need a library card 'cause I'm checking you out?"

This one caused the most laughter, and Lindsey found it impossible not to chuckle as well.

"Wait, wait, I've got one," Scarlett cried. "At last, we're fine-ly here."

The entire group went silent. No one even cracked a smile. Scarlett looked miffed and then said, "Oh, come on. Library fine? Fine-ly as in finally? That was a good one."

Sensing that they were teasing their friend, Lindsey patted Scarlett's shoulder and said, "It's all right. You just have to believe in your shelf."

"Pah ha ha ha," Nick burst out laughing, and the others joined in, looking delighted.

"Really?" Scarlett asked. "The librarian is getting more laughs than me."

"She works with books, Ginger," Harrison said to Scarlett. "She's bound to be funny."

This set the others off again, and Scarlett rolled her eyes. Lindsey leaned close to her and said, "I believe I have a book of puns around here if you're interested."

Scarlett gave her a conspiratorial wink. "Yes,

please. It is game on for the rest of this trip."

Lindsey left them to arrange their seats at the table. When she reached Sully, he grinned at her and said, "I like them."

"Me, too," she said. "It's a shame we don't have the same love of millinery in the States. A hat shop in Briar Creek would be so charming."

"Hat shop? I would love that. Think of what they could do for my story times!" Beth said as she and her fiancé, Aidan Barker, joined them.

"You could be the Mad Hatter," Aidan chimed in.

"Or the Five Hundred Hats of Bartholomew Cubbins," Lindsey said.

"And it's the lesser known Seussian book reference for the win," Beth said. She held up her fist for a knuckle bump, which in her formal wear seemed ridiculous, but Lindsey banged knuckles with her, and Beth wiggled her fingers and did the exploding noise.

As always, Beth was very much in touch with her inner child. Even when it came to dressing for tonight's event. While Lindsey and Sully had not purposefully coordinated their clothes, Beth and Aidan clearly had. Beth was wearing a flouncy pale gold dress, and her black hair, which she had been growing out for months, was pulled up and away from her face with wide curls falling from an ornate clip at the crown of her head. Aidan, meanwhile, was wearing black dress pants with a white dress shirt, over which he wore a brown vest and a blue blazer.

Lindsey tipped her head to the side as she considered them.

"Call me crazy, but you two look to have a 'tale as old as time' thing happening."

Beth grinned at her and then looped her arm through Aidan's and said, "See, I told you people would get it."

"I don't get it," Sully said.

"Oh no, don't—" Lindsey began, but it was too late.

Beth started to sing the famous song from the animated film. Aidan shrugged at Sully and then opened his arms. Beth stepped into them, and they waltzed over to the dance floor. When they arrived, Charlie, who was onstage waiting to start playing, caught the gist of Beth's song and began to play the refrain softly on his guitar. In a matter of moments, the people who had been seated began to fill the rented parquet dance floor, including the hat makers.

"Ah, *Beauty and the Beast*. Now I get it," Sully said.

"Oh, they're dancing already," Nancy said as she and Violet arrived together. Dressed in spectacularly glittery cocktail dresses, they barely paused to greet Sully and Lindsey, grabbing their table number from Carrie before rushing out onto the dance floor.

Ms. Cole and her date, Milton Duffy, followed them with Paula and her date, the high school librarian, Hannah Carson. The library staff were all sharing a table, and Lindsey walked them over to it. She had made certain this morning that it was on the opposite side of the room from the table that Olive was sharing with the rest of the library board and some of her friends. Lindsey didn't want to risk a scene from Olive if she was brought into close proximity with Paula, or Lindsey, for that matter.

Sully was called away to help Ian and Mary in the kitchen. With a quick kiss to Lindsey's forehead and instructions that she was to call him if needed, he disappeared down the hall that led to the staff break room where they had set up their catering base of operations.

"The music is too loud. Who arranged the balloon pillars here? They're in the way. And who put you in charge of greeting the arrivals? They couldn't hire professional valets?"

Lindsey felt her shoulders shoot up to her ears as Olive's voice shredded her nerves like a cheese grater. She sucked in a deep breath and slowly turned around.

"Hello, Olive," she said.

In a stunning beaded black ball gown, Olive stood with her group of lady friends, the ones known around town as the "mean girls," gathered around her. Olive's entourage stared at the room in front of them with matching looks of displeasure.

Oh boy.

Olive didn't speak to Lindsey. She looked her over from head to toe and turned away as if Lindsey was too insignificant for her to be bothered to acknowledge. It was the cut direct, like something out of a Georgette Heyer novel. That stung. Lindsey didn't like Olive, but the slight was jarring, mostly because it was incredibly juvenile when she had thought they could at least be civil for the library's event.

"I'll escort you to your table," Lindsey said.

"No need," Olive said. She swept past Lindsey with her three friends, Amy Ellers, LeAnn Barnett and Kim MacInnes, following her as they marched through the room in a petite parade of middle-aged female outrage that had no known point of origin.

"Well, they left a bitter nip in the air," Carrie said as she returned from escorting another party and joined Lindsey.

"Is there frost on me?"

"Just a touch on your hair and your eyelashes." Carrie smiled. "You'll thaw."

"Let's hope Olive does, or it's going to be a very long evening," Lindsey said.

She turned to face the main room, checking to see where Paula was in relation to Olive. They were across the room from each other as planned, but still, Olive was glaring at Paula all the same. Lindsey's gaze met Ms. Cole's, and the lemon gave her a small nod. Ms. Cole understood that she was to keep Olive away from Paula and vice versa at all times.

Given that Ms. Cole had not been overly fond of Paula as a new hire, Lindsey appreciated that the lemon was stepping up to protect her. It reminded Lindsey of her relationship with her brother, Jack. While they could trash-talk each other with impunity, if anyone else did it, there was hell to pay.

"Incoming," Carrie whispered, bringing Lindsey's attention back to the door.

Walking through the balloon pillars was another large group. She didn't recognize anyone as a local except Willow Devaney.

Willow had moved to Arizona ten years ago when her husband, a professor, had gotten a job at the university in Tempe. Recently, she had reappeared in Briar Creek. Everyone had assumed she was visiting, but as the weeks wore on, it became apparent that Willow was home to stay.

No one knew what had happened in her marriage, but she wasn't wearing a wedding ring, and when anyone asked about her husband, she deflected the question like a verbal ninja. Lindsey had only helped her a couple of times at the library, but she had come to learn that Willow was hooked on romantic comedy movies and was working her way through the library's extensive collection.

"Hi, Willow," she said. "Welcome to Dinner in the Stacks."

"Thank you, Lindsey." Willow took Lindsey's hands in hers and gave them a gentle squeeze. "The library looks amazing. I could smell Ian's cooking as we approached the doors, and my mouth started watering."

"I know. I'm glad it doesn't smell like this all the time or I'd never get any work done," Lindsey said.

"Well, with any luck, my new workplace *will* smell like this all the time," Willow said.

Lindsey gave her a considering look. "Does this have anything to do with all of the small business books you've been checking out lately?"

"Yes!" Willow cried. "Lindsey, these people are from Fairy Tale Cupcakes in Scottsdale, Arizona, and we're talking about me opening a franchise."

"Here? In Briar Creek? No way!"

"Way!"

"Hey, Mel, Tate, come look at this movie collection." One of the women in Willow's group was standing by the large shelf of movies that the library carried. She was wearing a smart copper-colored dress, and her long dark hair was twisted up on her head in a large round bun.

"Angie, this is fantastic," the man called Tate

said as he joined her. "It's even bigger than my personal collection."

"Oh, look, they have *Desk Set*," a tall blond woman said. She turned to the dark-haired man beside her. "Joe, we should borrow this to watch at the Beachfront Bed and Breakfast."

"You probably need to have a card," he said.

"I bet Willow has one," she said.

She glanced over, and Willow gave her a thumbs-up. Then she leaned close and said to Lindsey, "That's Melanie Cooper, in the mint green dress. She's a Cordon Bleu pastry chef, and the handsome guy beside her is her boyfriend, Joe DeLaura. She owns the bakery with those two, Tate Harper and Angie DeLaura, who are about to get married. The other two guys are Marty Zelaznik, the bald one, and Oz, er, Oscar Ruiz, the young one, and they work for the bakery. The group seems to have a preoccupation with quoting movies, but otherwise, they are really quite nice."

"I thought we were here to open a franchise and see the leaves change. I don't want to be inside watching a movie that came out when I was in my twenties. What's the point?" Marty asked. He sounded grumpy. He was thin and a bit stooped over in the shoulders, but he wore his navy suit well, and his shoes were polished to a noticeable high gloss that matched the sheen of his bald head.

"Oh, what are you thinking?" Oz said. His shaggy hair covered his eyes and he wore black Converse sneakers, which worked surprisingly well with his black suit. He frowned at the older man. "Marty, you know they're going to—"

Whatever he'd been about to say was cut off as Angie said, "The point? It's *Desk Set*. Hepburn and Tracy? Takes place in a library?"

" 'I don't smoke, I only drink champagne when I'm lucky enough to get it, my hair is naturally natural, I live alone . . . and so do you,' " Mel said.

" 'How do you know that?' " Tate continued the dialogue.

" 'Because you're wearing one brown sock and one black sock.' " Lindsey finished the movie quote.

The group of cupcake bakers turned to look at her, and Lindsey smiled. "Big fan of that movie."

"Lindsey Norris, library director, these are the owners of Fairy Tale Cupcakes," Willow said.

"That's 398.2," Lindsey said as she shook hands with each of them in turn. "I like it."

The bakers looked confused, except for the young man. He nodded, and his shaggy hair parted to reveal a pair of pretty eyes. "Dewey Decimal number for fairy tales. Nice."

The group all turned to look at him with expressions that ranged from impressed to disbelieving.

"Oz, how did you know that?" Angie asked.

"What?" he asked. "You guys don't know your Dewey Decimal numbers? That's just sad."

"That's not it, bro," Marty said. His bushy eyebrows lowered. "I mean, I could understand if you knew 641.8, you know, baking cupcakes? But fairy tales?"

A slow flush crept up into the young man's face, and he said, "Lupe likes the happily-ever-afters."

"Ah, his girlfriend schooled him," Tate said. He shared an understanding look with Joe.

"That explains it," Joe agreed. He looped an arm around Mel's waist and pulled her close. "It's amazing the things a guy will do for his gal."

They shared a look, and Lindsey noticed the sparkly rock on Mel's finger. Huh. It looked like weddings were in the air.

"If you'll come with me, I'll show you to your table," she said. The group followed her to table four, right next to the hat-shop people. Lindsey suspected the two groups would likely become fast friends.

She passed Carrie, who was escorting Sully's parents to the table they were sharing with some neighbors. Sully had grown up on Bell Island and his parents still lived there. Lindsey quickly exchanged greetings with his parents and noted that Mr. Sullivan held out Mrs. Sullivan's chair for her, and Lindsey realized it was small wonder Sully was such a considerate man. He'd had a terrific role model.

As she left them, she scanned the room and noted that most of the tables had filled up. It looked like they'd be starting the event any moment. She tried to ignore the butterflies in her belly that threatened to flutter off with her powers of speech. She could do this. She'd done it before, several times now. No big deal. Really.

The feel of a malevolent gaze on her back caused Lindsey to turn around, and she found Olive Boyle staring at her as if hoping she'd trip, walk into a wall or fall into a black hole and never return. When she met Olive's glare with a hard stare of her own, Olive smirked as if she knew exactly how much Lindsey hated public speaking and she was going to enjoy every moment of her suffering.

A sense of foreboding washed over Lindsey, making her heart race and her palms sweat. She couldn't help feeling that something bad was going to happen. She tried to tell herself that she always felt that way before getting up in front of an audience and that nothing bad ever did actually happen. It was cold comfort.

She began to obsess about Olive's smirk. Was there something wrong already? Did she have lipstick on her teeth? Visible sweat stains?

What if she said "um" too much? Truly, it was a nightmare. Lindsey tried to shake the dark feelings off, but this felt different. It felt dangerous, and she didn't know what to do about it.

6

"Oh my God," a woman cried as Robbie took the stage to start the festivities. "That's Robbie Vine, yeah?"

Lindsey turned her head to see Fee, one of the hat-shop girls, staring wide-eyed at Robbie as he took the stage to assume his master of ceremony duties. The rest of the group at the table looked equally gobsmacked, especially Nick, the man in the purple velvet.

"I'd read in the *Daily Mail* that he was living in Connecticut, but I had no idea he was living here. He's here! It's really him! How do I look? Is my tie crooked? What about my hair—is it holding up? Oh, why didn't I wear my red satin suit? Mrs. Parker, why didn't you tell me he was going to be here?" Nick cast her a fretful look.

Nick's partner, Andre, shook his head. He looked like he was trying not to laugh.

"Oh brother," Sully said. "Having his own countrymen fawn over him is going to pump the ham's humongous ego up into the stratosphere."

"Maybe," Lindsey said. "But don't forget, he has Emma now. She can be very grounding."

They both glanced over to where the police chief sat. She was at the same table as Mayor Hensen and several other department heads for the town. The head of facilities leaned over to say something to her, but Emma was so focused on Robbie, she didn't hear him.

"Or not," Sully said. His tone was dry, and Lindsey grinned at him.

"And now I'd like to bring up the lady of the hour, Lindsey Norris," Robbie announced from the stage.

"What?" Lindsey's head snapped up. She hadn't been paying attention. She wasn't ready! She felt as if her entire circulatory system had morphed into Splash Mountain and her blood was sloshing all over her insides, making her feel faint.

"Hey," Sully said, cupping her chin and holding her gaze with his steady blue one. "Just talk to me. You've got this."

Lindsey blew out a breath and nodded. She stood on legs that had the consistency of over-cooked noodles and made her way to the stage. She feared she'd trip and pulled her skirt out of the way to navigate the three steps up onto the dais. Charlie and his band were hanging out toward the back, and he nodded at her in encouragement as she approached the podium.

She put her hand on her stomach. There was no doubt about it. She was going to throw up. She'd probably make the front page of the weekly *Briar Creek Gazette*. She could see the headline now: *Local Librarian Blows Chunks at Fund-Raiser!*

"There now, love, you can do this," Robbie said softly so that the mic didn't pick up his voice. "Just picture them all naked."

She frowned at him. "Not helping."

He grinned. "Really? The mental picture of me naked does nothing for you?"

Lindsey laughed, which she suspected was exactly what he was going for. She drew in a deep breath and stepped up to the mic.

"Good evening, everyone," she said. "Welcome to the library's annual Dinner in the Stacks."

Her voice wobbled with nerves, so she cleared her throat and then scanned the crowd until she found Sully. He winked at her and gave her a slow smile that curved his lips up and crinkled the corners of his eyes. Suddenly, nothing seemed so terrifying.

"I'm delighted to say we have guests in attendance from as far away as Arizona and Great Britain. Who knew the love of books could cross continents and oceans? We did."

Sully nodded, letting her know she was doing just fine. She felt a genuine smile on her lips as she continued speaking about the library, the programs and equipment that the money from the dinner would provide, as well as some of the library's larger achievements over the past year, from the number of attendees at the story times, to the teens' makerspace creations, the programs for seniors offering help with medical paperwork, and so forth. She tried to keep it short but heartfelt and was relieved that she didn't hear any snoring at the end of it.

The applause when she finished seemed genuine and not just polite, so Lindsey took it as a win and turned the podium back over to Robbie.

"Well done, ducks," he smiled at her. "You may have a place onstage as yet."

"No, thank you," she said.

Arriving back at her seat, she allowed herself to melt into Sully's side for comfort, and he placed a swift kiss on her head.

"You were terrific," he said. "The library couldn't ask for a better advocate."

"Thanks," she said. "Focusing on you made all the difference."

Robbie entertained the crowd for a few more minutes and then dinner was served. Ian and Mary had outdone themselves with their signature clam chowder and a variety of seafood dishes, from bacon-wrapped scallops to stuffed cod. Their volunteer waitstaff moved quickly and efficiently through the room serving all of the tables, making Olive's observation that they were too pedestrian for her completely ridiculous.

The knot of nerves that had tied up Lindsey's insides began to loosen. Charlie and his band were playing soft background music. The sound of conversation, the clink of silver on plates and laughter swelled around the room. She thought they just might get out of this event unscathed.

A murmur in the room was the first indication that something wasn't right. Lindsey glanced at the tables to see what was happening. Out of the corner of her eye, she tracked motion and turned to see Olive Boyle moving toward the dais. Without breaking stride, Olive climbed the steps and approached the podium.

She glanced over her shoulder at Charlie and his band and made a slashing motion across her throat. They did a quick halt to the music, which felt abrupt and awkward. She then tapped the mic, making it squeal and everyone cringe. This did not deter Olive in the slightest.

"Good evening, everyone." Her voice boomed into the mic. The room fell quiet as the guests turned to see what was happening. "Sorry to interrupt your dinners, but as I am the president of the library board, I felt it was important for me to address you, even though I was not formally invited to do so."

The rebuke was clear, and Lindsey glanced across the table at Carrie Rushton, whose eyebrows had risen up to her hairline.

"Now I want to extend my deepest thanks to our director, Lindsey, for all of her . . . er . . . hard work. It really is a remarkable achievement for her to be here working in our public library when she has absolutely no background in serving the public." Olive's gaze found Lindsey in the crowd. While her expression was benevolent, Lindsey could see the calculating glimmer in her eyes. "Isn't that right, Lindsey? You were an academic librarian, weren't you?"

It was true; her specialty had been rare books. Feeling cornered and not liking it one bit, Lindsey gave her a vague nod. Olive seemed to take this as a victory.

"What is that miserable cow up to?" Beth hissed from across the table. She looked like she was about to get up and storm the stage, but Aidan had his arm about her, keeping her in her chair, for which Lindsey was grateful. If they could just get out of this without a scene, she'd be happy to take the hit for the team.

"Of course, when you flee your career because you discover your fiancé in bed with one of his students, well, rash decisions do happen, like taking a job you're not qualified for," Olive continued. She gave a feigned laugh, and the only ones who joined her were her mean-girl friends.

Lindsey felt a hot flush stain her face. It was common knowledge that she had come to Briar Creek on the heels of being laid off, due to budget cuts, and a bad breakup. She felt her heart pound in her chest, and angry tears began to well up in her eyes, not from sadness but from impotent rage. Olive was trying to humiliate her, but Lindsey would be damned if she'd let her. She blinked and forced the tears back and her chin up.

The blanket of awkward hanging over the room was positively suffocating. The dinner guests were dead quiet, and Lindsey could feel people looking from her embarrassed face to Olive's triumphant one in confusion and dismay. This was clearly payback for Lindsey's insistence that Olive leave her staff alone. Fine. She made eye contact with Olive and gave her a challenging look. Bring it.

"Is that all you did? Get a new job after a man did you wrong?" a voice piped up from the crowd. "Oh, sweetie, you're not even in the big leagues."

Lindsey turned her head to find Scarlett Parker addressing her from two tables over.

"I had to flee the country when I found out my boyfriend was cheating on me with the wife he said he'd left! I threw his anniversary cake at him, and the incident was filmed and went viral," she said. Her entire table was laughing as she pantomimed throwing a cake like a pitcher on the mound. "I'm well known as the party crasher. Maybe you've heard of me?"

A ripple of whispers spread throughout the room. Of course everyone knew who she was. Lindsey had watched the video herself when she was mad at her ex, like, fifty times. It was very cathartic. Someone in the room began to clap, and soon the crowd joined in. Scarlett rose from her seat and gave a deep curtsy.

Olive, realizing she had lost the room, shouted into the microphone, "Of course, with no supervisory experience, it was only to be expected that Ms. Norris would make rather poor hiring choices."

"Is this a roast?" Robbie asked in bewilderment. His stage voice carried to every corner of the room. "It's not on my program as such, plus, I thought they were supposed to be funny."

Olive glared at him, and he raised his hands in surrender.

"These unfortunate hires have brought outsiders into our community," Olive said. "But that's why we have a library board to protect the residents of Briar Creek."

Uh-oh. Lindsey glanced over at Paula. She looked as if all of the blood had drained from her face. Hannah leaned over and took her hand. Lindsey wanted to assure her that it would be okay, but she had no idea where Olive was going with this and she feared the worst.

"For example, we have a town employee with no experience working in a library, who doesn't even look the part of a mild-mannered librarian." Olive paused as if she was planning a big reveal.

Sully patted Lindsey's hand and then slipped out of his seat. He stealthily worked his way toward the front of the room. Lindsey was half afraid he was going to bodily haul the woman offstage and half afraid he wasn't.

"They make the most wonderful employees, don't they?" another voice interrupted Olive.

This time it was Mel, the cupcake baker from Arizona. She gestured at the two men seated at her table, Marty and Oz, who worked in her bakery.

"My best employees had little to no experience and look nothing like cupcake bakers." She lifted her glass of wine in Lindsey's direction. "Way to think out of the box. Clearly, this community is lucky to have you."

To Lindsey's bemusement, the rest of the room lifted their glasses to her as well. She gave a small, nervous smile and glanced back at the stage.

Two bright spots of color were blazing on Olive's cheeks, and it was clear she was about to lose her composure completely.

"No, no, no," she shouted. She glared at Lindsey and then at Scarlett and Mel as if furious with them for ruining her moment. "I'm the president of the library board. Me. I am the one who decides who is hired and who is fired and how things—"

Pop! The sound cut out on Olive's microphone. Sully was standing beside the dais with a power cord dangling from his grip. He nodded at

Charlie, and the band kicked in much louder than they had been all night.

The audience, uncertain of where Olive had been going with her speech, began to applaud as if she'd gracefully ended her rambling talk instead of being unplugged mid-tantrum.

Olive whipped around and glared at Sully, who twirled the plug in his hand and glared right back.

"If you don't kiss that man when he gets back to this table, I will," Ms. Cole said.

This startled a laugh out of everyone, including Ms. Cole's boyfriend, Milton, and the tension that had been ratcheting up eased. Olive had been effectively shut down, and it was clear to Lindsey that she had to get that toxic woman removed from the library board—the sooner the better.

"If you'll excuse me, I need to go have a chat with our library board president," she said.

Lindsey put her napkin on the table and strode across the room to where Olive was stepping off the dais, looking furious.

Lindsey did not care. She grabbed Olive by the elbow and half carried, half dragged her to the side of the room.

"Let me go or I'll file an assault charge," Olive spat.

"Just helping you when you appeared to trip," Lindsey said. "Because I'm nice like that."

Olive yanked her arm out of Lindsey's grip and turned to face her.

"What do you want?"

"An explanation," Lindsey said. "What was that?"

"That was me, looking out for this library and this community," Olive said. Her black beaded dress sparkled under the lantern light, and Lindsey was momentarily dazzled.

"From me?" Lindsey asked. "What did I ever do to you that you feel the need to come after me and my staff in the guise of a concerned board member? I've been here for over two years, and you never came into the library, not once, until you got yourself appointed to the board. What gives, Olive?"

"I don't like you," Olive said. "You bicycle through town with your long, flowing blond hair, and everyone talks about how wonderful you are. Well, I know better. I know your kind. You're just a little princess, letting everyone think you're so nice and sweet when you're really just a husband-stealing tart!"

Lindsey stared at her and blinked. Then very carefully, she said, "I've never stolen anyone's husband. Ever."

Olive waved a dismissive hand. "Doesn't matter. That's your type."

Lindsey clasped her hands to keep herself from strangling Olive. "That's no excuse to go after my staff."

"Actually, it is. Because if I can prove that you

hired someone who is potentially dangerous, then I can get rid of you, too."

"Dangerous?" Lindsey scoffed. "There is no one on our staff who is a danger to anyone."

Olive gave a delighted laugh. "You really don't know, do you? You have no idea the monster you've shoved into our lives. Oh, this is even better than I'd hoped."

"Monster? What are you talking about?" Lindsey cried.

"Excuse me." Kelsey Kincaid, the florist, passed by them with two glasses of wine in her hands. She looked distinctly uncomfortable to be in the vicinity of their spat, and Lindsey wondered if she was also leery of Olive coming after her about her flowers again.

"I'm talking about that loathsome woman you hired. Your clerk, Paula Turner. She can't continue to work in the library."

"Why not?"

"Because I have it on very good authority that she is a violent criminal," Olive declared.

7

W hat? I don't believe you," Lindsey hissed.
She glanced at Kelsey, who had most definitely still been within earshot when Olive spouted her ridiculous accusation. To her credit, Kelsey didn't show it, and Lindsey was grateful. The last thing she needed was anyone giving credence to Olive's poisonous lies.

"I don't need you to believe me," Olive said. "I have proof."

"Proof? Don't be absurd. Paula is one of our best employees. I won't have you targeting her for your own malicious amusement. You can't make up lies about my staff and try to have them fired. I won't allow it."

"I'm not lying," Olive said. "Ask her. Ask her about her past. Clearly you didn't before, since it was your incompetence that got her hired in the first place. I heard all about it. She and your dog saved a litter of kittens, whoop-de-do—that's not proper protocol for hiring someone, and I am going to see that you lose your job over it."

"Really?" Lindsey asked. "Because after the stunt you just tried to pull, I am planning on having you removed from the library board."

Olive smirked at her. "That's never going to happen."

"Oh, no?"

"No, because I have made it my business to know everyone's secrets," Olive said. "They can't remove me from the board, because if they do, I'll tell all."

"You're vile," Lindsey said.

"And you're unemployed, or at least you will be soon enough," Olive said. She swished away in her gown, looking so confident that it took all Lindsey had not to step on the back of her dress and trip her.

This was a nightmare. Lindsey had hired Paula on the spot when she'd found her in a rainstorm, saving a mama cat and her kittens with Lindsey's dog, Heathcliff, by her side. Maybe it wasn't standard operating procedure, but Lindsey had felt that anyone who put aside a job interview for a position they desperately wanted to rescue a family of cats from drowning, well, she didn't think there was much more that she needed to know about the person.

Of course the human resources department had run a background check, and Paula's references had been verified by Lindsey. There was nothing to indicate that Paula was anything other than what she seemed, a twenty-something woman looking to begin a career in library science. How could Olive accuse her of being a violent criminal? Surely, it would have come out when they did their background check.

No, this was just Olive being vindictive and mean, pushing people around just because she felt like she could. Well, it wasn't going to work with Lindsey. She had never tolerated bullying, and she wasn't going to start now.

When she arrived back at her table, the party was in full swing. Some people were dancing to the smooth groove Charlie and his band were playing, while others werc checking out the donated auction items. Robbie was pacing, getting ready to do his auctioneering bit. The noise was festive and bubbly. If Olive's intent had been to ruin the fund-raiser, then she had failed spectacularly.

Since no one else was upset by Olive and her hollow accusations, Lindsey refused to let the woman get to her. Paula as a criminal was crazy talk. She found Sully waiting for her, and when he held out his hand to lead her to the dance floor, she let him.

There was something calming about being in Sully's arms. With his broad shoulders and calloused palms, he made her feel safe and secure. She knew that no matter what happened he would be there, just like he'd been the one to hush Olive up in his own quietly effective way.

"Nice work unplugging Olive tonight," she said. "Thank you."

He pulled her in close and kissed her forehead. "No one messes up my girl's party."

Lindsey sighed and rested her cheek on his shoulder. She wished it was that simple, but she suspected it was going to get worse before it got better.

"Are you all right?" he asked, leaning back to study her face. "It looked pretty heated between you and Olive a minute ago."

"It was." She blew out a breath. "I tried to make it clear that her behavior was unacceptable, but she is determined to make trouble. I don't like it, but I'm going to talk to the mayor and see if I can get him to step in and remove her from the board."

"I think I can help make that happen," Sully said.

"Really?"

"Yeah, just go with it," he said.

With that, Sully put his hand on her hip and spun Lindsey, which was a pretty flashy move for their level of dancing, right into the vicinity of Mayor Hensen and his wife.

"Oh, pardon me," Lindsey said.

"Not at all." The mayor smiled at her. "You have quite the turnout tonight, Lindsey. Good job."

"Everyone loves the library," she said.

"Oh no, this is my dancing time," Mrs. Hensen said. "No shoptalk, you two."

"You know they can't help it, Mrs. H.," Sully said as he joined them. "These dedicated-public-servant types just don't know how to let loose. Come with me, we'll show them a thing or two."

Mrs. Hensen's eyes went wide, and without overthinking it, she dropped her husband's hand and took Sully's.

"Oh, now, hey—" the mayor protested.

"Back in a jiff," Mrs. Hensen said as Sully danced her away.

Smooth, the sailor was very smooth—Lindsey had to give him that. She turned back to the mayor. He hesitated only a moment before offering her his hand. Lindsey stepped into his arms, and together they moved around the dance floor in the most awkward swaying waltz ever witnessed in Briar Creek.

"Mayor Hensen," Lindsey began, but he interrupted.

"I can't remove Olive Boyle from the board," he said.

"What? Why? And how did you know I was going to ask you that?"

Beth and Aidan came careening in from the right, and Mayor Hensen weaved to the left just in time.

"Because it's pretty obvious that she's got it in for you," he said. "What did you do to tick her off?"

"No idea," Lindsey said. "Why can't you remove her?"

"Because she's a vindictive shrew and I don't

want her malevolence pointed in my direction during an election year," he said. "She could ruin me with her malicious gossip."

Lindsey heaved a sigh. "So, you're saying your political career is more important than my job."

"It sounds so rude when you say it like that," he said.

"Hmm," Lindsey grumbled.

She knew she could push him. She could force the issue, but to what purpose? He would resist. There would be tension between his office and her department. Other departments would get into the fray.

Small-town politics never went well when one department went rogue. If she wanted their support, she was going to have to figure out how to disarm Olive and keep her from threatening anyone else.

"What if I can find out her endgame?" Lindsey asked.

"Meaning?"

"You have to have heard the rumors," Lindsey said. She lifted one eyebrow at him and the mayor stumbled. Only her nimble reflexes got her toes out of his stomping range.

"I have no idea what you're talking about," he said.

"She's going to make a run for mayor," Lindsey said. "That's why she keeps getting on all of these boards and commissions. She wants to know all of the players. Probably, she's out to discover everyone's secrets so she can use them as leverage when she tosses her hat into the ring."

The mayor's shoulders hunched forward. He looked like a big kid trying to shield his favorite toy from being snatched by a bully. It wasn't going to work—not with Lindsey and not with Olive.

"If I find out for sure that she's after your job, will you help me get her to back off from the library?" Lindsey asked. "She's targeting my staff, and I just can't have that."

"I thought after your last near-death experience you'd given up sleuthing."

"I have," she said. "This is more like regular library work—you know, fact-finding."

"All right," he said. "I admit that I'm curious to see what she's planning. Find out what she's got cooking, and I'll do what I can to keep her away from you and yours."

"Thanks, Mayor Hensen." Lindsey smiled at him, and he returned it.

Sully twirled the mayor's wife back into his arms and reclaimed Lindsey.

"How'd it go?" he asked.

"I'm on my own until I do some fact-finding," Lindsey said. "He wants to know for sure that Olive is gunning for his job before he'll make a move to remove her from the library board."

"So, where are you going to start?"

"I think it has to be with those mean-girl neighbors of hers. They've got to know what her plan is, especially since they're always together, traveling in their pack of rude condescension."

She glanced over Sully's shoulder and saw Olive sitting with her friends. She was looking quite pleased with herself. When the youngest one in the pack, Amy, tapped Olive's arm and pointed to Lindsey, Olive snatched up her glass of champagne and lifted it in Lindsey's direction.

Olive wrinkled her nose as the bubbles tickled, then she gave a wicked, merciless laugh—the sort that could have inspired the Brothers Grimm to write about wicked witches and made the hair on Lindsey's neck stand on end.

Why was Olive after her? Had she done something? Lindsey thought over the past few years, trying to remember any unpleasantness between her and Olive. Had she inadvertently irritated her? And why would Olive ever think that Lindsey was a husband stealer? That was just mental.

Sully turned them to avoid colliding with his sister, Mary, and her husband, Ian. Mary looked amazing in a white gown that draped becomingly over her baby belly, and Ian looked delighted as ever to be with his wife.

"If there's anything I can do to help, just ask," Sully said.

"I will. I promise," she agreed. "You know, if

she was only coming after me, I wouldn't mind so much, but she's set her sights on Paula, and I can't have that."

"That's what makes you a good boss," Sully said. "You look out for your people. Any idea why she has it in for Paula?"

Lindsey thought about confiding in him, but when she glanced over his shoulder and saw Paula, sitting at their table, looking anxious, Lindsey couldn't share what Olive had told her. It was so vicious and Lindsey was so certain it was completely untrue that she didn't want to give credence to Olive's nastiness by saying it out loud.

"Personality clash?" she suggested. "That and I think she might be using her to get to me."

Sully nodded. "I can see how Olive might not approve of Paula. I don't agree with it, but I can see it. Then again, I can see Olive being like that with just about anyone."

"She really is awful," Lindsey said.

"But why come after you?" he asked.

"No idea."

The music slowed to a stop, and they broke apart to applaud. Sully put his fingers in his mouth to give a raucous whistle, and Charlie grinned at them from the stage.

"We play weddings, bar mitzvahs, funerals, too," Charlie joked. The crowd laughed, and the band broke into their next song.

Lindsey and Sully took the opportunity to walk to the other side of the library and check out the auction. Robbie was killing it, driving up the bids with witty banter, fibs and the occasional threat. He was lively and fun and worked the crowd over while entertaining them at the same time.

Lindsey spent the rest of the party mixing and mingling with all of the guests while keeping one eye on Olive. It made for a stressful evening, and when the auction ended and people started to head for home, she felt herself begin to relax for the first time all night.

As the last of the guests straggled to the door, Lindsey was quite sure she had a blister on her heel, and her back hurt from standing for so long. She was hobbling as she walked, and when she smiled, it felt forced. Honestly, she could not wait to be in her pajamas with her book.

With just the staff and a couple of their dates left in the building, she pulled the doors shut and turned the lock. They would do a quick cleanup tonight, and then Lindsey would come back tomorrow to meet the town's cleaning crew for a more thorough Sunday wipe down before opening hours the following Monday.

She had just started across the room when a fist rapped on the glass door. She turned back around to see LeAnn, Amy and Kim standing there. There was no sign of Olive. Lindsey had the brief thought that Olive had sent her posse to do her dirty work, but maybe she was just being paranoid.

She bent down and unlocked the doors and manually pried them open a crack.

"Did you forget something?" she asked.

"We can't find Olive," Kim said.

"She said she'd meet us outside by the car after the auction ended, but that was a half hour ago, and she's not there," LeAnn added.

Lindsey pulled the doors open wider and gestured for them to come in.

"She wouldn't have left, would she?" Lindsey asked.

"Not without us," Amy said. She pushed her trendy rectangular-framed glasses up on her nose and gave Lindsey a hard stare. "We all came together, and the car is still out there."

"Did she meet someone?" Lindsey asked. She couldn't imagine anyone being crazy enough to hook up with Olive, but she didn't want to be rude and say as much.

"No. She's in here. She has to be," Amy said. She gave Lindsey an impatient look as if she thought Lindsey was being difficult on purpose.

"What's going on?" Beth asked as she joined them.

"Olive is missing," Lindsey said.

"Maybe she just caught a ride home on her broomstick," Beth said, low enough so that only

Lindsey could hear her. Lindsey quickly turned her laugh into a cough.

When she glanced up, Olive's friends were staring at her as if they expected her to produce Olive out of thin air. Lindsey's blister hurt, and she was feeling cranky. She turned away to address the room.

"Listen up, everyone. Olive Boyle's party is looking for her," Lindsey announced. "Could everyone check the bathrooms and study rooms and make sure she hasn't gotten distracted?"

While Olive's friends waited in the front of the building, the staff split up to search. Wanting to avoid Olive, Lindsey decided to the check the fiction area, assuming that it was highly unlikely that Olive would be browsing for a good read at this late hour.

She was almost all the way to the back of the shelving units when she heard a gasp. Someone was back there. She hurried forward, scanning the spaces between the tall shelves as she went. When she rounded the corner to the second-to-last unit, she stumbled to a halt.

Crouched on the floor, holding one of the steak knives from dinner, was Paula Turner, and lying on the ground at her feet was Olive Boyle.

8

Paula's eyes were huge. She glanced at Lindsey, and the knife fell out of her fingers and landed on the carpeted floor with a soft thump.

"I just found her! I swear!" Paula said.

Lindsey blinked and raced forward, falling to her knees as she pressed her hand to Olive's chest, feeling for a heartbeat, breaths, anything that would indicate she was alive.

"No, no, no," Lindsey cried. She'd seen enough death, been through enough tragedies. She desperately wanted this not to go that way.

Olive's skin was still warm, but her body felt as if it was softening, as if her life essence was pooling out of her like the puddle of blood that soaked into the floor. Her face was slack, her eyes open and staring at nothing. There was no pulse in her wrist, no rise to her chest, no breath coming from her lips.

There was nothing. Olive Boyle was dead.

"I need to call an ambulance." Lindsey lurched to her feet, planning to race back to her office and make the call.

"Don't leave me." Paula jumped up, too, and Lindsey nodded.

"Let's get help," she said. She turned on her heel and hurried to the end of the row. She stepped out and slammed into Amy Ellers.

"Oh!" Amy staggered back.

"Sorry." Lindsey held out her hands to steady Amy, and Amy's eyes went wide.

"You're covered in blood!" Amy cried.

Lindsey looked at her hands. They were shaking and streaked with red. She dropped them to her sides.

"Do you have your phone? I need you to call an ambulance," she said. "Quickly."

"Why?" Amy demanded. "What's going on?"

She pushed past Lindsey and peered down the row at Olive's body. Her spine went rigid, and she let out an ear-piercing shriek. Lindsey reached out to her, but Amy jumped away from her bloody hands, slamming into a shelf and knocking the books to the ground.

"What's happening?"

"What was that noise?"

"Oh my God, is that blood?"

Everyone in the building came running toward them, shouting questions. Lindsey felt her heart pound in her chest, and her ears were ringing. She was struggling to process what was happening, and the crowd rushing at her made it even more difficult.

"Stop!" She held up her hands to ward them off. She spotted Sully in the crowd.

"Call the police and an ambulance," she said to him. "Olive Boyle has been stabbed."

"Are you all right?" he asked. He snatched his phone out of the inside pocket of his suit jacket.

She gave him a jerky nod to let him know that none of the blood was hers. He spun away from the gathering crowd to speak into the phone.

"What happened?" Kim demanded.

"Is she dead?" LeAnn pulled Amy away from the shelf and wrapped a protective arm about her.

"Yes, I think so," Lindsey said. Her voice wasn't much more than a puff of breath.

The three of them stood silently in front of her, their eyes wide as they took in the horror of the scene before them. Lindsey glanced over her shoulder and noticed that Paula wasn't there. She had slipped away before the crowd arrived. Lindsey wasn't sure what to make of that, but she suspected it was a wise decision.

The staff members were all talking at once. Lindsey raised her hands to get their attention, but when she remembered the blood on them, she lowered them.

"Can someone please go unlock the front door?" she asked. "We're going to need to let the EMTs in."

Beth and Aidan hurried back through the library. They passed Robbie and Emma, who were just stepping out of the break room, looking decidedly mussed.

"What's the ruckus?" Robbie asked.

"Emma, I need you!" Lindsey cried out, relieved to see the chief of police was still on the premises.

Emma snapped to attention immediately. Her cop's sixth sense must have alerted her that something was very wrong.

She dropped Robbie's hand, lifted the hem of her gown and broke into a run. Robbie followed her, looking faintly bewildered. Emma elbowed her way through the remaining staff and Olive's friends.

"Police! Move aside," she said.

Everyone stepped back, and Lindsey knew she had never been so grateful to see Emma in her life.

"This way," she said. She hustled Emma back toward Olive.

From a distance Olive looked to be a pool of glittering black. In the dim nighttime lighting, her dark beaded gown blended with the blood that saturated the carpet beneath her.

Emma bunched her skirts around her knees and knelt down, examining Olive. Lindsey saw her stare at the bloody knife lying on the carpet and then at Olive. She did the same vitals check that Lindsey had. When she sighed and glanced at the delicate gold watch on her wrist, Lindsey knew she was marking the time of death as best she could.

"When did you find her?" Emma asked.

"Just a few minutes ago," Lindsey said. She didn't mention that Paula was actually the one to discover Olive. She would tell her, but not here, not with all of these people listening.

"What have we got here, love?" Robbie joined them, kneeling down beside Emma.

She shook her head at him. "*I've* got the victim of a homicide. You have nothing except an errand. Could you grab my purse from Lindsey's office? I have a pair of gloves in there."

"Right." Robbie stood and hurried away.

"Tell me exactly how you found her," Emma said to Lindsey.

"Just like this," Lindsey said. "I put my hand on her chest to see if she was breathing, but she wasn't. No heartbeat either."

"Let me see your hands." Lindsey held them out, and Emma nodded. "Tell Sully to keep everyone here in the building, then go wash up. I'm going to call in a crime scene unit."

Lindsey nodded and turned to go.

"Oh, and Lindsey," Emma called her back. "I hope you're going to stick to the promise you made a few months ago not to investigate crimes anymore. I know it will be especially challenging since it's on your turf and all, but I'd like your reassurance that you'll stay out of it."

"Don't worry about me," Lindsey said. "I've learned my lesson. This case is entirely yours."

Lindsey had Sully take watch over the staff and their guests who remained in the library while she went to clean up. She went to use the unisex staff bathroom that was adjacent to the break room but found the door locked.

She knocked. No one answered, as if whoever was inside hoped she would just go away. There was only one person it could be.

"Paula, it's Lindsey. Let me in."

Seconds ticked by before she heard the door unlock and it was pulled open. It was Paula. She looked wrecked. Her hair was mussed, her eyes were puffy and the end of her nose was red. It was clear she'd been crying.

"Are you all right?" Lindsey asked.

"No, not even a little."

Lindsey smiled at Paula's usual candor.

"I'm going to wash up, okay?" she asked.

Paula nodded and stayed in the room with her while Lindsey scrubbed the remnants of Olive's blood from her skin. As the water turned pink and swirled down the drain, Lindsey felt the saliva in her mouth pool beneath her tongue. The urge to throw up was almost more than she could shake off.

"Barfing helps," Paula said.

Lindsey expelled a breath that was somewhere between a grunt and a laugh.

"I'm sorry I ditched. I just couldn't—"

"It's all right," Lindsey said. "The first time

you see a body like that, hell, anytime you see a body like that, it's bound to take you out at the knees."

"Yeah," Paula said. She glanced away while Lindsey used a paper towel to dry her hands.

"Paula, did you see anyone or hear anything before you found Olive?"

"No, there was no one, just her," she said.

Lindsey studied her tear-ravaged face. She believed her. She stepped forward and put a hand on Paula's shoulder.

"Take as long as you need, but I'd better get back," Lindsey said. "You'll need to talk to Chief Plewicki and tell her exactly how you found Olive. Will you be okay to do that?"

Paula nodded. It was a lie. They both knew it, but Lindsey didn't have time to push her. She needed to get back to the crime scene and help Emma in any way she could, minus any investigating. That she would not do.

When she returned to the main part of the library, she found the library staff and Olive's friends sitting in the new book area where there were comfy chairs. Sully was standing beside the doors, making certain no one left without Emma's okay. When he saw Lindsey, he opened his arms and she stepped into them.

Engulfed in his warmth, it was the first time she realized how icy cold her skin had become. He must have felt it, too, because he shrugged out of his jacket and slipped it over her shoulders.

He rubbed her arms while he studied her face. "Are you all right?"

"Not really," she said. "I know Olive and I had our differences, but I never would have wanted anything like this to happen to her."

"Really?" Amy Ellers asked. She rose from her seat and approached Lindsey and Sully, looking like she was spoiling for a fight.

"Yes, really." Lindsey stepped back from Sully and stood straighter. She understood Amy was hurting, that her friend was dead, but Lindsey wasn't going to be harassed.

"I find it very convenient that you were the one to find her," Amy said.

LeAnn and Kim rose from their seats and flanked Amy. All three stood with their arms crossed over their chests, looking like they were standing in judgment of Lindsey.

" 'Convenient,' " Lindsey repeated. "That's not the word I would use."

"Yeah, try *traumatizing,*" Beth said. She rose from her seat and moved to stand beside Lindsey.

"Or *horrific,*" Ms. Cole added.

Much to Lindsey's surprise, the lemon moved to stand on her other side. She was oddly touched to have her staff stand up for her even though it wasn't likely to help the current situation.

"Given that Olive humiliated you at your own

gala, I'd say that gives you a motive," LeAnn said. She tossed her head, making her severe chin-length bob emphasize her words.

"To kill her?" Lindsey gaped. They were serious.

"Everyone knows she was planning to have you replaced," Kim said. She planted her hands on her curvy hips and narrowed her eyes at Lindsey. "Killing her would have saved your job, plus how did you know exactly where to find her body?"

Lindsey felt her eyes go wide. *What?!*

Both Beth and Ms. Cole began to sputter in her defense, while Sully tried to calm everyone down, but only one voice could be heard over the outrage.

"Lindsey didn't find Olive's body. I did!" Paula shouted.

The room went still, and Lindsey felt her stomach drop into her feet. She turned to find a very distressed Paula, standing off to the side with her hands clenched into fists like she was preparing for a fight.

"Lindsey, Paula, I'd like to speak with you both in private." Emma interrupted the altercation, looking from one group to the other as if daring anyone to try anything. No one did.

9

Lindsey led the way to her office. Out of the corner of her eye, she saw Paula duck her head and hug her arms into her belly. She looked terrified.

Emma sat on Lindsey's desk while Lindsey and Paula sat in the visitor chairs facing her. Emma looked pale and tired, and Lindsey remembered that tonight had been her night off, but then a public servant was never really off duty.

"I need you both to tell me exactly what happened," Emma said. "Paula, since you were the first to find Ms. Boyle, I'd like you to go first."

Paula nodded. "Her friends showed up looking for her while we were cleaning." She paused to look at Lindsey, who nodded. "We all split up, and I took the fiction collection, thinking there was no way she'd be back there."

Emma held up her hand. "Why look in a place you didn't think she'd be?"

Paula looked at Lindsey, but this time Lindsey didn't nod. It was up to Paula to decide what to tell Emma. The truth would come out, and Lindsey hoped Paula would choose wisely, but she wasn't going to take the decision away from her.

"Olive Boyle had it in for me," Paula said. "Those remarks she made at the dinner tonight about Lindsey hiring someone from outside the community who wasn't qualified? Yeah, she was talking about me."

"Oh," Emma said. She waited, clearly letting Paula think through what she wanted to say.

"I was trying to avoid bumping into her again," Paula said. "Instead, I found her body. Some irony there, huh?"

"Was she already dead?" Emma asked.

Paula turned a sickly shade of green and nodded. She closed her eyes for a second as if she could will the grisly discovery away and then opened them with a sigh, obviously resigned to the fact that she could never unsee the horrible discovery.

"I knelt beside her, and something dug into my knee," Paula said. "I picked it up before I realized it was a knife, a steak knife, and that whoever had killed her had probably used it to stab her." Paula swallowed hard before continuing. "That's when Lindsey arrived."

Emma turned to look at Lindsey with her eyebrows raised. "Lindsey?"

"Yes?"

"When I asked you to tell me how you found her, you said, 'Just like this.'"

"Yes."

"You didn't mention Paula."

"No."

"Why not?"

"Because you asked me if that was how I found Olive," Lindsey said. "You didn't ask me if I found anyone with her."

Emma pinched the bridge of her nose as if to ward off a headache. She turned to look at Paula.

"We bagged the knife," she said. "Picking it up will mean it likely has your fingerprints on it."

Paula looked stricken. "I didn't think about that."

"Didn't you?" Emma asked.

"No!" Paula cried. She looked panicked, and Lindsey reached over to take her hand in hers.

"It's okay," Lindsey said. "Mistakes happen."

"Especially when people who have no business being near a crime scene blunder into one," Emma said.

She sounded mad. Lindsey couldn't blame her, but at the same time, it wasn't Paula's fault. There was no way she could have known that someone would murder Olive.

"There's nothing we can do about that now," Lindsey said. "Paula had to check on her to make sure she was okay. I'm sure she couldn't comprehend what had happened until it was too late."

Emma nodded. "You're right. Sorry. Okay, I want you both to tell me everything you remember from the time her friends showed up looking for her until you found the body."

There wasn't much to tell. Both Paula and Lindsey had been cleaning the library with the others when Amy, LeAnn and Kim arrived, looking for Olive. The staff had separated to search for her, and only a few moments passed before Paula found her and then Lindsey found Paula with her.

"And where did you say you were when the friends arrived?" Emma asked.

"I had just locked the front door," Lindsey said.

"And I was picking up the circulation desk, you know, cleaning it up since it was the beverage station," Paula said.

Emma studied them both. She looked as if she was choosing her words very carefully.

"So, it seems that Olive Boyle's speech tonight was directed at you two, and she made it sound as if she had a grudge against you both. Why?"

"No idea," Lindsey said. "When I confronted her, she pretty much admitted that she hated me, and she called me a husband stealer, which I've never been." She paused to collect her thoughts before adding, "As far as I know, neither of us ever had anything to do with her that would cause her to want to take our jobs."

"I haven't," Paula agreed. "I barely even know the woman. The only thing I could figure was that she didn't approve of my hair or my tattoos."

Lindsey waited for her to add something more, such as Olive fabricating stories about her past, but Paula didn't say anything. Lindsey wondered if Paula even knew the length Olive had been prepared to go to with her lies.

"Trying to get you sacked over tattoos and purple hair dye seems a bit like overkill," Emma said. Then she cringed. "Sorry, I can't believe I just said that. There was this crew of Londoners at the dinner tonight, and they, well, never mind."

"Punny, were they?" Lindsey asked.

"Yes, along with being a bit obsessed with my boyfriend," Emma said. She met Lindsey's gaze. "It was quite a turnout tonight. Do you happen to know if we have a list of all the people in attendance?"

"No, we don't," Lindsey said. "We only have the names of the guests who purchased the tickets."

"Were any tickets bought with cash?"

"Just by some of the staff," she said.

"I'll need the list then," Emma said.

"Carrie Rushton was in charge of the ticket sales; I'll see if I can get the list from her."

"Did Carrie have any altercations with Olive Boyle?"

"Not that I know of, but I wouldn't be surprised. It might be simpler if you asked who didn't have a beef with Olive," Lindsey said. "She told me herself she made it her place to know everyone's secrets and to use them to get what she wanted."

"Was she threatening you?"

"Is it a threat or a warning when someone tells you they're going to replace you?" Lindsey asked. "I didn't take her very seriously, but I can't think I was the only one she felt this way about. She may have threatened the wrong person."

Emma's boobs began to vibrate. Both Lindsey and Paula stared at her and then at each other.

"Hang on. I need to take this," Emma said. She reached into the top of her dress and pulled out a smartphone. She studied the screen before she slid her thumb across the display, held it up to her ear and said, "Chief Plewicki."

"Yes, sir," she said. There was a pause, and she said, "No, sir. Absolutely, I'll call you when I know something."

She ended the call and looked at both Lindsey and Paula. "You're free to go. The state police's crime scene unit is here along with Detective Trimble. I need to brief them on what's happening."

With that she rose from her perch on the desk and made for the door. Lindsey and Paula both stood and walked with her.

"Is this the part where you tell us not to leave town?" Paula asked.

"It is," Emma said. "And just so we're clear that this is coming from me and my office in an official capacity—don't leave town, either of you."

Paula and Lindsey watched her walk away in her swishy black satin dress. Paula staggered back into Lindsey's office and slumped onto a chair, looking like she might pass out.

"Stay with me, Paula," Lindsey said.

She patted her arm and then raced to get a cool cloth for the back of Paula's neck and a cold glass of water. Poor Paula. As if finding Olive wasn't traumatic enough, being questioned by Emma and realizing she had inadvertently compromised the crime scene had to have her rattled as well.

As Lindsey returned to her office, she found Paula sitting forward in her chair with her head hanging between her knees.

"I'm sorry," she said. "I can't seem to shake this woozy feeling."

"You've nothing to be sorry for. Tonight has been extremely traumatic."

She put the cloth on the back of Paula's neck and set the glass of water on the desk for when Paula might need it.

"I screwed up," Paula said. "I shouldn't have touched the knife, but I was so shocked. I wasn't thinking. Oh my God, Emma is going to think I did it! Everyone is going to think I'm a murderer!"

She pressed her fingertips to her temples, looking as if she was trying to keep herself from completely freaking out.

"You can't worry about what others will think,"

Lindsey said. "Even if they do, I was right there with you, so they'd have to accuse me of it as well."

Paula glanced up at her. It was clear that she didn't think this was as helpful as Lindsey did, and Lindsey had to agree, although she didn't say as much.

Given that Olive had called her out in front of all of the guests at Dinner in the Stacks, would it really be surprising if everyone looked at Lindsey as the murderer? The thought was disturbing, and she felt the need to go and help Emma with the investigation in any way that she could.

No, nope, she wasn't going to do it. After almost getting herself and others killed last spring, she'd made a promise to herself and to Sully that she would not investigate any more murders, and she wouldn't stick her nose into any business that wasn't library business.

Of course, technically, with Olive being on the board and the murder happening in the library, Lindsey could make the argument that it was library business. Very much library business, in fact, but she didn't think Sully would go for it, and she really didn't want to worry him any more. They were in a really good place in their relationship, and she feared that investigating a murder might damage it.

So, no more asking questions, doing research or, as some liked to say, being a buttinsky. She was going to live a normal and safe life, leaving all of the crime solving to Emma and the police department. Really, she was.

When Paula was steady on her feet, she and Lindsey left the office to join the others. Everyone there had been questioned, and Emma had announced that they were free to go. Aidan and Beth were going to take Paula home, since her date, Hannah, had left earlier in the evening as she had to coach the high school cross-country team early in the morning. The rest of the library crew had rides. It was a subdued group that left the building.

Because they were too shaky to drive, Robbie offered to take Olive's friends home. As the three friends left the building, they looked shocked and distraught, as if they couldn't wrap their heads around what had happened.

As director, Lindsey stayed behind to make certain the library was locked up after Olive's body was removed to the mortuary. She and Sully stayed out of the way, sitting on the edge of the dais on the far side of the main room.

Sully didn't say anything but sat beside her with his hand on her back in a comforting show of support that she appreciated so much, since it felt like it was the only thing keeping her from falling apart.

They watched as the body bag was taken from the building. Lindsey felt her heart thump hard in her chest at the sight. Life was such a fleeting thing, and it could be cut short so swiftly. She shivered, and Sully pulled her into his side.

When Robbie returned from driving Olive's friends home, he trailed Emma, trying to help even though she told him repeatedly to go away. He made his way over to Lindsey and Sully and sat on her other side.

"Not the end to the evening I had hoped," he said.

"No," Lindsey agreed. "You did an amazing job with the auction though. It was the most money we've ever raised."

"Nice work," Sully said.

Robbie frowned at him. "Are we mates now?"

"If you mean friends, maybe," Sully said. He gave Robbie a considering look. "A big maybe."

"I can live with that," Robbie said. He glanced at Lindsey. "So where do we begin?"

"Begin what?"

"Our investigation," he said. "Obviously, it's time for the dynamic duo to help solve this case."

"And our friendship is over," Sully said. "Lindsey doesn't investigate anymore."

"What?" Robbie looked shocked. "I thought that was just a lot of codswallop because you almost got killed."

"Not codswallop," Lindsey said. "I meant it. I'm out. You need to find a new partner."

"But—"

"Aren't you dating the chief of police?" Sully interrupted. "Surely, if you're going to play detective, it should be with her."

"Emma gets cranky about my being a civilian and an actor," he grumbled. "She says I'm not qualified, even though I played Detective Inspector Gordon on *Masterpiece* for years. I'm a method actor, you know. I learned quite a lot about being a detective to convincingly play that role."

"Well, DI, you're on your own," Lindsey said. "Or maybe you've been promoted. You were my sidekick, the Watson to my female Sherlock, before. Now it's time to find your own sidekick."

Robbie rubbed his chin. "You might be right. But it won't be the same without you, pet. I don't wear skirts nearly as well as you do."

Lindsey smiled, and Sully shook his head at Robbie and said, "Please don't try."

"There's the love from sailor boy that I've been missing," Robbie said.

Lindsey glanced between the two men, and as she did so, she saw Emma walking toward them. She looked grim, and Lindsey felt a sense of foreboding creep over her skin like a wintery draft. Something was wrong, very wrong.

"Lindsey, can I have a word?" she asked.

"Sure." Lindsey waited.

"Alone," Emma clarified.

"I'm sure anything you have to say to Lindsey,

you can say to us," Robbie said. "We'll keep it in the strictest confidence."

"Absolutely," Sully agreed.

"No," Emma said.

The two men looked at each other. Emma had given them nowhere to take their argument. Lindsey rose to her feet and made a mental note to practice her firm *no* for the next time she was asked to volunteer for something she didn't want to do. Truly, it was like a roadblock. Even Robbie couldn't figure out how to navigate around it.

Emma led Lindsey to the far side of the room. It was surreal to be dressed in party clothes and have the chief of police wanting to talk to her about the murder of the president of her library board. If an elephant in a tutu came dancing through the room right now, Lindsey would be so relieved, because it would mean she actually was dreaming and this horrible evening wasn't real. No elephant appeared. It was real.

"When I spoke to you and Paula earlier, she said that when Olive's friends arrived, she was cleaning up the circulation desk," Emma said.

"That's right," Lindsey agreed.

"Well, according to Ms. Cole, *she* was cleaning up the circulation desk," Emma said.

"They might have been working on it together," Lindsey said. She felt her stomach sink like an anchor.

"No, because when I asked Ms. Cole if anyone

was with her, she said no," Emma said. "When I interviewed the staff to see if they remembered who was where and when, no one mentioned seeing Paula anywhere."

"She was probably confused," Lindsey said. "Maybe she was working in the break room or taking a cigarette break."

"Does she smoke?" Emma looked hopeful.

"No," Lindsey said. "But it could be something like that."

Emma heaved a heavy sigh. "I know you want to protect your staff, I do, but, Lindsey, Paula lied to us about where she was. Maybe she had a good reason, but it doesn't look good. I'm going to have to interview her again, but I wanted to warn you to be extra careful around her."

"You don't really think—"

"As of right now, she is my prime suspect," Emma said. "And just so we're clear, yeah, I really do think she could be our murderer, but then again I think that about everyone.

10

When Sully dropped Lindsey off at home, he offered to stay with her, but she knew he had an early morning boat tour to give, and she suspected she would be tossing and turning all night, trying to process what had happened, and she didn't want to keep him up.

"Call me if you need me—anytime," he said. He waited while she unlocked the front door to the house where she rented a third-floor apartment.

"I will. I promise," she said.

As soon as she pushed the door open, a black ball of fur, otherwise known as her dog, Heathcliff, came dashing out of his dog sitter's first-floor apartment, wagging his tail and rising up on his back legs so he could hug her knee.

"Hey, buddy." Lindsey dropped her keys and her purse and bent over to hug her dog. As if he sensed her distress, he licked her face, and Lindsey smiled, releasing him so she could wipe the slobber off with the back of her hand.

"If you didn't have him, I wouldn't be comfortable leaving you alone," Sully said. He bent down, and Heathcliff wagged his way over to his favorite male person. The boys had a lovefest of their own, and then Sully stood to enfold Lindsey in his arms one more time.

He pressed a kiss against her hair and said, "Lock the door behind me."

"I will," she said.

He gave her one more squeeze and a lingering kiss and then he was gone. Lindsey shut and locked the door behind him, almost changing her mind and calling him back, but she resisted. When she turned to look up the stairwell to her third-floor apartment, she wondered if it was always this dark and creepy or if it was just tonight.

Nancy had left the door to her first-floor apartment open, so Heathcliff could greet Lindsey when she arrived. Lindsey knocked on the doorjamb to let Nancy know she was there on the off chance she hadn't heard Heathcliff barking.

"Come in."

Lindsey followed the sound of Nancy's voice, which mingled with the scent of cinnamon on the air to lead her right to the kitchen where Nancy was finishing a batch of molasses cookies. Nancy was known throughout the village for her cookie-baking skills. Not surprisingly, there was a plate of cookies and a couple of mugs of cocoa sitting on the island counter as if waiting for Lindsey.

"I gather you heard the news," Lindsey asked.

"Everyone heard," Nancy confirmed. She put her cookie sheet down, took off her pot holders and leaned over the counter to give Lindsey a hug. "I was so upset I didn't know what to do with myself, so I started baking. Olive Boyle made a lot of enemies in this town, but still, to murder her—that's vicious."

Nancy shook her head as if she couldn't fathom how a person could ever take another's life. Lindsey was right there with her. She sipped the hot chocolate and was immediately soothed.

"Sully's recipe?" she asked.

"Always," Nancy said. "Where is he? I thought he'd come in with you."

"He has an early tour of the islands," Lindsey said. "I didn't want to keep him up."

Nancy nodded. "We do seem to have a lot of autumn visitors this year, from all over the world no less."

Lindsey put down her cocoa and picked up a cookie, then she put it down, her eyes wide. "Do you suppose one of them murdered Olive?"

"No!" Nancy protested. "I don't think so. I mean the ones at the dinner all seemed so nice, but I guess anything is possible."

"It is, isn't it?" Lindsey asked. She bit into her cookie. Crunchy on the outside, chewy on the inside. Perfection.

She hadn't thought of it before, but Nancy was right. Olive might have been murdered by a total stranger, one of those Londoners, maybe, or those people from Arizona. Who knew how far Olive had spread her poison?

"It's a good thing you've made a promise not to investigate anymore, huh?" Nancy asked. Her look was sly.

"Yeah, I suppose it is," Lindsey agreed. She put the remnants of her cookie back down. A smear of the sugary glaze Nancy drizzled on the cookies stuck to her finger, and she licked it off. "It's just—"

An image of Olive's body flashed in Lindsey's mind and she shivered.

"Just?" Nancy asked. She sipped her cocoa and pushed Lindsey's mug in her direction, encouraging her to have more.

Lindsey picked it up and stared into the froth on the top as if the creamy chocolate could give her answers. She only wished. She took a sip, letting the cocoa warm up her insides.

"You left before we discovered Olive's body," Lindsey said. "You didn't by any chance notice her with anyone, say, one of my staff, maybe, having an argument on your way out, did you?"

Nancy frowned. She stared at the pile of cookies before her as if willing them to give her an answer.

"I'm sorry. I left with Violet, and we were busy cooing over the trip for two to Paris that she won in the auction. Why do you ask?"

"No reason." At Nancy's dubious stare, she added, "Really. I made a promise I would leave these things to the police, and I intend to keep it."

"Of course, dear," Nancy said. She tipped her head to the side and studied Lindsey. "You look tired."

"I am," she said.

Exhaustion hit her like a heavy feather pillow to the face. The desire to be unconscious suddenly overrode any other need, even the one to stuff her face with Nancy's amazing cookies, and that was saying something.

"Here." Nancy handed Lindsey her mug and then bagged a dozen cookies for her. "Take these and go hit the sack. Things will be better in the morning."

"Will they?" Lindsey asked.

"No, but you'll have gotten some rest, and everything is always more manageable when you've had some sleep."

Lindsey gave her landlady a one-armed hug. "Thanks for watching the boy."

"My pleasure," Nancy said, and she walked them to the door.

The two flights of stairs in her dress and heels were too daunting to contemplate, so Lindsey kicked off her shoes in the foyer and left them on the bottom step. She would collect them in the morning. Then she grabbed her handbag and her keys and made the slow climb upstairs, sipping her cocoa as she went.

When she reached the second-floor landing, she paused to nibble a cookie and finish her rapidly cooling cocoa while Heathcliff waited patiently by her side. Her neighbor Charlie popped his head out and smiled when he saw her.

"I was waiting for you," he said. He gestured to the cocoa and cookies. "Aunt Nancy was waiting for you, too."

Lindsey held out the bag for him to take a cookie.

"Thanks," he said. He chomped it down in two bites. "So, we heard about Olive Boyle."

"Grisly news travels fast."

"She was a pretty hateful old bat," Charlie said. "I don't wish ill on anyone, but I can't pretend that I'm heartbroken either."

"Charlie, while you were there breaking down your equipment at the end, did you notice anything weird?"

Charlie tossed his stringy black hair and tipped his head to the side. It almost looked like he was trying to identify a song he heard playing, but there was no sound other than Heathcliff's nails on the hardwood floor while he paced back and forth waiting for Lindsey.

"Nothing that I would call weird, exactly," he said. "More like annoying."

"Oh?" Lindsey raised her eyebrows.

"Yeah, what's going on with Kelsey Kincaid and Devon Strickland?" he asked.

"You mean Kelsey the florist and Devon the landscaper?"

"Yeah, are they a thing?"

"Um, I don't know," Lindsey said.

"Well, that's not very helpful," Charlie said.

Lindsey held up the bag of cookies, and he took another.

"I take it you were preoccupied with Kelsey and Devon and didn't notice much else?" she asked.

"She danced with him like four times. The guy can't even play an instrument," Charlie stated, clearly dumbfounded that Kelsey could find a non-musician attractive.

"Okay, then, good talk. Night, Charlie," Lindsey said. She patted him on the shoulder and headed up the stairs.

"If you hear anything about Kelsey and Devon, let me know," he called after her.

"Roger that," Lindsey said.

"Roger? Who the heck is Roger?" he asked. "She's not dating some guy named Roger, too, is she?"

Lindsey paused in the middle of the stairs and glanced down at Heathcliff. He sat at her feet as if understanding that she needed to finish her conversation with Charlie.

"No, that was *roger* as in *okay*. You know, *roger that,* like a fighter pilot, military speak."

"Oh." His face turned a bit pink, and he nodded. "Sorry, she's just got me all . . ."

Lindsey thought about Sully and how he got

her in a tizzy at times. "No worries. I totally get it."

Charlie grinned at her, and it transformed his face. How had Lindsey never noticed how handsome he was? Maybe he stood a shot with Kelsey after all.

"Smile at her like that when you ask her out," Lindsey said. "She won't say no."

His smile snapped into a frown. "I never said I was going to ask her out. There's criteria involved, you know. Non-negotiable stuff."

Lindsey began walking again and called out, "Yeah, yeah, I know, like does she prefer the Beatles or the Rolling Stones. Big criteria there."

"Are you mocking me?" he called after.

Lindsey leaned over the rail so she could see him. "Yes."

"Well, at least you admit it," he grumbled.

"Good night," she called out. She unlocked her door, and Heathcliff dashed in, eager to sniff around their one-bedroom apartment to make sure everything was exactly as they'd left it.

Lindsey followed him and locked up. She bagged her dress in an old dry cleaning bag, thinking she never wanted to wear it again. Even if she had it professionally cleaned, she couldn't in good conscience donate it to charity. She left it on the floor by the front door, resolved to figure it out tomorrow. Then she took a scalding shower as if the hot water could burn the horror of the night out of her mind, but of course, it couldn't. Nothing could.

She bundled herself up in her robe and took the last of the cookies with her as she snuggled up on her couch. Heathcliff immediately jumped up beside her and stretched his length along her legs with his chin draped over her ankles.

It was comforting being in her own space with her dog. The night was dark and chilly, but they were safe inside. She chewed a molasses cookie and pondered the events of the night.

Olive was dead. At that stark thought, the cookie got lodged in Lindsey's throat, and she had to hack and wheeze a bit before she could suck in a decent breath. Her eyes watered, and she felt a sob bubble up in her throat.

She had seen dead bodies before—in fact, she had seen more than her share—but this was different. This death made her feel tainted somehow, as if she were an accomplice to whoever had killed Olive because Lindsey had felt such animosity toward the woman herself.

It made her feel awful, truly, purely terrible, as if her own anger had caused Olive's death. Lindsey wasn't sure how to process these feelings. She could take no joy in Olive's murder, but like Charlie, she wasn't terribly distraught either. Olive had been a vicious woman who enjoyed making everyone around her suffer. When a person threw out that sort of karma, was it any surprise when something terrible happened to them?

She glanced at the clock on the wall. It was late, and she was exhausted, but still, she stayed on the couch eating cookies. She couldn't stop thinking about the dinner, revisiting who had been where and when as if she could find the puzzle piece that was out of place, rearrange it and have the answer to who killed Olive Boyle.

It wasn't that simple, however. There were too many players in this drama, and too many unknown entities. They'd had so many out-of-town visitors. How could she know who might have used the dinner as an opportunity to kill Olive? Was it a stranger? Or worse, was it someone she knew? Someone she trusted?

She shivered even though she wasn't cold. She told herself it didn't matter, because she wasn't going to investigate. Sure, she was curious, and she felt a certain responsibility, because the murder had happened in her library, but she had promised that she wouldn't butt into any investigations anymore.

Having faced down the barrel of a loaded gun just a few months before, Lindsey had a new appreciation for her life and how much she wanted to keep on living it. The thought of losing her life because she was overly inquisitive did not appeal to her in the least.

She reached into the bag for one more cookie.

It was empty. She sighed. It was just as well. She needed to go to bed. The library was closed tomorrow, but a specialized cleaning company would be there to try and get the bloodstains out of the carpet. She felt the cookies in her belly burble in protest.

She slid off of the couch to get ready for bed. Once she'd checked the apartment, brushed her teeth and assisted Heathcliff up onto the foot of the bed, she tried to settle in and sleep. Nancy was right—everything was better after a good night's rest.

She lay there, waiting, willing the drowsiness to overtake her. Instead, she kept flashing on Paula's face when she had looked Emma right in the eye and said she'd been working on cleaning the circulation area. She had lied, and Lindsey had no idea why. She didn't want to think it, but she could only figure one reason for Paula to have lied about her whereabouts: because she had murdered Olive Boyle.

11

Lindsey stared at the bakery case. She needed to eat something, but what muffin paired best with bloodstained carpet? She went with the pumpkin chocolate chip, knowing full well she wasn't going to eat it.

She had left Heathcliff with Nancy and dressed in her warm wool jacket and jeans before she biked to the library to meet the professional cleaning crew who was arriving to see what they could do about the flooring where Olive Boyle had been stabbed to death.

The thought of hot coffee and a muffin had lured her to the bakery counter located in the small-town grocery store that she passed every day on her way to the library. Although, she suspected that today she didn't want coffee and a muffin as much as she wanted to stall her arrival at the library.

Climbing back onto her bike, she looked out at the pier. Sure enough, Sully's tour boat was loading up, and even at a distance she could tell that some of the people boarding were the Londoners and the Arizonans she had met the night before. She briefly wondered if there was a murderer in their midst.

She shook her head. Nope. Not going there. Really.

She pedaled slowly to the library and locked up her bike on the rack by the back door and let herself in, deactivating the alarm as she went. The cleaners were coming in an hour. She wasn't generally the jumpy type, so she found it odd that being in the deserted darkened building suddenly gave her the heebie-jeebies.

Lindsey took a deep breath and tried to calm the beat of her heart, which felt heavy in her chest. She stood still, listening to the silence of the library, a quiet in which she usually found comfort. A shiver started at the base of her spine, and she moved over to the main set of light switches and flicked every single one on.

"Hello?" she called out.

Not surprisingly there was no response.

She scanned the room. No shadows moved. There was no noise, not the sound of footsteps or of someone breathing; still, she felt unsettled. She slid, with her back against the wall, into her office, where she shut and locked her door even while telling herself that she was being ridiculous.

She sat in her chair and went to take a restorative sip from her coffee, when her phone chimed, causing her to jump and shriek and spill coffee on her pants.

She snatched up her phone. It was Robbie.

"Hello," she answered, relieved to have someone to talk to, as it made her feel less alone.

"Hello, pet, do me a favor and unlock the front doors," he said.

"You're here?"

"Right out front," he said.

"Oh, thank God," Lindsey muttered. She hurried out of her office and dashed across the lobby to get to the main entrance.

"What was that?" he asked. "I couldn't hear you."

"Nothing," she said. She waved at him through the glass door. She ended the call and knelt down to unlock the doors. They whooshed opened, and Robbie stood there, smiling at her. Lindsey grabbed him by the hand, as if he might try to run, and dragged him into the building.

"What's got you all in a fizz?" he asked.

"I'm not," she protested. "Okay, it's just a teeny bit unnerving to be here by myself after last night."

Robbie glanced from side to side. "It is eerily quiet, isn't it?"

They both stood still, listening. The silence was thick, as if weighted down by the tragedy that had occurred.

"Ms. Norris?"

"Ah!" Lindsey started and whirled back around to find a man in a hazmat suit standing in the doorway.

"Sorry, ma'am. I'm John Solis with the cleaning company," he said. He was covered from neck to toe in yellow coveralls and was holding a face mask in one hand.

"You're early," she said.

"Is that a problem?"

"No, not at all. Sorry, I'm a bit jumpy," she said.

He gave her a sympathetic look. "Completely understandable. Can I bring my crew in and get started?"

"Sure, I'll walk you over to the . . . er . . . area," she said.

They turned to walk to the stacks when there was a shout from outside. Lindsey turned back to see Kili Peters, a reporter, racing toward the front door with a cameraman at her back.

"No, just no," Lindsey said.

She hurried forward, trying to shut the door, but the rest of the cleanup crew arrived at the same time, and she couldn't shut out Kili without shutting them out as well.

"Lindsey, don't you do it. Don't make me go through the mayor!" Kili shouted.

Lindsey's shoulders slumped. Kili was a petite, blond, buxom reporter that Lindsey had tangled with before. Kili, pronounced just like the fruit but with an *l* instead of a *w,* was known for latching onto a story and sensationalizing it to the point of no return. She had reported on events surrounding the town of Briar Creek and the library before, and it never went well for them.

132

She had a vindictive streak, and shutting her out would likely only make her even more doggedly determined to report on them in a negative way.

"Fine," Lindsey said. She looked at Robbie. "Keep her here and do not say anything."

With that, she gestured to the cleaners to follow her and led them back to the area where Olive had been found. The sight of the dark stain under the stark fluorescent lighting made her breath catch and her heart pound. Would there ever come a time when she wouldn't walk amongst these shelves and feel sick? She doubted it.

"If you need anything, Mr. Solis, I'll be up front," she said.

"Don't worry," he said. "We'll take care of this for you. More than likely we'll have to remove the existing carpet and put in a fresh piece."

"That's probably for the best. Thank you."

They nodded at each other, and Lindsey turned and hurried back to the front, hoping she could do whatever damage control would be required to keep Kili from slandering the library or hampering them with a slew of bad press that would take months for her to counter. She remembered the first time she and Kili had tangled. Lindsey had been fairly new to the small town and found her library in the center of what was little more than a smear campaign. It had been a learning experience she could have lived without.

"Kili," she said as she approached. She noticed that the reporter was staring at Robbie, looking starstruck. Maybe they could get out of this alive after all.

"Lindsey," Kili said. She tossed her hair and tugged on the lapels of the jacket that framed her figure to its best advantage.

"Why are you here?" Lindsey asked.

"Duh." Kili looked at her as if she was too stupid to live and gestured in the direction where the cleaners had gone.

"Fine, let me rephrase that." Lindsey blew out a breath to give herself a moment to gather her scattered patience. "What did you hope to learn here today?"

"Learn?" Kili blinked at her.

"You're an investigative reporter," Lindsey said. "Aren't you supposed to be digging into Olive's life, looking for clues, tracking down witnesses, interviewing suspects?"

"Yeah, that, that's what I'm doing," Kili said. She took her cell phone out of her pocket and used the reflective surface to check her teeth and hair.

"Over my dead body," Lindsey muttered.

"Really?" Robbie asked.

"Sorry."

"Let's go, Micah," Kili said to the cameraman.

The burly man, wearing a headset, hefted the

134

camera onto his shoulder and aimed it in their direction.

"In five, four, three . . ." Micah counted down.

Lindsey had no intention of being interviewed, and she dove for cover. When Robbie stood there, looking ready for his close-up, she grabbed him by the arm and yanked him down behind a waist-high shelving unit with her.

"Two . . ."

"You are not answering any questions on behalf of the library," she hissed.

"One. And rolling," Micah said.

"But the camera," Robbie protested.

"No."

"Cut!" Kili snapped. She stomped forward and leaned over the shelving unit to peer down at Lindsey and Robbie where they squatted. "Very mature."

Lindsey leaned to the right to glance past her. When she saw that the red light on the top of the camera was off, she rose to standing. Robbie followed her.

"Sorry, but I'm not giving an interview right now," she said. "I would have to get permission from the mayor—you know that."

"Yeah, I suppose, if you're determined to follow the rules. Plus, you really need to do something with this," Kili said. She used her index finger to make a circle around her own face. Lindsey took this to mean that her lack of makeup was frowned upon. Kili turned to Robbie and batted her false eyelashes at him. "How about you, big guy?"

"Uh . . . well . . . I . . ." Robbie hedged.

"No. He doesn't work here," Lindsey said. "He can't speak for the library."

"No?" Kili asked. She sidled closer to Robbie. "How about as a resident then? You could be my man on the street."

Robbie tipped his head to the side as if considering this. Kili waved her hand behind her back at the cameraman to get ready as she pressed herself against Robbie's side.

"Robbie, don't—" Lindsey began, but Kili interrupted her.

"Just think what a refreshing angle it would make," Kili said. "World-famous, stunningly handsome heartthrob tells the viewers what it's like to live in the murderous shoreline town of Briar Creek with a lame-duck chief of police."

A smile spread across Robbie's face as he got caught up in her description of his role.

"Yeah, let's hear your thoughts on the lame duck," a voice said from behind Micah.

Lindsey turned to see Emma standing there in her chief of police uniform with her arms crossed over her chest, which was probably a good thing, as it kept her from using her Taser on Robbie.

"Em! You're here." Robbie's eyebrows shot up in alarm.

"And just in time," she said. She pushed past Micah and moved into Kili's personal space. "Back away from my boyfriend."

"Boyfriend?" Kili looked outraged, and then the reporter in her became intrigued. "The actor and the officer— Oh, this is delicious. Do tell and don't leave out any details. Did you meet when she nabbed you for a drunk and disorderly?"

"No!" Robbie protested. "What sort of bloke do you think I am?"

"Enough," Emma said. She moved forward, forcing Kili and her cameraman back until they were on the outside of the library looking in. "There will be an official press conference at the station later today. Any questions you have will be answered then."

"But—"

Emma manually pulled the doors shut and then crouched down to lock them.

"How did she manage that?" Robbie asked Lindsey. "We couldn't scrape those barnacles off for the life of us."

"Power of the badge," she said.

"Ah." He nodded.

"The cleaners are here?" Emma asked.

"Yeah, they've already started," Lindsey said.

"How are you holding up?"

Lindsey shrugged. She didn't have it in her to force a smile or lie and say she was fine. She wasn't.

"That's why I came by," Emma said. She looked over her shoulder at Kili and Micah who were stomping back toward their news van. "And just in time, apparently."

"You know I would have had your back, love, don't you?" Robbie asked.

"I believe you would have tried," Emma said. "But reporters, especially that one, are tricky. This is an ongoing investigation, so I would prefer it if you direct any inquiries to me."

"Absolutely," Lindsey said.

"Sure thing," Robbie agreed. He studied Lindsey and then glanced out the door. When the news van pulled away, he put his arm around Emma's shoulders and pulled her into his side and swiftly kissed her hair. "How are you?"

"I've been better," she said. "The mayor is on my behind to solve this case, and despite the two hundred plus people that were here last night, I've got nothing substantial."

She glanced at Lindsey, and Lindsey knew she was thinking that she had nothing substantial except Paula. Lindsey stared her down. Her clerk was not involved in this. She knew it all the way into the marrow of her bones.

There must have been something on her face that waved Emma off, because she pushed away from Robbie and said, "I'm just going to check in with the cleaning crew."

Lindsey and Robbie watched her go.

"All right, spill it," Robbie said.

"What?"

"What, what? The tension between you two is so dramatic it comes with its own soundtrack," he said. "What's going on?"

Lindsey considered him for a minute. Could she tell him? Should she tell him? No, she couldn't. He was involved with Emma romantically, so as far as Lindsey was concerned, when it came to confiding in him, his loyalty was compromised.

Besides, she wasn't getting involved in this situation, and if she told him what was happening, he would take it as a sign that she needed to investigate, and he would badger her until she gave in. She couldn't let that happen.

"I don't know what you're talking about," she said.

"Little tip, love," Robbie said. He looked disappointed in her, which bothered Lindsey more than she wanted to admit. "When you lie to someone, you should really maintain eye contact."

He walked away in the same direction Emma had taken, leaving Lindsey alone by the front door, wondering how many relationships she was going to ruin by refusing to get involved.

12

Lindsey spent the following Monday afternoon sitting at the reference desk, wading through the online time slips for her staff to make sure they were filled out correctly before she forwarded them over to the human resources department at town hall.

Ann Marie, the library assistant who usually manned the desk, was on break. Lindsey didn't mind covering for her, as she felt that it kept her reference skills sharp.

She had just finished signing hard copies of a couple of leave slips and sealed them in an interoffice envelope when Mr. Chesterton, a native Creeker, approached the reference desk.

He was a mild-mannered older gentleman, known throughout Briar Creek for his award-winning apple pie. Every year for the past three years, his pie had won the blue ribbon at the annual harvest festival. Lindsey had been one of the judges last year, and she could testify that his pie was the best she'd ever tasted. Truly, it had an amazing butter and brown sugar crumble crust that was top-notch.

"Hi, Mr. Chesterton," she said. "What can I help you with?"

Of medium height, with a thick head of brown

hair that was just turning gray, Mr. Chesterton favored khaki pants and dress shirts and was always soft-spoken but with a dry wit that Lindsey had come to enjoy.

"I am actually here on behalf of Mrs. Chesterton," he said.

"Oh, all right," she said. She put the envelope aside and gave him her full attention.

"She is an avid fan of the author Lori Wilde," he said. "And while the online catalog says her latest book is in, I couldn't find it on the shelf."

"Did you try the romance section?" Lindsey asked.

"Yes, it's not there," he said.

"Let me look up the record and see if I can track it down," Lindsey offered. She opened up the catalog and typed in the author's name. She turned the monitor so that it faced Mr. Chesterton and asked, "Which title of hers are you looking for?"

"You mean is my wife looking for," he corrected her. "That one, right there."

He pointed, and Lindsey clicked on it. She checked the date that it had been returned to see if that would tell her where it might be if not on the shelf.

"It looks like it came back two days ago, so while it is checked in, it might not be on the shelf yet. Things have been . . . hectic, and we're running a little behind on our shelving," she said.

"I'll go check the sorting carts and be right back."

"Thank you," he said.

Lindsey hurried into the sorting area, which took up a large counter in the workroom. Sitting on stools, fine sorting trucks of books before they took them out to shelve, were two of the library's current pages, Heather and Perry. They seemed to be in a heated discussion and didn't notice Lindsey when she arrived.

"I'm just saying that I don't think she did it," Perry said.

"Well, you don't really know what a person is capable of, do you?" Heather argued. "Remember Dylan's mother."

"Yes, but she was crazy," he argued.

"But she didn't look it until we knew she was," Heather said.

"Only because we weren't paying attention."

"I'm paying attention now, believe me."

"Ahem." Lindsey cleared her throat, and they both jumped. "Hi. I'm looking for a romance by Lori Wilde."

"I'm nonfiction," Perry said.

"I've got genre fiction," Heather replied.

"Excellent. Thanks," Lindsey said. She moved to check over the cart Heather was working on. She debated not saying anything to the teens, but she just couldn't let it lie, not if they were talking about Paula and thinking the worst.

"Got it," she said. She took the book off the cart

and said, "Mrs. Chesterton will be very happy."

Perry and Heather exchanged a look, and Perry started to laugh.

"What?" Lindsey glanced between them.

"The romances Mr. Chesterton checks out aren't for Mrs. Chesterton," Heather said.

"I don't understand," Lindsey said.

"My mom is friends with Mrs. Chesterton," Perry said. "They both love crime novels. Mr. Chesterton is the one who loves the romance."

"Are you sure?" Lindsey asked. She had always thought Mr. Chesterton was more of a spy-novel guy.

"Oh yeah," Perry said. "Watch him when he leaves. He'll start reading before he even reaches the sidewalk."

"Huh," Lindsey said. "Is it weird that I think that's utterly charming?"

"No," Heather said. "I think it's lovely, too."

Lindsey smiled at her.

"Well, I don't," Perry grumbled. "It's not fair making me read Jane Austen just to get you to go out with me."

Lindsey glanced between the two. She knew Perry had been pining for Heather for a while, but she didn't realize a relationship was in the works. She turned to Heather and gave her a thumbs-up. "Nice. What Austen novel did you start him on?"

"*Pride and Prejudice*," she said. "I see a lot of Colin Firth's Mr. Darcy in him."

Lindsey studied Perry with his wavy dark hair, aristocratic nose and arching eyebrows. Yes, it was there just beneath the surface.

"Don't worry," she said to Perry. "It's a great book, and then you can read *Pride and Prejudice and Zombies*, which you'll really love."

"Zombies? Why didn't they put that in the first one?" he asked. "It would totally rock with zombies. I think if I read that one it should count as close enough."

"No." Heather rolled her eyes, and Lindsey laughed.

"Listen, guys, on a more serious note, I don't know what you were talking about when I came in, but I want to be very clear that we don't gossip about staff," she said. Both teens sobered immediately. "Also, I would like it if you would believe the best in a person until there is absolute evidence to prove otherwise."

"All right."

"Okay."

They both looked guilty, and Lindsey felt badly about that, but if the situation were reversed and they were the ones in the questionable circumstance, she would protect them just as fiercely.

"Neither of you have anything you need to tell me, do you?" she asked. "You haven't seen or heard anything that causes you concern?"

"No, Ms. Norris," Perry said.

"No," Heather said. "Sorry about . . . you know. It's just, I'm a little paranoid since I've thought the best of others before and been really, really wrong."

Lindsey nodded. She knew the feeling. She tried to quiet the uneasy voice inside of her that said she needed to be cautious with her loyalty to Paula. She glanced through the glass window that overlooked the circulation area. Paula was working beside Ms. Cole. Her face was pale and wan, and she looked as if she hadn't slept in days.

Lindsey wondered if she should send her home to rest, but she suspected that Paula wouldn't rest until she was no longer a suspect. She could relate.

"For what it's worth, I know how you feel," Lindsey said as she turned back to Heather. "But Paula needs our support now, and until we know otherwise for certain, let's give her that. Okay?"

Heather nodded. Lindsey glanced at Perry, and he nodded, too.

"All right, I'm back out to the desk if anyone needs me," she said.

She left the break room, cut through the circulation area just to see if everything was okay—it was—and then found Mr. Chesterton perusing the romance section for more titles. He had several written by prominent authors Delores Fossen, Holly Jacobs, and Nancy Warren in his hands, and when Lindsey handed him the book

146

he'd requested, he added it happily to his pile.

"Well, I think this should keep my wife busy," he said.

"Yes, that's quite a terrific selection you have there," Lindsey agreed. She bit the inside of her cheek to keep from smiling. "If I find any other titles that I think she'd like, I'll be sure to put them aside for her."

"I know she would appreciate that," he said. "Thank you, Lindsey."

"My pleasure," she said, and she meant it.

She settled back down at her desk and opened up the latest issue of *Library Journal*. She watched from afar as Mr. Chesterton checked out his books, and just because Perry had told her to, she found herself watching him as he left the building. Sure enough, he was read-walking his way up the sidewalk with the Lori Wilde novel open in his hands. Lindsey snorted. Dang, if Perry hadn't been right. Mr. Chesterton was the romance reader. Huh.

She was halfway through an article about how to catalog self-published books when she heard a ruckus coming from the front of the library. She stood to see who was making the commotion.

Oh no, it was Olive's three friends, Amy, LeAnn and Kim, and they looked to be zeroing in on Paula. This could not be good.

Lindsey hurriedly left the desk. She had worn heels and a skirt today for a meeting she'd had at the town hall. The meeting had been canceled, leaving Lindsey in her grown-up clothes, which were not nearly as comfortable for breaking up altercations as slacks and boots were.

"We know what you did," Amy hissed at Paula.

She was leaning over the desk into Paula's personal space, while Paula stood frozen, like a mouse afraid to move in front of a snake lest it strike.

"I didn't—" Paula protested.

"Liar!" LeAnn accused.

"That's enough," Ms. Cole snapped at the women. "You are in a library, and I expect you to comport yourselves as such."

Lindsey blinked. Good ol' Ms. Cole. Only she would be more outraged that they had raised their voices than that they had accused someone of murder. If the situation weren't so tense, she would have laughed.

Instead she used her frostiest tone when she approached the group. "May I help you?"

"Yes, you can," Amy said. "I want her fired and arrested."

The sheer ridiculousness of the statement made Lindsey shake her head and give Amy a squinty look. "Yeah, I'm a librarian. The whole arresting people thing—that's more of a police matter."

Amy ignored the sarcasm. "Why is she still here? You need to get rid of her. She could be a danger to us all."

"Then one might suggest you leave," Ms. Cole said.

"Why, you—"

"Stop." Lindsey put both of her hands up as if she could ward them off by sheer willpower. "Do not harass my staff, any of them. If you have a need to use the library, you are welcome. If you do not, I am asking you to leave."

"Our friend was murdered here," Kim spat.

"I'm sorry for your loss. I truly am," Lindsey said. "But coming in here and throwing accusations—"

"See? I told you so. She's in on it," LeAnn sniped.

"Excuse me?" Lindsey shook her head as if she was hard of hearing.

"We've been talking, and it seems to us that since it was the two of you who found her, it was probably the two of you who murdered her," Amy said.

"What?!" Lindsey and Paula said together.

"See how they are?" Kim said. She wagged a well-manicured finger between Lindsey and Paula.

Lindsey gave Paula a wide-eyed look, and Paula looked back at her as if she had no idea what to say or do. When her lips trembled, Lindsey had had enough.

"I can assure you that if there was any indication that either of us were involved in

Olive's murder, we would have been arrested by now," she said. "We haven't been, so clearly we're not involved."

"Olive wanted to replace you," Amy said. "What happened? Did she tell you she was going to have you fired so you freaked out and stabbed her?"

"No!" Lindsey snapped. She felt her heart beginning to pound in her chest, and she knew it was because half of Amy's statement had been true. Olive had told her she was going to try and replace her.

"And what about you?" Amy turned on Paula. "Olive said she knew something about you, something she was planning to share at the dinner. Did you kill her before she could?"

"N-no, I didn't. I swear," Paula said.

A single tear spilled out of her eye, and Lindsey felt all of her own outraged emotion shift from herself to Paula. If they wanted to come after her, fine, but they would leave her staff alone.

Lindsey moved forward until she was looming over the three women. Now she was glad she'd worn heels—go figure.

"Back off," she said.

"We have every ri—"

"No, you don't," Lindsey said. "You have no right to speak to my staff or me like that. Now, you will leave on your own, or I will call security and have you escorted out of the building in handcuffs if need be."

The three women glanced at one another. They were clearly unsettled by Lindsey's firm tone.

"Fine, but this isn't over," Amy snapped. She turned on her heel and led the way out of the building.

As soon as the doors whooshed shut behind them, Lindsey collapsed onto the circulation desk. She'd had to face down a few patrons in her time, but never ones accusing her of murder.

After a few beats, Ms. Cole asked, "We have security?"

"No," Lindsey admitted. "But they didn't know that."

A rare smile lit up Ms. Cole's normally stern countenance, and she said, "Well played."

Lindsey was still processing that when Paula stepped forward. She handed Lindsey an envelope and said, "I had a feeling this sort of thing was going to happen. I won't let it happen again. Thanks for taking a chance on me, Lindsey, but I quit."

13

W hat is this?" She opened the envelope and noted that it was a letter of resignation. "Paula, no, please don't."

"I'm sorry. I just can't face that every day," she said. "Everyone's going to think I killed Olive, and I didn't."

"We know that," Lindsey said. "And we won't let anyone accuse you of anything so vile."

"You can't stop gossip," Paula said. "It's vicious and mean, and people thrive on it."

"You're right, and it's a pity," Ms. Cole said. "It's difficult to stop gossip but not impossible."

"You have a suggestion?" Paula asked her.

"Yes, you keep your head held high and a stiff upper lip, and you forge on, showing no emotion. Bullies always look for a weakness to exploit. If you don't have one, then they can't touch you."

Lindsey couldn't argue with this sound advice. She could not imagine anyone being stupid enough to try and bully Ms. Cole. She was a force of nature, and her stern demeanor alone scared the patrons into behaving.

Paula, however, was a different employee altogether. She was friendly and approachable and took her time with people, determined to get them what they needed. As public servants went, she was one of the best.

"She's right," Lindsey said. "You shouldn't give up what you love because someone is trying to drive you out."

"I appreciate that," Paula said. "But the situation is complicated. Every time I help someone, I wonder if they think I'm a killer. It's only a matter of time before you're asking for my resignation. This will save us both the awkwardness."

"Now why would I go and do that," Lindsey asked, "when you haven't done anything wrong?"

"Because like those ladies who were just in here, people will expect it, probably demand it," Paula said. She rose from her seat, looking like she was getting ready to leave the library for good.

Ms. Cole and Lindsey exchanged an alarmed look. Ms. Cole snatched the letter out of Lindsey's hand and tore it into tiny pieces.

"Hey!" Paula protested. "You can't do that."

"Looks like I just did," Ms. Cole said. "Your resignation is refused."

Lindsey had no idea what to say. If Paula wanted to quit, could Lindsey really force her to stay? Ms. Cole clearly had no issues with doing so.

"But—" Paula stared at the lemon wide-eyed.

"Paula, you have nothing to worry about," Ms. Cole said.

Paula cast her a dubious look that expressed her opinion that the lemon was an encyclopedia shy of a full set without her having to say so.

"You don't," Ms. Cole insisted. "Lindsey will find out what happened to Olive Boyle."

"What? No!" Lindsey balked. "I don't do that anymore."

"Don't be ridiculous." Ms. Cole frowned at her. "Of course you do."

"No, I made a vow after I almost got my head blown off that I would not be a buttinsky anymore," Lindsey protested.

"That was then and this is now," Ms. Cole said. "Things have changed. This is one of your staff who needs help. You have to step up. It's what you do."

Ms. Cole looked bewildered, as if she couldn't reconcile the image in her head of Lindsey being an investigator with the woman before her saying "no" and looking all professional.

"But I—" Lindsey wanted to argue. She wanted to insist that she couldn't do this, but one look at Paula's distraught face and she felt her resolve crumble like a cookie dunked in milk. "All right, well, I don't suppose it would hurt anything if I asked a few questions."

"Woo-hoo!"

Lindsey spun around to find Robbie standing behind her.

"How long have you been standing there?" she asked.

"Long enough to know that you're back in the game," he said. He rubbed his hands together, looking eager to start with the detecting.

"No, no, no," she said. "You're getting that look in your eye, and the answer is no."

"Oh, come on," he argued. "Look at the poor girl. She's scared out of her wits. You have to help her."

He gestured at Paula, who was watching the two of them with a decidedly hopeful glint in her eye. How could Lindsey refuse to help one of her staff? She couldn't.

"Fine," she said. They all smiled, so she felt compelled to add, "But if there is a hint of danger, even a mere suggestion of it, I am tapping out."

"Absolutely," Robbie said. "That is a perfectly reasonable response."

Lindsey stared at him. She did not trust his happy little grin, so she added, "I mean it."

"Of course you do," he said. "Now, let's have tea and discuss the case." He took Lindsey's elbow and began to lead her away but turned back to Paula and said, "Don't you worry, pet. We've got this."

Paula beamed at him. It was the first time Lindsey had seen her smile in days. Okay, so that was something.

"I'll start the kettle," Robbie offered. "You get the biscuits."

He set off toward the break room, and Lindsey shook her head. She shouldn't encourage him; she knew she shouldn't. She could only imagine what Emma was going to have to say about this. The mere thought made her sweat a little bit.

Ann Marie finished her break and took over the reference desk for Lindsey, leaving her no choice but to go forage for cookies, because biscuits in Robbie-speak meant cookies. When she arrived back at her office, she found Robbie sipping tea while he thumbed through one of the gossip magazines.

"You don't make the headlines for your shenanigans like you used to," Lindsey said.

"Shenanigans aren't really my thing anymore," he said. "Now that I'm a dad, I am trying to set a better example."

"Uh-huh," she said. "Don't you miss it? Being in the spotlight, having everyone follow you around and care about what you wear, what you eat and who you're dating?"

"Not even a little," he said. He poured a cup of tea, put in milk and sugar just the way Lindsey liked it and handed it to her. "Actually, I was thinking I might retire from the limelight permanently."

"You mean give up acting?" Lindsey asked. Her eyes were wide. In the year she had known him, he had left town several times to film various projects. It never occurred to her that he might leave the business.

"There's more to life," he said. He gave a careless shrug.

Lindsey narrowed her eyes. "Such as?"

He sipped his tea and met her gaze over the rim of his cup. That was it? He wasn't going to say anything more. Lindsey wanted to call foul, but she had a feeling that until he wanted to share what was going on, she would get nowhere. She'd have better luck trying to figure out who killed Olive Boyle.

"Okay, suit yourself," she said. "If you don't want to share your feelings with a dear friend . . ."

He picked up a cookie and finished it in two bites. Obviously, guilt trips were unfamiliar excursions for him, and he completely missed the boat. Whatever.

She glowered at him and took a restorative sip of her tea. The sweet heat spread through her, and she felt herself relax. She would find out what was going on in Robbie's world, and the best way to do it would be to observe him over the next few days while they tried to figure out who might have had a reason to kill Olive. Or rather, who out of all the people who had a reason to kill Olive was the one who actually did it.

"Let's get to work, shall we?" Robbie asked. "I've been thinking about who might have had an interest in killing Ms. Boyle, and I've come up with a list of names."

"You have?" she asked. She was surprised he'd forged ahead on his own. She took a cookie and bit into it. After she swallowed, she asked, "How does Emma feel about your list?"

"She won't discuss it with me," he said. "Bloody maddening."

Lindsey smiled. "All right, then, let me have it. Who's on your list?"

"Suspects in no particular order," Robbie said. He pulled a folded-up piece of paper out of his pocket and smoothed it open on his lap. "Milton Duffy."

"What?" Lindsey cried. "Milton? That's crazy! Why would he want Olive dead?"

"She took his position as the president of the library board," Robbie said. "Milton had that position for how long? Ten years?"

"About that," Lindsey said. "But trust me, while we were all surprised at how the vote went, he wasn't upset. He conceded graciously."

"Ah yes, that's what he showed on the outside," Robbie said. "Maybe on the inside he was seething with the injustice of it all, and at the dinner when she took the stage, his rage overtook his calm demeanor and he stabbed her."

"No. And what injustice are you talking about?" Lindsey asked.

"I'm glad you asked," he said. "I talked to the only board member who voted for Milton, Lydia Wilcox, and she seemed to think that the other board members were coerced into voting for Olive because Olive had dirt on all of them."

"It's true. Lydia was the only one who voted for Milton," Lindsey said. "At the time, I thought it was loyalty, but if what she says is true . . ."

She pondered this information. She had thought it was weird when Milton lost his position as president of the library board, since the board had always seemed to be very friendly with no infighting, no grudges, no power struggles, nothing, until Olive Boyle made a play for the president position. Still, she didn't see Milton as a murderer.

"Milton is a yogi," she said. "I don't think you can be a yogi and be a murderer. They're mutually exclusive, aren't they?"

"No idea. Just throwing out the suspects as they came to me," he said.

"Let's move on then," Lindsey said.

"After talking to Lydia, I had to put the other board members on the list," he said. "What sort of goss could she possibly have on them, and how far would they go to keep it a secret?"

"That would be Curt Delaney, Stuart Humphries and Susan Kershaw," she said. "They're all wonderful people, active in the community, donate their time to the library and to other causes. What could Olive possibly have had on them?"

Robbie shrugged. "Everyone has secrets."

Lindsey blew out a breath. "Maybe I don't want to dig into this. Maybe I don't want to know these things about my community."

She reached for another cookie, knowing full well that she was now comfort eating.

"We don't have much choice," Robbie said. "It's that or sit on our hands waiting for the police to solve the case."

Lindsey raised her eyebrows in question.

"Yes, I believe Emma can solve the case, but she's hampered by the very laws she upholds, you know, like warrants and procedure and all that folderol, while we are not."

"Good point," Lindsey said. "Besides, if you think about it, we're really just doing informational recon, and as the library director, I have insights into the gathering of information."

"Exactly. You have an advanced degree," he said. "It'd be a shame not to use it."

"Who else is on your list?"

He gave her a sheepish look.

"No, sir, you did not," she said.

"Sorry, but she did try to humiliate you in front of all the dinner guests," he said. "And for accuracy's sake, it was noted that even before the gala, you were heard to say to Olive . . ." He glanced at the paper before adding, " 'I'll choke you out.' "

Lindsey gasped. "How do you know I said that?"

"Everyone knows you said that. Small community, tongues wagging—really, are you surprised?"

Lindsey huffed out a breath. "Great, so I'm investigating myself."

"And Paula," he said.

"Whoa, whoa, whoa," she said. "I thought the whole point of this"—she gestured between them—"was to help her."

"It is, but we have to treat her just like anyone else," he said.

Lindsey put down her tea and her cookie and pressed her temples with the tips of her fingers.

"Who else?"

"I added her three friends, Amy, LeAnn and Kim," he said. "Did you notice that when we found Olive, not one of them shed a single tear?"

"I didn't," she said.

"I suppose it's the acting thing. I'm always studying people's reactions to use in my work," he said. "Theirs were not normal."

"Do you think they weren't really Olive's friends?" Lindsey asked. "As in, maybe she coerced relationships with those women the same way she bullied her way onto the library board, assuming Lydia's suspicions are true."

"It does seem to be her modus operandi," he agreed.

They were both silent, sipping their tea.

"Who else?" she asked.

"I did a little digging and found out she has an ex-husband and a sister," he said. "If Olive was as awful to them as she was to everyone else, it could be either of them."

"And usually a person is murdered by a family member or an ex," Lindsey said. "The statistics show that most murders are committed by a person the victim knows, usually following an argument."

"Didn't you have an argument with Olive after she took over the stage at the dinner?" Robbie asked.

Lindsey stared at him. "I would consider it more of a discussion. Besides, murderers who use a knife usually have a very high level of anger for the victim. At most, I was irritated."

"If you say so."

Lindsey chose to ignore him.

"Maybe we should start with her ex-husband," she suggested. "I can't imagine divorcing Olive was a pleasant experience. Who knows what bitterness lingered."

Robbie nodded. "We're going to need to have a reason to contact him—for that matter we need an address."

Lindsey frowned. "Leave the reason up to me."

"You have a plan?"

She nodded. "I just need to run it by a few people."

Robbie grinned at her. "We can go see him as soon as we locate his whereabouts then?"

"I'll make the time."

"Excellent."

"One question," Lindsey said. "Isn't Emma going to be angry with you for interfering in an investigation?"

"Nah, she'll be fine. She's been telling me to get a hobby."

"She probably meant photography or boating," Lindsey said.

"Ugh, those sound positively dreary," he said. "She can't want me to be bored to death, can she?"

"No, but I don't think she wants you to put yourself in danger or compromise her investigation either," Lindsey said.

"It'll be fine." Robbie waved a hand at her. "So long as I keep her in the loop and don't take any unnecessary risks, we're good. What about your merman?"

"Yeah, what about me?"

Lindsey's head whipped to her office door to find Sully standing there. His arms were crossed over his chest, and the expression on his face was seriously unhappy.

14

"What is this I hear that you're investigating Olive Boyle's murder?" he asked. "We talked about this, and you agreed no more."

"I know, but there are extenuating circumstances," she said.

Sully looked at Robbie. "I'll bet."

"Don't scowl at me, mate," Robbie said. "She has a mind of her own."

"How did you hear about this anyway?" Lindsey asked. "I thought you had a big boat tour."

"I did," he said. "We just got in, and Ronnie met me at the end of the pier to tell me that you and Robbie were planning to look into the murder."

"How did Ronnie know?" Lindsey asked. Ronnie was Sully's octogenarian office manager, who wore her poufy hairdo in a dashing shade of cranberry and had the attitude to match.

"Apparently, Hillary Macintyre was in here and heard you talking, and she told Krista, her server at the Blue Anchor; who told my sister, Mary; who called Ronnie; who told me."

"Sheesh, that news spread faster than a case of the flu," Lindsey said. She looked at Robbie. "That means Emma's likely heard, too."

"Huh, fancy that. Look at the time," Robbie said. He pushed up his sleeve and glanced at his bare wrist. "I'd best go find my girl before she puts a warrant out for my arrest. Lindsey, I'll talk to you later. Sailor boy, don't get all knotted up now."

"Says the over-actor," Sully said. He shifted so that Robbie could get by him and then stepped into Lindsey's office, shutting the door behind him.

"Got a minute to explain in greater detail?" he asked. He leaned against the door, making it clear that he had plenty of time.

Lindsey glanced at the clock. Her break was over, but since the current situation centered around the murder of the library board president and directly involved herself and her staff, she felt like she could justify the time spent talking about it.

"Paula handed in her resignation," she said.

Sully took Robbie's vacated seat, leaning forward with his elbows on his knees, giving her his full attention.

"Ms. Cole ripped up her resignation letter and told her that I would figure out who killed Olive Boyle and that she wasn't to quit her job or worry," Lindsey said.

Sully's eyebrows rose, so she knew even he got the significance of Ms. Cole being the one to offer Lindsey up as the person most likely to figure out what had happened. Ms. Cole had criticized Lindsey repeatedly for being, as she put it, "a buttinsky."

"I know I promised not to investigate anything anymore," she said. "But I don't think I can walk away from this without at least trying to help."

Sully rose to his feet. He looked agitated. He opened his mouth, like he wanted to say something, and then closed his mouth. He paced to the corner and back. He looked at her then looked away and then resumed pacing.

Lindsey stayed right where she was. She didn't say a word but let him work it out for himself. She finished her cookie. He paced. She washed the cookie down with some tea. He stopped in the middle of her office and put his hands on his hips while he stared down at her.

"Okay."

Sully was the original big, strong, silent type. The kind of guy whose mere presence made Lindsey feel safe and secure. He always had an air of having things under control. Maybe it was because he spent his life on boats, focused on taming the sea, which made the rest of life's trials seem not so difficult. She didn't know. What she did know was that she had expected a heck of a lot more than "Okay."

"Okay what?"

"Okay, I get that this investigating thing is a part of who you are," he said.

"But?"

"But I don't think I can stand back and watch you put yourself in harm's way again," he said.

Lindsey felt her heart sink into her shoes. She had known this. It wasn't a surprise. He had said before that he didn't like that she put herself in danger. She just hadn't realized what a deal breaker it was. Sully was breaking up with her. Could she really blame him?

"I see," she said. Her voice was little more than a rasp, and she cleared her throat, trying to sound stronger than she felt. "I understand."

One of his eyebrows lifted higher than the other. "What do you understand?"

"That you don't want to be involved with a woman who puts herself in jeopardy," she said. "That's perfectly reasonable."

"I think so," he said. "Which really only gives us one solution."

"Yeah," she said.

She glanced down at the top of her desk and willed herself not to cry. He was about to dump her for the second time, and she was going to handle it like a champ, show no emotion, make a clean break—yeah, she was the lying-est liar of pants on fire liars.

This time their breakup was going to crush her, and she'd be lucky to get out of it with any dignity intact. Still, she couldn't fault him. He'd always been very clear about his dislike of the risks she took, and she couldn't in good conscience ask him to just put up with it.

She waited, but he didn't say anything, so she forced herself to glance up at him and meet his gaze when he broke her heart into a million pieces.

"The solution is that you and Heathcliff are going to have to move in with me—permanently," he said.

"I underst— Uh, what?" she asked.

"The only way I am going to be okay with this is if I know that you're safe under my watch," he said. "And the only way I can keep an eye on you is if you live with me. So there it is, our solution."

Lindsey gaped at him. Live with Sully? Every single cell in her body cried, *Yes!* It felt that right. Still, she said nothing as she tried to process this unexpected turn of events.

His blue gaze was steady, and then he winked at her. "Surprised you, didn't I?"

"I can honestly say I didn't see that coming."

"You didn't think I was going to break up with you, did you?"

"Well . . . yes."

He shook his head at her as if he couldn't believe that she didn't know him better than that.

"I just got you back," he said. "I'm not letting go of you—not now, not ever."

Lindsey rose from her seat and circled the desk.

She stood right in front of him. She met his gaze, resisting the urge to hug him close. She was still on the clock, after all.

"There are some things you should know, things I may not have been completely open about while we were dating, but if we live together, you'll find out," she said.

"Such as?" he asked. He gave her a considering look.

"I occasionally, like daily, use the floor as a hamper," she said.

"Ah, we're going for full disclosure here. That's fine, so I guess I have to admit I leave the seat up sometimes. Okay, more than sometimes," he said.

Lindsey laughed.

"I eat ice cream for dinner," she confessed.

"I drink milk straight out of the carton."

"I sing in the shower."

"I talk in my sleep."

She grinned at him. "I think I can work with that."

"Me, too," he said. "So, is this a yes?"

"Yes."

He grinned at her. A slash of white teeth and a curve of his lips just before he put his mouth on hers. It was swift and sweet, and Lindsey leaned against him for just the briefest moment.

"Want to talk it over at dinner tonight?" he asked.

"Sounds like a plan," she agreed.

He planted one more kiss on her and then left, closing the door softly behind him. Lindsey watched him wave at Beth and the other staff members as he made his way out of the building. She was going to live with him. Despite all of the stress and confusion of the past few days, she felt a bubble of happy float up inside of her.

It was really nice to have something to look forward to, especially if this investigation went wrong and she found herself or Paula in jail for a crime neither of them had committed.

She glanced out of her office window at Paula. Now that she had a future she desperately wanted to hang on to, it seemed even more imperative that they find the real killer, meaning she couldn't dodge it anymore. She had to demand answers.

Paula was going to have to explain about the letter of resignation, the lie she told about where she was right before they searched for Olive, in addition to a comment she made that Lindsey hadn't been able to let go of. Paula was going to have to come clean and tell her everything. There was simply too much at stake.

Lindsey walked out to the circulation desk, and when Paula glanced up, she smiled and said, "Can I talk to you for a moment?"

Paula's face was instantly wary, but she nodded and followed Lindsey into her office. Lindsey shut the door and gestured for Paula to take a seat while Lindsey sat on the edge of her desk. Paula clasped her hands in her lap as if to keep herself from fidgeting or maybe because she just needed something to hang on to and the only reliable thing she could find was herself. That broke Lindsey's heart just a little bit.

"Don't look worried," Lindsey said. "I just need to be clear on some things."

Paula stared at her. Her eyes were huge, as if trying to track an incoming hit.

"When you handed me your resignation, you said, 'I won't let it happen again.' What did you mean?"

Paula unclenched her hands and ran them up and down her thighs. She blew out a breath and turned her head away. Lindsey waited. She didn't want to pressure Paula, but if she was going to help her, she needed to know everything.

"When I was fourteen, I was . . ." She paused and took a breath. She held it for a few seconds and then blew it out as if it could pull the words loose. She continued on the same breath, "I was attacked by my stepbrother. He tried to . . . I fought him off . . . but he was too strong . . . he chased me into the kitchen and the only weapon I could find to defend myself was a knife. I stabbed him in the shoulder. No one believed me . . . that he tried to hurt me."

Her voice broke, and a shiver ran from the

top of her head all the way through her body. Lindsey didn't say a word. She held her breath and waited.

"Not even my mother."

"Oh, Paula." Lindsey felt her insides clench tight.

"Yeah, my mother didn't want to give up her new husband, and my stepfather refused to believe that his son . . . Well . . . long story short, I was sent away to live in a foster situation."

"Did you go to jail?"

"No, the state argued to lock me up for two years, but the judge—I think she believed me—put mc on probation for three years, and I had to do community service and go for a psych eval," she said. "My foster family was strict, but at least I was safe. I don't want to go through that misery all over. That's what I meant. I don't want to have people not believe me—not again."

"I'm so sorry." Lindsey moved and sat in the chair beside her. She wanted to hug her. She wanted to give her the love her own mother should have given her, but this was a work environment, so instead, she put her hand on Paula's shoulder and gave it a bracing squeeze. "Thank you for telling me."

"I didn't want anyone to know," Paula said. "Ever."

"But somehow Olive Boyle found out," Lindsey said. "Is this what she was talking about at the dinner when she referred to you as a violent criminal?"

"Probably," Paula said. "It's the only time I've ever been in any sort of trouble. I didn't kill my stepbrother, but I did hurt him pretty badly. It was self-defense."

"I hope you hurt him badly enough that he never tried to victimize another person ever again," Lindsey said. "That was very brave of fourteen-year-old you."

Paula glanced down at her hands. "Thanks."

"Now I hate to ask, but I need to know where you were right before we all went looking for Olive," Lindsey said.

Paula's eyes went wide again, and she paled. "I don't know what you mean."

"You weren't picking up the circulation desk like you told Emma and me, were you?"

Paula hung her head. "No."

"Where were you?"

"Hiding."

Lindsey felt her heart beat hard in her chest. Oh no, was this the moment that Paula confessed? Lindsey had been so sure she was innocent.

"I walked Hannah out to her car, because she had to leave early, and when I came back, I heard Olive calling my name," Paula said. "I was afraid. I didn't know what she was going to say or do, so I thought if I hid, then she'd give up and go away."

"Where were you?"

"I was in the storage closet at the back of the building. I waited until I thought she was gone. When I came out, well, I cut through the fiction area and that's when I found her."

Lindsey let out a shaky breath. Paula hadn't even known they'd been looking for Olive. What a shock that must have been.

"It's okay," Lindsey said. The lie held as much substance as dandelion fluff, and Paula clearly wasn't buying it.

"No, it's not." Paula's face crumpled with anguish. "Don't you see? If I hadn't hid from her, she wouldn't be dead. Whoever killed her only got her alone because she was searching for me and I hid."

Paula dropped her head into her hands and sobbed. This time, Lindsey didn't hesitate. She hugged Paula close and let her cry it out all over her shoulder. To carry such a load of guilt. It wasn't fair—not when Paula had suffered so much.

"Is that why you lied about where you were?" Lindsey snagged a tissue from the box on her desk and handed it to Paula.

"Yes, I didn't want everyone to know it was my fault," she said. She took the tissue and dabbed her nose and eyes. "If I hadn't been such a coward . . ."

"No, if Olive hadn't been such a bully, you

175

wouldn't have run away from her. This is not your fault. Listen, we're going to figure this out," Lindsey said. "I don't want you to worry. You're not alone this time, and you have people who believe you. I promise."

Lindsey spent the rest of the afternoon going over Robbie's list of suspects. Given the situation, she called an emergency meeting of the library board for the following afternoon. To her relief, everyone agreed to make time in their schedule to attend.

Next, she left her office to go find Milton. The library was Milton's home away from home, and not just because he'd been on the board, held a chess club there, or because his current ladylove, Ms. Cole, worked there. No, he had always been a fixture in the library, doing his yoga quietly in a corner. He brought a certain Zen to the place that Lindsey had never appreciated more than now.

His favorite spot to practice yoga was in one of the corners of the building where the floor space was clear and the tall windows looked out on the town park and the ocean beyond. Lindsey strode past the shelves toward that space. To her surprise, when she found Milton, he wasn't alone.

"Do you think that's healthy, all that blood rushing to his head?"

"Search me, but if he can do it, so can I."

"Marty, don't—"

"Don't worry, I got this."

Lindsey stepped into the cleared space to see an older, bald gentleman and a young man with a floppy head of black hair standing a few feet away from Milton, who was in the midst of a meditative inversion known as sirsasana, or a headstand to non-yogis.

"Hey, Oz, grab my feet," the bald man said.

"Aw, man, do I have to?"

Before Lindsey could stop him, the old guy bent over and put his hands on the ground. Then he kicked up his heels in the young man's direction. Caught off guard, the young man took a heel to the chin and went down with a grunt. The old guy fell on top of him, and the two of them landed in a tangle of arms and legs and swear words.

"Oh!" Lindsey cried. "Are you all right?"

She desperately did not want to have to fill out an incident report given that her last one had been about a murder. She could happily wait several more years before having to turn in another.

"Hey, I found them!" Mel, the cupcake baker from Arizona, called to Angie, her dark-haired friend, as the two women joined Lindsey by the windows. "Marty, Oz, what are you doing?"

"Getting kicked in the face by our guru here," Oz said. He shook his shaggy head.

"Hey, if you had caught my feet, I'd be all Zen

right now like that guy," Marty groused. "You harshed my mellow."

"Dude," Oz said. The one syllable carried an entire rebuke.

Lindsey glanced at Mel and Angie. They were clearly trying not to laugh and failing miserably.

"Are they always like this?" Lindsey asked.

"Yes," the two women said together.

Marty brushed himself off and reached out a hand to pull up Oz. "Better question, is he always like this?" He pointed to Milton, and Lindsey nodded.

"Hey, we heard that the woman who spoke at the dinner the other night was murdered here in the library. Is that true?" Angie asked.

"I'm afraid so," Lindsey said.

All four of the bakery people stepped away from her. Lindsey raised her eyebrows in surprise.

"Sorry, it's nothing personal," Mel said. "But not our circus, not our monkeys."

With that the group of bakers scuttled out of the library, leaving Lindsey puzzling after them. But really, she couldn't blame them. How often did cupcake bakers come up close and personal with murder? Probably never.

She approached Milton, who had not even cracked an eyelid during her exchange with the bakers, and crouched down beside him. If he was in some deep transcendental meditation, she didn't want to interrupt him. She settled in to wait, sitting with her legs folded to the side to accommodate her skirt. She pulled her phone out of her pocket to check her messages.

"Are they gone yet?"

"Ah!" Lindsey jumped and glanced at Milton to see his eyes open as he regarded her. "Yes, they're gone."

Milton took in a deep breath, and then as he exhaled, he moved out of his inversion until he was sitting on the ground beside Lindsey.

"I thought that old guy was going to do himself an injury," he said. He didn't acknowledge that the "old guy" was likely the same age as he was, and Lindsey opted not to mention it either.

"Me, too," she said. Then she laughed. "Good thing he managed to land on the young one."

Milton smiled. He gazed at her for a moment and then said, "But that's not why you're here."

"No."

"Is this about Olive Boyle?"

Lindsey nodded. She wasn't sure how to ask what she had in mind, but she had to clear Milton from Robbie's list for her own peace of mind if nothing else. She considered Milton her friend. She was going to go for blunt and hope he forgave her the harshness of the question.

"So, Milton, did you by any chance murder Olive Boyle?" she asked.

15

W hat?!" Milton cried. "Lindsey, I'm shocked. How can you even think that?"

"I don't," Lindsey said. "I'm just crossing you off the list of people who had an issue with Olive."

"What list?" he asked.

"The one Robbie made up," she said.

"And he put me on it?" Milton sounded outraged. "He knows I'm a pacifist."

"I'm on the list, too," Lindsey said. "If that helps at all."

Milton's shoulders dropped, and he ran a hand over his neatly trimmed silver goatee. "Actually, it does."

"I don't believe that you hurt Olive," Lindsey said. "Not at all, but Robbie spoke with Lydia Wilcox, and she suspects that Olive manipulated the rest of the board into voting for her."

Milton glanced away. It hit Lindsey then that she wasn't telling him anything he didn't know.

"You knew?"

"They came to see me," he said. "Olive did blackmail them. That's what she does . . . er . . . did."

"Over the library board presidency?" Lindsey

asked. "But it's such a nothing job. Oh, sorry, that came out wrong."

Milton shrugged. "Don't be. I had the same thought myself. But it turns out Olive had bigger plans. She told the library board members who did vote for her that she would remember their loyalty when she won the job of mayor next year."

"Wow, so it was true. She was planning a mayoral run." Lindsey blinked. She could not imagine the rich, spoiled, petulant Olive Boyle as mayor. She'd set their little town back fifty years at least.

"She just wanted to get on some of the local boards to prove her leadership before she went for the big job," Milton said. "I suspect she unconsciously felt that being mayor would sate her need for power, and she was willing to do whatever it took to get there. How's that for scary?"

"It's terrifying," Lindsey said.

"Agreed."

"Well, that's a game changer," she said. "And my list of suspects just got longer."

"And it includes the mayor," Milton said.

"Do we know if he knew about her plans?" she asked. "When I talked to Mayor Hensen at the dinner, he was still trying to keep out of her sights."

"Rumor has it, she threatened the mayor and his right-hand man, Herb Gunderson, in a private meeting they were having about taking down the fencing in front of her McMansion and opening the beach to the public," Milton said. "I believe she called Mayor Hensen a waste of space and vowed to take his job. Whether he took her seriously or not, I don't know."

"Either way, it had to be awkward."

"To say the least."

"How many people know about that meeting?"

"As of right now, probably the whole town."

"So, the library was just a stepping stone to greater things. Huh, I should have figured it wasn't her love of reading or people. But if the library board was a nothing position for her, then why was she so set upon going after me and my staff?"

"Well, it could be that she was systematically trying to get rid of anyone who was in tight with the mayor," he said.

"I never considered the mayor and myself that close. I mean we're cordial, but we're not weekend barbecuing together or anything."

"No, but from the outside looking in, it's easy to see that you and the library make him look very good. She probably didn't want that happening while she was running against him," he said.

"Thanks, Milton." Lindsey rose to her feet and squeezed his shoulder. "We'll figure it out."

"Am I off the list now?" he asked. "I never even gave you my alibi."

"Oh, right," she said. "Where were you when Olive was stabbed?"

"Waiting for Ginny, rather Eugenia . . . um. . . Ms. Cole," he said. "I was warming up the car for her since we were about to—"

"No!" Lindsey held up her hands in a stop motion. "Details are not necessary."

". . . go home and have tea," he finished.

"Oh."

"Just so."

"I'm going to go back to work now," she said.

Lindsey pointed behind her and beat a hasty retreat to her office. Milton had been dating Eugenia, aka the lemon, for about a year, but Lindsey had a feeling that no matter how much time passed, she would never get used to it. Thus, she'd likely keep stepping in it if she wasn't more careful.

As she rounded the circulation desk, she couldn't even look at Ms. Cole. How sweet that Milton called her Ginny. But sheesh, had she really thought Milton was going to disclose an intimate moment with the lemon? She was an idiot. Still, the idea mortified.

She stepped into her office just as the phone rang. She glanced at the display. It was Robbie. Oh no. She wondered if Emma had actually locked him up and he was calling for bail.

"Everything all right?" she asked, not even bothering to say hello.

"It's brilliant, actually," he said. "I was on my way to see Emma but saw those harpies of Olive's and decided to follow them instead. They are having a glass of wine at the Old Orchard Country Club. Come meet me and we can interrogate them."

"Amy, LeAnn and Kim?" Lindsey clarified.

"The same," he said. "And, frankly, they look quite conniving."

Lindsey glanced at the clock. The Old Orchard Country Club was on the outskirts of town, maybe a fifteen-minute bike ride from where she was. She did have to drop off the envelope of leave slips at the human resources department in the town hall, so it would just be a little, okay, a lot out of her way.

"I'm on my way," she said. "Stay out of sight until I get there."

"Don't you worry. I'm just the chap in the hat, holding down the bar," he said.

Lindsey grabbed the interoffice envelope, her sneakers, her handbag and her jacket and dashed out the door.

"Going to the town hall," she called as she popped her head out of her office. "I have my phone. Call me if you need me."

Ms. Cole nodded to signify that she'd heard while Paula gave her a faint smile and waved.

Shrugging into her jacket, Lindsey hurried out the door to the bike rack in the back of the

185

building. Dumping her handbag into the basket, she slipped off her heels and slid into her sneakers. She unlocked her red Schwinn cruiser and sped off as fast as she could.

Normally, she would have enjoyed a brisk ride with the wind in her hair and the breeze reddening her cheeks with a bite of cold, but at the moment it felt as if everything was too far away and she couldn't get there fast enough. She hopped off the bike while it was still moving, dumped it on the ground and hurried into the town hall. She ran into the human resources office and tossed her envelope into their intake basket.

"Hi, Lindsey, how are you?" Marcia Burges asked.

"Good, I'm good," Lindsey answered as she hurried back out the door. Marcia was lovely, but she did like to chat, and Lindsey had no time. "I have the new Fixer-Upper Mystery by Kate Carlisle coming in. I'll be sure to put it aside for you."

"Oh, yay, I just love the TV movies they've made out of her books, don't you?" Marcia asked.

"Never miss them!" Lindsey cried.

She let the door close behind her, and she raced back to her bike. She hefted it up and pushed off the curb. Now to get to the country club before the mean girls finished their wine. She pedaled hard all the way to the road that ran along the shore. She was out of breath and sweating, but still, she didn't slow down.

At the country club, the parking valet raised one eyebrow at her as she rode right up to his station and hopped off, handing him the handlebars so she could grab her handbag. She then switched out her sneakers for her heels.

"Take good care of it," she instructed with as much dignity as she could muster.

"Yes, ma'am," he said. She watched as he wheeled it over to his booth while shaking his head.

A doorman held open the large glass door for her, and she hurried inside. The massive entryway was old and stately with paneled walls and a fireplace. A staircase led upstairs to the floor above and Lindsey hurried past it, knowing from a previous visit that the club's restaurant and lounge were down the hallway toward the back of the building.

The hallway had painted portraits of some of the outstanding members over the years. Basically a rogues' gallery of stuffy old men.

There was one portrait toward the end that caught her eye, and Lindsey paused. With a bushy red mustache and wearing an old-fashioned golfer's cap with a pom-pom on top, "Happy" Lawrence smiled down at her as if he was amused by all of the club's goings-on. The date on the painted portrait was 1872.

Lindsey grinned. Maybe the old and stuffy ones had come after him because, judging by the glint in his eye, she would have put good money on Happy being a real cut-up.

She passed the restaurant, which was empty, as the waiters scrambled to set the tables for dinner. A glance through the door and she could see through the far windows out onto the golf course beyond. Golf. She straight up didn't get it. She'd heard it once described as "a good walk spoiled," and she'd never been able to think of it any other way.

The double doors to the lounge were ahead, and she slipped through them, trying not to draw any attention to herself. It appeared a group had just come in from the course, as they all stood around the bar having a deep discussion about the treacherous pond by the seventeenth hole.

Lindsey followed the line of the bar until she spotted a man sitting by himself wearing a cap. Robbie! She hurried over and slipped onto the empty stool beside him.

"Have they seen you?" she asked.

"Not yet," he said. "Luckily, this crew arrived and have been making quite the ruckus about a duck stealing a ball in the pond. Sounds like fiction to me."

"How did you get a drink and manage to linger until I arrived?" she asked. "Are you a member?"

"God, no," he said. "Like Groucho Marx, I'd never be a member of any club that would have me, but people just assume I'm a member because, well, I'm me."

Lindsey shook her head at him. "It's just a totally different world that you live in, isn't it?"

"What do you mean?" he asked.

"You can go wherever you want, do whatever you want, and no one questions it because you're Robbie Vine, famous actor," she said. "I can't even imagine being able to have that sort of access to the world."

"Huh, you think it's my fame?" he asked. "I always thought it was my extraordinary good looks."

Lindsey snorted.

"Really?" he asked with a feigned look of hurt. "It's not that funny."

She waved her hand at him. "Stop. Be serious. Where are the mean girls?"

Robbie jerked his head at the mirror behind the bar. It was angled so that it picked up the reflection of a booth nestled in an alcove in the corner. The mirror made it possible for Lindsey and Robbie to see the women but was at an awkward angle for the women to see them.

"How do you want to play this?" Lindsey asked. "Should we approach all casual-like and see if we can engage them in conversation?"

"No offense, pet, but I don't see them talking to

you," he said. "I think I'll have better luck on my own."

Lindsey thought about her earlier altercation with them. The three friends had made it pretty clear that they thought Lindsey had a solid reason to murder Olive, given that Olive had announced her plan to hire a replacement for Lindsey. In all honesty, if the situation were reversed, she would have found herself suspicious, too.

"Agreed. Let's use our phones so I can listen in on your conversation," she said.

Robbie nodded and pulled his phone out of his pocket. He called Lindsey and she answered. He then turned the volume off on his phone and slipped it into his shirt pocket so it would act as a microphone.

"Stay here," he said. "And keep your back to the ladies so they don't recognize you."

"Do we need a signal in case you get into trouble?" she asked.

A rocks glass was in front of him. He lifted it, and the smell of Jameson wafted up into Lindsey's nose. He tossed it back, and Lindsey looked at him warily.

"Nah. Don't worry, ducks. I've got this," he said.

She watched as he wobbled his way over toward the mean girls' table. Oh, brother. She had a bad feeling about this.

She pressed her phone to her ear, listening

intently. Robbie, in his usual larger-than-life way, paused beside the women's table.

"Well, hello, lovelies. Fancy finding a flock of pretty birds amidst all of these warthogs," he said.

Lindsey watched his reflection in the mirror as he didn't wait for an invitation but pushed his way into their booth.

"Hey, we're trying to talk here," Amy Ellers, the youngest of the group, complained. She waved her eyeglasses at him as if to admonish him. She had a heart-shaped face, pretty but not extraordinarily so; her black hair was cut in short layers around her face; and her eyes were sharp on Robbie since she was holding her trendy eyeglasses, a bit like a weapon. With glasses or without, Lindsey got the feeling Amy didn't miss much.

"Good thing I happen to be a fabulous conversationalist then," he said. "Love, has anyone ever told you that your eyes are the color of melted caramel?"

Lindsey rolled her eyes when she heard one of the women giggle. It wasn't Amy, who shoved her glasses back onto her nose as if they formed a barrier of protection between them.

"Go away," Amy snapped. "You're as tenacious as a sourdough."

"Did you just call me bread?" Robbie asked.

"No, where I come from, it's what you call old-timers who outstay their welcome."

191

"That's not very nice," Robbie said. He made to leave with an exaggerated sigh of disappointment.

"No, please stay," Kim MacInnes said. She had the typical middle-aged woman's requisite dyed blond hair, which she wore in a big knot on the top of her head. She was well-rounded with generous curves and dressed to show them off to their best advantage. She had a heavy hand with the makeup, as if long lashes and red lips could distract from the wrinkles puckering her lips and eyes.

"Sure, why not?" LeAnn Barnett asked. She was the oldest of the three. Skeletally thin, with light brown hair cut in a severe chin-length bob, and an overbite that wasn't hidden by her thin lips. She had an air of defeat about her that hung on her shoulders like an overcoat that was too big.

"Excellent. What are we drinking?" Robbie asked. He picked up the bottle of wine on their table and studied the label. "Here, mind if I borrow these?"

Lindsey watched in the mirror as he deftly snatched Amy's glasses from her face.

"Hey!" she protested.

Robbie squinted at the label through them. He frowned and handed them back to her. "Not much of a prescription there, love, is there?"

Amy shoved her glasses back on and snapped,

"They're for seeing distances, not close-up."

"Ah." Robbie nodded, sounding unperturbed. "What are we drinking to then? Wealth? Power? Eternal youth?"

Kim giggled. Amy glared. LeAnn stared morosely into her glass.

"To the memory of our friend, Olive, if you must know," Amy said. Her tone was condemning. Robbie seemed not to notice.

"Ah, that was a tragedy," he said. "Have the police offered any ideas as to who they think might have done it?"

"None," Amy snapped. Her voice sounded equal parts disgusted and frustrated. "Of course when you are besties with the chief of police that probably gets you a pass."

"Oy, what are you saying there?" Robbie sounded irritated.

Lindsey watched in the mirror as Kim wrapped an arm around him, trying to soothe him. He wasn't having any of it, however, and leaned aggressively over the table toward Amy.

"Briar Creek's chief of police is one of the finest in the state," he said. "She would never let a criminal go, whether the person was her friend or not."

Amy glared back. "Says you."

"Damn right, says me," he snarled.

Lindsey wondered if she needed to step in. Robbie was letting his defense of his girlfriend get in the way of his interrogation. While she appreciated the sentiment, she really didn't want to miss the opportunity to find out more about these women and their relationship to Olive.

"She saved your life a while back, didn't she?" LeAnn asked. She was giving Robbie a curious glance.

"Yeah," he said. He seemed to realize he was on shaky ground. Not many people knew that he and Emma were a couple, and he'd lose his chance to question these women if they figured it out. "So, I feel a certain loyalty there."

"Perfectly understandable," Kim said. She wrapped herself more tightly about him. "I, for one, am going to thank her the next time I see her."

Robbie seemed to clue in to the fact that Kim's intentions were more than friendly, and he eased himself out of her grip.

"So, you haven't told me, who do you suspect in the murder of your friend Olive?" he asked.

The three women exchanged a glance as if trying to decide whether to talk to him or not. Finally, Amy shrugged.

"It won't matter if we tell him," she said. "Given what we told her, I'm sure Chief Plewicki is on her way to the library to take her into custody right now."

Lindsey felt her heart triple thump in her chest. Who? Who was Emma going to arrest? She clutched the phone closer to her ear, trying to hear over the rushing sound in her ears.

"And who would *she* be?" Robbie asked.

"That library girl Paula Turner, of course," Amy said. "Olive had something on her, something bad that would cost that nosy librarian her job for hiring her and ruin Paula Turner at the same time. I'm sure Paula killed Olive to shut her up, and the police think so, too."

Lindsey dropped the phone from her ear. She didn't wait to see what Robbie was going to do or how he was going to extricate himself from those women. She had to get back to the library. Pronto!

16

Lindsey thrust a ten-dollar bill at the valet as he parked her bike in front of her. She checked her messages, feeling her panic ebb when she saw a new text from one of her staff. She read it quickly with great relief. Still, she knew a situation was brewing, and she needed to be there. She hopped on her bike, hoping she could get back to the library in time.

While pedaling, she tried to call the circulation desk, but the call went right to the recorded message that announced the library's hours. The same thing happened when she called the reference desk. Beth wasn't answering her cell phone, and Lindsey had a moment of panic that the entire library had fallen into a sinkhole while she was gone, because she could not for the life of her figure out why no one was answering their phone. Maddening!

She cut through the neighborhood, trying to shave some time off of the ride. She was hot and sweaty and the last hill about killed her, but she didn't stop pedaling or pause to catch her breath. She had just pulled out onto Main Street, when a car pulled up alongside of her and she recognized Robbie's strawberry blond head as he leaned over the console from the driver's side and glanced at her through the open window on the passenger's side.

"Did you hear?" he asked.

"Yes," she cried. Then she gestured at the library up ahead. "Go!"

With a nod, he stepped on the gas and sped right up to the large stone building at the end of the street. He parked in front and jogged up the walkway just as Lindsey pedaled to a stop in front of the building. Barely taking the time to grab her purse, she ditched the bike on its side and bolted into the library.

She was sucking in great gulps of air, and her heart was beating triple time. She had to pause to bend over and catch her breath.

"There's no time for that," Robbie cried.

He grabbed her elbow and dragged her forward into the main room of the library. Lindsey would have argued that breathing wasn't something a person needed to make time for, but she had no breath.

When they approached the circulation desk, it was to find Emma having a stare-down with Beth. With her black hair in two pigtails on the top of her head, while wearing a red sweatshirt with black dots on the back and a pair of strap-on black wings on her back, Beth looked about as intimidating as a ladybug possibly could, which was to say not very.

"Beth, I understand your concern, I do," Emma

said. "But this isn't negotiable. I'm here to speak with Paula. Now where is she?"

"Wait!" Lindsey panted. "Let's talk."

Emma spun around to see Lindsey with Robbie. Her eyebrows rose, but she didn't say anything about the two of them being together and obviously out of breath.

"We were racing," Lindsey explained anyway.

"Racing?" Emma asked.

"Yeah," Lindsey wheezed. "His car versus my bike. Big fun."

Robbie looked at her, and she nudged him with her elbow.

"Right, racing," he said. He rubbed his hand over the sore spot on his side and gave her a look to let her know she didn't need to poke him that hard.

Sorry. She mouthed the word then turned back to Emma.

"What can I help you with, Emma?" she asked.

"I'm looking for Paula, actually."

"Sure, okay," Lindsey said. "She should be around here somewhere. Follow me. We'll find her."

She ignored Beth's outraged flap of wings and Ms. Cole's huff of displeasure. They didn't know that she'd just received a text from Paula, telling her that she'd be taking some personal leave time effective immediately.

Emma was in uniform and had her radio in a holster on her shoulder. Without taking her eyes off of Lindsey, she said, "Suspect is in the building. Are all points of entry being monitored?"

"Yes, Chief," several different voices responded.

Lindsey felt her heart sink. This was serious. Paula may have put off the inevitable, but she was going to be taken into custody, and there was nothing Lindsey could do about it.

"Can we talk first?" Lindsey asked.

"It won't change anything," Emma said.

Lindsey nodded. She led the way to her office, and Emma fell into step beside her. When Robbie would have joined them, Emma turned back and said, "Not you."

"But—"

"No."

As soon as the door closed after them, Lindsey turned to face the chief of police. She crossed her arms over her chest as if that gave what she was about to say more authority.

"Paula didn't murder Olive," Lindsey said.

"Can you prove that?"

"No."

Emma studied her. It was her cop face. The one that didn't miss even the smallest facial tic.

"You knew, didn't you?" Emma asked. "About her past?"

It was pointless to lie. Lindsey nodded. "She told me about the incident with her family just this morning."

"Incident? She stabbed her stepbrother," Emma said. "She was taken from her home for it."

"She was defending herself from assault by him," Lindsey argued.

"That's not what her parents said," Emma argued.

"Yeah, it seems her stepfather couldn't believe his son would do anything like that," Lindsey said. "I'd be curious to see how the stepfather has treated her mother all these years. You know, any calls for a domestic disturbance."

Emma studied her and then gave a slow nod. "I'm ahead of you on that one. There have been calls, and the husband has been taken into custody a few times, but the wife never presses charges."

"And Paula grew up in that. Still think the stepbrother didn't attack her?"

"That's a fair question, which would be easier to answer if I could talk to Paula."

Lindsey couldn't argue the reasoning. Still, she had questions. "How did you find out about Paula's past? I didn't think there'd be a record of it if she was a juvenile," Lindsey said.

"I didn't go through the courts," Emma said. "I got an anonymous tip, and then I started calling people where she went to high school."

Lindsey stared at her for a moment. "A tip? Isn't that convenient?"

"I don't turn away information, no matter where it comes from. Besides, she lied about where she was just before Olive was found, so I did some digging into her background, which I would have done with or without the tip," Emma said. "But because of the tip, I spoke with one of her old teachers, one who was more than happy to share, because she believed Paula had been wrongly accused and that her parents were worthless. She argued quite strongly on Paula's behalf. Now here's a question for you: Why didn't you tell me all of this as soon as you found out?"

"Would it have made any difference or would you just have arrested her sooner?" Lindsey asked.

"I'm not arresting her. I'm taking her in for questioning," Emma said. "There's a difference."

"Not to Paula."

"I'll be as gentle as I can, but this is a murder investigation, Lindsey. I have to do my job. I have to find out who killed Olive Boyle. Besides, by questioning her, I'm protecting her."

"How do you figure?"

"If she's straight with me, then I can remove her from my suspect list," Emma said. "She'd be cleared."

"Maybe, but given that she's been wrongly

accused before, I doubt that's a risk she wants to take."

Emma studied her for a moment. "How did you and Robbie know I was here?"

"We were out and about." Lindsey went for vague. "I heard that you were coming here and wanted to see what was up."

"Uh-huh, so you ran *into* the building?" Emma asked. "Most people run away when I show up."

"Well, I wanted to talk to you," Lindsey said.

"Who told you I was coming here? Robbie?"

Lindsey shook her head. "It's not important."

"It is to me," Emma said. "The last thing I need is people spreading rumors."

"Fine. Olive's friends seemed to think you were going to arrest Paula for murdering Olive."

Emma frowned. "When were you hanging out with Amy, LeAnn and Kim?"

"We weren't hanging out exactly," Lindsey said.

"What was it exactly?"

"It was more like Robbie ran into them at the country club, and while he was chatting them up, I listened through my phone," Lindsey said.

"Oh. My. God." Emma scrubbed at her face with her hand as if she could wipe away the stupid. "Why would you go anywhere near them?"

"Because . . ." Lindsey had nothing. There was no answer to this question that would not make Emma less cranky with her.

"You're investigating Olive's murder, aren't you?"

"Um, no . . . Maybe . . . Yeah," Lindsey said. She dropped into her seat behind her desk as the exhaustion from the bike ride and the stress of the past few minutes took her out at the knees.

"I didn't want to, but Paula . . . and Robbie . . ."

"Yeah, I get it," Emma said as she sat in the chair across from her. "The man gets me to do things . . . Well, never mind."

"If you're interviewing Paula, I have to ask: Am I a person of interest in Olive's murder as well?" Lindsey asked. "I mean, I was there when the body was found, too."

"Everyone is a person of interest until I have the perp locked up," Emma said.

"Not exactly the comforting answer I was looking for."

"Well, I haven't locked you up yet, so there's your comfort."

"Any word from the medical examiner?"

"Not yet, and even if there was—"

"You wouldn't tell me," Lindsey finished for her. She glanced at the clock. She figured enough time had passed by now.

"Um, as to your looking for Paula," she began.

Sensing she was about to hear something she'd rather not, Emma sat up straight in her chair.

"What?" she asked.

"Paula sent me a text saying she was taking some personal time," Lindsey said.

"You knew this and you kept me here chatting?" Emma cried as she jumped to her feet. "You know I could throw the book at you for impeding an investigation."

"She was gone before you got here," Lindsey said. "And you won't do that."

"Won't I?" Emma raised an eyebrow.

"No, because I think you don't believe Paula is guilty any more than I do," Lindsey said.

The two women stared at each other. Lindsey held her breath. Emma could be legitimately furious with her, could even take her in if she chose, but Lindsey suspected what she said was true. Emma didn't really believe Paula was the killer. It was too convenient, too easy, almost as if someone was using Paula and her past to cover their own tracks.

"I'm going to have to bring her in sooner or later."

"Go for later," Lindsey said. "Surely, there are other leads to follow."

"I'm not sharing any with you," Emma said. She studied Lindsey for a moment. "Are you going to Olive's funeral tomorrow morning?"

"She was the president of the library board, and I'm the library director. I think I have to go."

Emma was silent for a moment and then said, "A lot of murderers go to their vic's funerals."

Lindsey met the police chief's steady brown gaze. She wasn't sure what Emma was trying to say, but it made her uncomfortable. Then she saw the wicked twist to Emma's lips.

"You're teasing me? *Now?*"

Emma shrugged. "You're running around town with my boyfriend. Seems appropriate pay-back."

She glanced at Lindsey, tipped her head to the side and then put her finger to her lips. Lindsey watched as Emma stealthily crept to the door, which she yanked open in one smooth move. Robbie tumbled into the office and sprawled onto the floor.

"Oy, was that nice?" he asked.

"Eavesdropping?" Emma countered. She put her hands on her hips and glared down at him.

"Well, it's not like you answer my questions when I ask," he said. "Medical examiner, did you say?"

"Forget it," she said. "When I get the report, I am not sharing it with you. Detective Trimble and I will determine the best course of action after the report."

"Detective Trimble and I," Robbie mimicked her. It was not flattering. "I'll tell you what I'd like to do with Detective Trimble."

"Oh, wow, you're jealous," Lindsey said.

Robbie turned to face her. "I am not. I've never been jealous a day in my life. I don't get jealous."

"He did sound jealous, didn't he?" Emma asked, looking pretty delighted.

"Yes," Lindsey answered at the same time Robbie said, "No."

Emma grinned.

"I'll see you at the funeral tomorrow," she said to Lindsey. "In the meantime, please steer clear. I know you won't, but I feel compelled to say it anyway."

"I'll try," Lindsey said. It was the best she could do.

"And you," Emma rounded on Robbie. "What is this Lindsey tells me that you were at the country club, talking to Olive's friends? And don't tell me you were there for the golf—you hate golf."

"Maybe I changed my mind," he protested.

Emma led the way out the door, and he followed.

"You and Lindsey were butting into my investigation," Emma said. "And don't pretend you weren't."

"Fine," he said. "But if you would just tell me what's happening, I wouldn't have to now, would I?"

Lindsey watched as they kept arguing all the way out the front doors of the library and onto the sidewalk. The sparks flying between them were enough to light the small community for at least a week.

"Is it just me or do they enjoy that?" Beth asked. She had put away her wings but still had on her red sweatshirt with the dots.

"Oh, they do," Lindsey said. "I'll bet you five bucks he kisses her in five, four; wait, there he goes, never mind."

They both stared as Robbie raised his hands in frustration and then reached out, grabbed Emma's shoulders, pulled her close and planted one on her.

"Sucker's bet," Beth said. "Those two are made for each other."

"Since she didn't zap him with her Taser, I have to agree."

A ruckus in the children's area drew Beth's attention, and she hurried over to her side of the library, giving Lindsey a quick wave on her way.

Lindsey glanced back out the glass doors and saw Robbie and Emma walking down the sidewalk, holding hands. The sight made her happy way down deep. And not for nothing, but maybe Robbie could work his magic on Emma and get a sneak peek at the medical examiner's report when it came in.

There was so much they could learn from the examination: whether the assailant was male or female, left- or right-handed, how tall they were. And that was just the obvious stuff. Once the lab work kicked in, there would be so much more.

Lindsey could only hope that whatever the

medical examiner discovered, it cleared Paula from suspicion. What a nightmare for Paula to have put so much distance between herself and her past only to have it come roaring back up on her.

It wasn't right. It wasn't fair, and Lindsey was going to do everything in her power to see that Paula was allowed to keep her past private.

Olive Boyle's funeral was a packed house with a restless crowd, as if they were expecting some sort of spectacle like the murderer confessing or the police arresting someone in the middle of the eulogy. They were woefully disappointed. At the end of the service, the small church in the center of town regurgitated bodies like a seagull horking up its lunch.

From her spot at the back with the library board, Lindsey saw Olive's three friends sitting stiffly in the first pew, and behind them a man and woman who sat far enough apart to wedge two more bodies in between them. They were never introduced during the brief service, and Lindsey wondered if they were the ex-husband and the sister Robbie had included on his list of suspects. There was only one way to find out.

The reception after the service was held at Olive's house and hosted by her friends. When she arrived, Lindsey was surprised to find that the same people who'd crammed into the church were now shuffling into Olive's big house on the water. Given that Olive had not been well-liked—understatement—she couldn't figure why so many people had turned out. Free food? Free booze? Morbid curiosity?

Robbie walked beside her, since they'd taken his car, and he was wearing a somber dark suit that matched her standard black funeral dress. He scanned the crowd, studying the faces as if the killer would be visible to the naked eye. Lindsey couldn't fault him, since she was pretty much doing the same thing.

"Where's the buoy boy?" he asked as they stood in line to enter the house.

"Working," she said. "Autumn is a big season for boat tours around the islands with the leaves changing and all."

"He doesn't mind that you're here?" Robbie said. "I thought he was set on you not investigating anymore."

"We came to an understanding about that," Lindsey said. She glanced at him and then said, "We're moving in together."

Robbie halted in midstep and stared at her. In a perfect teen girl voice, he said, "Shut up."

Lindsey chuckled and then quickly stifled it. Funeral! She shrugged and said, "He says he can handle my investigating if he knows that at night I will come home to him where I will be safe."

"He's sickening," Robbie said with disgust.

"In the best possible way," Lindsey agreed.

The line began to move more quickly, and they hurried their pace. As they were climbing the front steps, Robbie leaned close and said, "I'm happy for you two. I really am."

Lindsey smiled at him. "Thanks."

Olive's house was massive. Perched right on the edge of the water with a view of the Thumb Islands and Long Island Sound, it was three stories of stone and glass. Lindsey couldn't even wrap her head around what the taxes and insurance must cost. As far as she knew, Olive didn't work, and even if she had won the job of mayor in the next election, it certainly wouldn't pay enough for this not-so-humble abode.

"Blimey, who do you suppose she had to kill to buy a place like this?" Robbie muttered.

"You!" Amy Ellers stood in the doorway, glaring at them. "How dare you show your face here?"

17

R eally?" Robbie asked. "I've been told my face is my best feature."

"Not you. Her!" Amy snapped.

Lindsey felt a hot flush creep into her face. Still, she refused to be cowed or bullied by accusations that were untrue.

"Olive was on my library board," Lindsey said. "We may have had our differences, but I certainly wished her no harm."

"Is that what you told yourself when you were stabbing her with that steak knife?" Amy asked.

"Whoa, easy there, pet," Robbie said. "There's no call to make unsubstantiated accusations like that."

"Isn't there?" Amy asked.

"No, there really isn't," he said. "Lindsey didn't hurt Olive, and you know that as well as I do. I can see that you're hurting, but taking it out on her won't bring Olive back."

Amy glared at them. She didn't say anything but instead jerked her head in the direction of the house, signaling that they could enter.

Once they crossed the threshold, Lindsey let out a sigh of relief. She had thought Amy was going to make a scene and deny them entrance.

Not that she expected to find some fabulous clue as to who had murdered Olive Boyle, but maybe they'd get lucky. Besides, as Emma had said, murderers did show up at their victims' funerals sometimes, so maybe they'd see someone who was singularly out of place.

For her own part, Lindsey found that she was uncomfortable with the one-dimensional image she had of Olive. Perpetually unhappy and rather unkind to everyone she met was how Olive was perceived. Lindsey couldn't help but hope that inside her house there might be a glimpse of something more, a softer, gentler Olive.

Much like the church, the house was standing room only. Lindsey saw Mayor Hensen in attendance. She couldn't decide if he actually looked relieved or if she was just projecting what she thought he was feeling. He had a big smile of very white teeth, so it was hard to tell, as she was usually blinded by the flash.

She scanned the room. Although she had been able to spot them at the church, she did not see the other members of the library board here. Milton was the only one in attendance, and he was standing beside Ms. Cole as they chatted with Carrie Rushton, who was representing the Friends of the Library.

Beyond the people, Lindsey surveyed the rooms. It was an open floor plan, so one room blended seamlessly into another. She looked at the art on the walls, the tabletops, the bookshelves. It was all very sparse, and very coordinated. The colors of the book spines on the shelves matched the colors used in the contemporary seascape hanging on the wall beside the bookcase.

There were no family photographs to be seen, no photographs of anyone at all, in fact. The house was as cold and as impersonal as Olive had been. Lindsey felt a shiver run over her skin. Maybe this was just in the formal downstairs area. Surely, above in her bedroom there would be something that signified a person had actually lived here.

"I'm going upstairs," she whispered to Robbie. "Cover me."

"All right. Wait, what?" he asked.

"Just do it," she said.

The staircase that led upstairs was near the front door. Lindsey dragged Robbie in that direction. When they spotted Kim MacInnes talking to Amy, Lindsey gave him a push, and Robbie broke into their conversation. He pivoted so that they had to turn their backs to the staircase to talk to him. He gave a small nod, and Lindsey took this as her signal to go.

She pressed herself against the wall and hurried upstairs. If anyone asked, she figured she'd just say she was using the bathroom. The rooms upstairs were massive, so there weren't many of them. She began looking in the master bed-room. It was an obsessive-compulsive person's dream. There wasn't a bit of clutter anywhere. Everything was shiny, clean and tidy. Even the clothes in the walk-in closet were hung in color-coordinated groupings and then broken into subsets by season.

There were no pictures on the dresser or the nightstand. The art hanging on the walls looked pricey but impersonal. There was nothing here. Lindsey moved on to the guest bedrooms and found more of the same. They were neat and tidy and completely lacking in personality. She passed the laundry room and approached the door to the final room on this level, Olive's office.

She stood outside and listened for a bit. She wanted to make sure no one was coming to use the bathroom. All was quiet.

She turned the knob and pushed open the door. A laptop was folded shut on top of a very nice antique cherrywood desk. She wondered why the police hadn't taken the computer. Wouldn't they want to go through all of Olive's emails and accounts to ascertain if there was someone in her life who posed a threat and wanted her dead? She wished she could ask Emma about it, but, of course, then she'd have to admit what she was doing. Nuts!

She checked the bookcase, hoping to see something that would signify Olive was the person who lived here. A tiny framed photograph caught her eye. She snatched it up, feeling like the worst sort of voyeur.

Inside was a picture of a handsome man and a lovely woman. It took Lindsey a second to place the woman. It was Olive in a wedding dress standing next to a man in a tuxedo. This must be her ex-husband. It seemed odd, trying to picture Olive married, even though here Lindsey was holding the evidence in her hand. Olive was of an age for having been married, and it made sense, since she didn't work, that a nice divorce settlement could have landed her this house.

So, what had happened to Olive's husband? Where was he? Why did she have a picture of him in her office if they were no more? Was he the man from the funeral? Lindsey couldn't tell since she'd only seen him from the back.

She glanced around the room. There was a pretty blue sweater draped over the back of the office chair as if this room was always cold and Olive liked to have a sweater available. It gave the space a more lived-in look than anywhere else in the house.

Was that why the one photograph of Olive with somebody else was in this room? Perhaps this was her sanctuary more than anywhere else in a place that was more a showplace than home. That bothered Lindsey.

She thought of her own apartment with

photos of her family and friends everywhere, Heathcliff's chew toys scattered, books stacked in every nook and cranny and her grandmother's afghan draped on the back of the couch.

It was messy, sure, but it was homey. Her thoughts then strayed to Sully and his house. His place had the same lived-in look right down to having some of Heathcliff's toys scattered across his living room floor. That thought made her smile. She took it as a sign that moving in together was the right thing to do.

A footstep sounded in the hallway, and Lindsey shook herself out of her reverie. It would not do to be caught upstairs in any room other than the bathroom. She replaced the photo on the bookcase and made her way to the hall. She paused at the door, listening for the footsteps she was certain she'd heard.

She waited, but there was no more sound. She eased out of the room and lingered in the doorway, glancing in both directions before she stepped out. Seeing no one, she moved forward toward the bathroom.

"Find what you were looking for?"

"Ah!" Lindsey yelped and jumped. LeAnn moved around the half-open doorway of the bathroom directly across the hall from her. Obviously, she had been waiting for Lindsey to come out of the office.

Lindsey put her hand over her heart and

gave LeAnn a weak smile. "You startled me."

"I'll bet. Funny how being caught snooping will do that to you."

"I wasn't," Lindsey protested. "I was just looking for the bathroom, and when I found it, someone was already inside. I didn't want to walk all the way back downstairs, so I was checking out the bookcase in the room right there. The librarian in me just can't pass up a bookcase."

"Is that so?" LeAnn asked. "Well, the librarian in you has also worn out her welcome. Let's go."

"But the bathroom." Lindsey pointed to the room behind LeAnn.

"I hear they have them at the public library," LeAnn said. "Probably, you could use one there since you're leaving now."

Lindsey had to give her points for not being a pushover. She debated asking her about Olive's ex-husband, but she doubted that LeAnn would be eager to tell her anything.

Together they made their way down the stairs. Lindsey scanned the visible faces for Robbie but didn't see him nearby. She didn't know how to enlighten him about her current predicament. She didn't want to text him in from of LeAnn. The ladies seemed to like Robbie, and if he could get information where Lindsey couldn't, then she didn't want to hamper his future ability to question these women by letting LeAnn know that he was her ride.

"What is this, an event for party crashers?" LeAnn snapped. She stomped down the stairs, passing Lindsey, who noted LeAnn was clenching her hands into fists at her sides.

"Get out!" LeAnn spat as she approached a man in an overcoat who was just coming inside. "You're not welcome here."

"LeAnn, you know that's not true," the man said.

He glanced up, and Lindsey caught her breath. Staring back at LeAnn was the man in the photograph, the man in the tux who'd been standing next to Olive in the tiny photo upstairs. Her ex-husband?

"It is true," LeAnn argued. "Olive was very clear about how much she loathed you. If she'd left us a list of people to ban from her service, you'd be on the top of it."

"Yeah, this week," he said. His voice sounded full of weary resignation. "You know what Olive was like—one minute she was running to me and the next she was running over me. When I married her, it was because I thought she'd never be dull. Turns out dull is highly underrated."

"Well, I'm sure you've discovered the joy of dull-hood with wife number two," LeAnn snapped.

"Leave Molly out of it. She's done nothing to you," he said. His tone held a strong note of warning, and a flash of unease passed over LeAnn's face.

"Fine," she said. "But we know it's true. Your wife isn't half the woman Olive was."

"The crazy half, for sure," the man muttered.

Lindsey almost laughed, but she didn't want to get tossed out just yet. She glanced at her phone. She had only a few more minutes before she had to get back to the library for the library board meeting.

A name. She needed this guy's name, before he was kicked to the curb just like her. He was here alone, but he wore a wedding ring on his left hand, verifying that he was still married to wife number two, so why had he felt compelled to attend the funeral of his ex, who, judging by what Lindsey knew of her, redefined the word *vengeance?*

"I'm going to pay my respects to some of our old friends," he said. "No matter what happened between Olive and me during our marriage and our divorce, she was my first love, and that means something."

LeAnn stared at him, and then she gave him a slow nod. "All right, Doc, but be quick."

Doctor! Lindsey wanted to pump her fist, but she didn't. With a nod, the man moved past her into the house.

Lindsey saw Robbie chatting up some other guests in the corner. She stared until he glanced up. When she caught his eye, she jerked her head in the direction of the door. He nodded.

"So, was Boyle Olive's married name?" Lindsey asked.

LeAnn just stared at her.

"Okay, then," Lindsey said.

LeAnn gestured to the door. "Good-bye."

Lindsey glanced over her shoulder to see Robbie making his way toward her. She stepped outside into the overcast, chilly day and was thankful that her black funeral dress had long sleeves.

She walked down the steps and waited for Robbie on the curb. Parking had been at a premium, and they had parked one street over.

"What did you get?" he asked when he joined her.

"Observed the doctor ex-husband," she said. "And you?"

"Found the sister, a Margaret Davidson," he said.

"Really? Was she at the service?"

They began to walk down the sidewalk to Robbie's car.

"The pew behind the mean girls, sitting next to the ex-husband," he said. "No seat of honor for her, as the two sisters are . . . were estranged. How about the ex? Did you get a read on him? Potential killer?"

"No idea. He's remarried, so I can't imagine what would motivate him," she said. "Although, he sounded . . . Well, it seemed as if he still had feelings for her."

"Did his wife come with him?"

"Nope."

"Interesting. So, who should we start with first?"

"I have a meeting with the library board this afternoon," she said. "Then I'm thinking I'd like to visit the ex-husband, Dr. Boyle I believe his name is. Even if he had no reason to kill her, it's odd that literally the only photo on display in the entire house is one of the two of them on their wedding day."

"Huh, I don't know what to make of that," he said. "Not one person in there seemed to have anything nice to say about Olive. Even her friends seemed to struggle with the task."

"Why do you suppose they were her friends then?"

"Honestly, the only thing the four of them seem to have in common is that they all live in big houses on this street," he said. He stopped walking and turned to look at Lindsey. His eyes were wide. "All four live on this street. All four are women, Olive and Kim are divorced, Amy is single, as far as I can tell, and LeAnn's husband hasn't been seen in months. So all four are seemingly living alone. It's like a strange sorority of sad single women."

"We need to find out more about the friends," Lindsey said.

"Kim seems to like me," he said. "I could start with her."

"Okay, but be careful," Lindsey said. "You don't want to put your relationship with Emma in jeopardy over this."

"Emma would understand," he said.

Lindsey looked at him as if he'd recently hit his head and lost some cognitive function. "No, she wouldn't."

Robbie shook her off, unlocking her door and opening it so she could climb into the car. They drove back to the library in silence, each mulling over their list of suspects.

"Pick you up after work?" he asked as he pulled up beside the library.

"Perfect," she said. "I'll have an address for the ex by then."

"See ya, Sherlock."

"Later, Watson."

Lindsey hurried into the library as Robbie sped away. Just stepping through the doors eased the tension that had been coursing through her since the funeral began this morning.

It had been uncomfortable to see no one moved to tears by Olive's death. Not that she enjoyed seeing other people's pain, but usually at a funeral there was a sense of loss and grief. With Olive's service, the overwhelming feelings had been morbid curiosity mingled with the feeling of relief. What a waste to live a life that only touched others in a negative way.

It also made the task of trying to determine who had murdered Olive more daunting. Usually, in a murder, it was hard to find a suspect, but this time there was an overabundance of people with a grudge, including her very own library board.

"How did it go with the board?" Robbie asked.

"Every single one of them had a solid alibi for where they were at the time of Olive's death," Lindsey said.

"So, annoying?"

"Exactly."

They were back in his car headed toward the nearby town of Guilford. Lindsey had tracked down Olive's ex-husband to a residence there. Doctor Boyle and his wife, Molly, lived in yet another large house by the water with their two teenage children.

Apparently, Kyle and Olive Boyle had divorced twenty years ago. According to the local papers, the divorce had been instigated by Kyle, and the settlement Olive had demanded had been astronomical. Lindsey couldn't help but think that if Kyle had wanted to murder Olive, it would have been when she was trying to gut his fortune, most of which had been inherited. Why would he kill her now?

Then again, if he didn't kill her, he might have a lead on who did. They just had to convince

Dr. Boyle to talk to them, and Lindsey had the perfect way to make that happen.

Robbie pulled into the circular driveway in front of the two-story white colonial with black shutters. Cornstalks and pumpkins decorated the shallow steps that led up to the wide wooden red front door.

Lindsey led the way, pressing the doorbell without hesitation. She and Robbie stood on the stoop, waiting. She strained to hear if anyone was approaching. It was late afternoon, and there were two high-end vehicles, one of which was a very luxurious looking minivan, if that was even possible, parked in the driveway, so she assumed Dr. Boyle was home.

Robbie opened his mouth to speak just as they heard someone unlock the door. A middle-aged woman, with long curly blond hair and big blue eyes, stared back at them as if she was trying to determine if they were selling something or not.

Robbie glanced between Lindsey and the woman and raised one eyebrow. Lindsey had told him that Olive had called her a husband stealer during their altercation at the Dinner in the Stacks event. Given the marked similarity between this woman and Lindsey, in height, build and hair color, it was not hard to figure out why Olive might have had an issue with Lindsey. She looked like his second wife.

"Hello, Mrs. Boyle," Lindsey greeted the

woman, assuming that she was in fact his wife, Molly, the one he had told LeAnn not to speak of when LeAnn snapped at him at the post-funeral reception.

"Hi. May I help you?" Molly asked. She looked at Lindsey and then at Robbie. She blinked. Her mouth opened and then it closed and then it fell open again.

"Oh my God! It's you!" She slammed the door in their faces. She yanked it open again and screeched, "Don't move!" Then she slammed it again.

18

Lindsey slowly pivoted her head to look at Robbie.

"Fan of yours?" she asked.

He shrugged with a look of complete bafflement, but she could see the pleased smile lurking just beneath the surface.

"It never gets old being you, does it?" she asked.

"Nope. Look on the bright side: my celebrity is going to get us in."

"Perhaps, or maybe arrested," she said.

The door was yanked open again, and the woman waved for them to enter. She was breathless and her hair was mussed. Her face was bright red, and she looked to be a bit winded. She had also managed to change from her oversize sweatshirt and yoga pants to a silk blouse and slacks, with pearls at her throat and fresh lipstick.

"Please come in. Can I get you anything, coffee, tea, a sandwich, cookies?" She bounced on her feet. "Can I please take a picture with you, Mr. Vine?"

The words came at them like gunfire, and Lindsey was still turning over the offer of a sandwich when the woman thrust her phone into Lindsey's hands and stood beside Robbie for a photo op. Lindsey took several pictures, and the woman snatched back her phone to look at them.

"My bunco group is never going to believe that I had Robbie Vine in my house!" She looked up from her phone to stare at them with delight.

Several awkward seconds passed—well, awkward for Lindsey. Robbie seemed to be just fine basking in the adoration of the woman who was equally happy to adore. When the lovefest showed no signs of breaking up, Lindsey felt it behooved her to get them back on track.

"We're actually here to speak with Dr. Boyle," she said.

The woman didn't even look at her. She just nodded and continued worshipping Robbie with her eyes.

"I loved you in that romantic comedy with Mila Kunis," she gushed. "You were so charming."

"Thank you, that's very kind of you," he said.

"And as DI Gordon on *Masterpiece*. I never missed an episode, Mr. Vine," she said.

"Lovely of you to say, and do call me Robbie," he said. He tipped his head down in what Lindsey knew was his humble look. Meanwhile his besotted fan looked like she might faint. Oh boy.

"Robbie, are you sure I can't make you some tea?" the woman asked, looking hopeful.

Lindsey heaved a long-suffering sigh. They were never going to get out of the foyer.

"Molly, who is it?" Dr. Boyle appeared in a doorway on the opposite side of the entryway. He glanced at his wife, who had yet to take her gaze off Robbie. In fact, Lindsey was pretty sure she hadn't even blinked. Dr. Boyle's voice was stern when he asked, "May I help you?"

"Hi, I'm Lindsey Norris . . ." she began, but Molly interrupted.

"This is Robbie Vine—in our house, standing mere feet away from me," Molly said. She didn't look at her husband when she spoke.

Robbie raised his eyebrows as if looking for backup. Molly's scrutiny had become too much even for him.

"I can see Mr. Vine," Dr. Boyle said. To his credit, he sounded amused instead of put out. Behind his wife he shrugged at them as if to let them know that he knew she was being weird but he had no idea what to do about it.

"Robbie," she said. "He said I could call him Robbie."

Molly continued to stare.

"Quite right," Robbie said. He sidled closer to Lindsey, as if he thought she might protect him. Lindsey shook her head at him. He was on his own with his new fan-slash-stalker.

"Yes, well, Dr. Boyle, we don't want to take up too much of your time," Lindsey said. "I'm sorry to say that it's an unfortunate circumstance that brings us here, but we wanted to talk to you

231

about a memorial for your ex-wife, Olive Boyle, to get your input."

Immediately Molly's back snapped straight and she ripped her gaze away from Robbie and stared at Lindsey as if just noticing her.

"Olive? You're talking about a memorial for Olive?" she asked. Her tone made it more than clear how she felt about that idea.

"Um, yes? I'm Lindsey Norris, the director of the Briar Creek Public Library, and this is my . . . associate, Robbie Vine. In light of recent events, we felt that a memorial would be an appropriate gesture of appreciation for her time spent as the president of the library board."

"Oh, so you appreciate bullying, belittling, coldhearted shrews, do you?" Molly asked.

"Molly." Dr. Boyle's voice held a note of warning. Molly didn't look like she gave two hoots about his warning.

"A memorial?" Dr. Boyle turned back to them, looking faintly surprised. "I'm not sure I understand."

"The library fund-raiser made an awful lot of money," Lindsey said. "I met with the board today, and we agreed that it seemed only fitting that we take a portion of that money and use it to honor Olive, since she was the president of the board and was mur . . . Well, she met an unfortunate end in the library that night."

Dr. Boyle winced, and Lindsey felt badly that

232

she couldn't have found a better way to phrase it, but really, what could she say?

"I'm sorry," she said.

He nodded as if to let her know he understood the difficulty of speaking about Olive's passing. He glanced at his wife and said, "I think I need to discuss this with them."

With obvious reluctance, Molly said, "Yes, of course. My personal feelings aside, no one deserves that end. Do come in and make yourselves comfortable."

She gestured for Lindsey and Robbie to follow her.

Unlike Olive's house, this was a home. Pictures of two children, a boy and a girl, were scattered everywhere, following their growth from birth to teenagers. Photos of the family of four graced the walls and furniture, and books and magazines were stacked on every surface, along with the odds and ends of life, such as shoes on the floor, a lip gloss on an end table, a knit hat half stuffed behind a couch cushion. The place smelled faintly of laundry detergent and cinnamon rolls. It was the sort of house that welcomed because it was well lived in. Lindsey liked it—she liked it a lot.

"Can I get you some coffee?" Molly asked.

"Yes, please," Lindsey said.

"That would be lovely, Molly," Robbie added.

Molly blushed a faint pink and giggled.

"We'll be in my study," Dr. Boyle said.

He led them down a short hallway into a small room. It had a large window that overlooked the side yard and a thick patch of woods that separated it from the house next door. A desk was in front of the windows, while a small couch and two armchairs filled the rest of the space. The walls were floor-to-ceiling bookcases crammed with medical texts. The librarian in Lindsey was impressed.

"Dr. Boyle," she began, but he interrupted.

"Please call me Kyle, since you're on a first-name basis with my wife," he said. He smiled at them and gestured for them to sit. Lindsey and Robbie took the couch while he sat in one of the armchairs.

"All right, and I'm Lindsey and you know—"

"Robbie," Kyle said. "Yes, I got that. My wife is quite taken with you."

"Sorry about that," Robbie said.

"Not at all," Kyle said. "Molly's a good woman. She deserves to have something to brag about at her card games. Thank you for humoring her."

"She's really very nice," Lindsey said. "Although I did get the feeling that she wasn't overly fond of Olive."

"No," Kyle agreed. "There was no love between them. Being the second wife was hard on Molly."

Both Lindsey and Robbie were quiet, waiting for him to continue. Kyle glanced out the window as if lost in thought and then back at them.

"Sorry, I'm still having a hard time processing the whole thing. Olive and I divorced twenty years ago, and yet she still managed to keep me dangling on a string. I do think she is the only thing Molly and I have ever fought about."

Lindsey could feel Robbie's gaze on her face and knew he was thinking the same thing she was. Had Molly gotten fed up with Olive's presence in her married life and murdered Olive?

"I'm sorry, that probably came out wrong," Kyle said. "Molly and I have been together for eighteen years, we have two beautiful kids and we love each other very much. Molly knows that her place in my life and my heart is secure. She would never harm Olive."

"Of course not," Lindsey said, as if she hadn't been thinking that very thing.

"That doesn't mean Olive didn't get on her last nerve," Kyle said. "Olive seemed to think that just because we were married at one time, she could still call on me for any emergency or crisis and I would take care of it. Because of my own ridiculous guilt for ending the marriage, I would always answer her call. It became a sticking point between Molly and me."

There was a rap on the door, and then Molly came in bearing a tray with four cups of coffee.

Robbie and Kyle rose to their feet, and Robbie took the tray from her hands, making Molly blush, and put it on the coffee table in front of her.

Molly handed everyone a steaming mug and took the empty seat near her husband's. Lindsey noted that Molly probably had about twenty years on her but that she would have resembled Lindsey even more closely when Olive had first met her. She thought about Olive's hostility. She couldn't believe that the woman had gone after her because of her resemblance to her ex-husband's wife, but given that Olive clearly had a vengeful soul, maybe it wasn't such a surprise.

"So, what sort of memorial for Olive were you considering?" Kyle asked. He stirred sugar and milk into his coffee before looking up at Lindsey.

Lindsey had put zero thought into the memorial. When she had used the same tactic to grill the library board about their where-abouts during the murder, they had come up with a memorial garden with a bench on the east side of the building. She decided to go with it now.

"We were thinking a small garden with a bench with her name engraved on it," she said.

Molly snorted. Kyle looked at her, and she shrugged. She gave them an apologetic smile and put her coffee cup back on the tray.

"Sorry, but I'm having a heck of a time imagining

Olive's name on a bench. It seems so personable, which isn't the first word that springs to mind when I think of her," she said. Then she sighed. "It might be best if you discuss this without me. I'll go get some cookies." She turned to Robbie and asked, "Do you like oatmeal raisin?"

"Love them," he said.

She nodded and left the room.

"Sorry about that," Kyle said. "She really has put up with a lot from Olive, so I can't blame her."

"How long were you and Olive married?" Lindsey asked.

"Eleven years," he said. "We met in college and were married right after, but being a doctor's wife is hard. I was in residency for much of our marriage, leaving her alone. It wasn't her fault . . ."

His voice trailed off, and Robbie and Lindsey exchanged a glance.

"What wasn't her fault?" Robbie pressed.

"She was lonely," Kyle said. He took a sip of coffee. "These things happen."

"She found someone to make her less lonely?" Robbie asked.

Lindsey was impressed with his tact but then remembered the British talent for understatement. Truly, it was a gift.

"Yes, after a couple of separations, one of which was over a year, we finally decided to call it quits," Kyle said. "We parted on friendly terms. I knew that our life together wasn't enough for her, and I was fine with it. I really just wanted her to be happy."

"But then you met Molly," Lindsey said.

"Yes, Olive didn't like that," he said. "It was a bit like she didn't want me but she didn't want anyone else to have me either."

"Was she always like that?" Robbie asked.

"Yes. I don't have a clinical diagnosis, but I do believe she had NPD, narcissistic personality disorder," Kyle said. "It made getting married again . . . difficult."

"Kyle, have the police been here?" Lindsey asked. She knew full well that Emma would have been here already, but she wanted to see if she could get Kyle to tell them what he'd told the police and maybe give them some insight into the police investigation.

"Oh yeah," he said. "The spouse, even an ex-spouse, is always pretty high up on the suspect list, or so they tell me."

"But you're not a person of interest, surely," Robbie said. He delivered the line with just the right amount of disbelief.

"No, my son had a football game—he's in the marching band and they play at halftime—and I was there in the stands, watching the whole time. I was surrounded by most of our town. You can't beat an alibi like that."

"No, you can't," Lindsey agreed. She felt as if they had just smacked into another dead end, not surprisingly, because she couldn't fathom a motive for Olive's ex-husband to have killed his ex-wife.

Kyle asked more questions about the memorial garden and bench the library was planning, and Lindsey answered as best she could as she'd only hit the library board with the idea that very day.

Both Lindsey and Robbie asked leading questions about Olive and who might have wanted to cause her harm, but Kyle obviously didn't like speculating about such a thing. And any talk about Olive's personality or her narcissism causing someone to want to kill her was met with uncomfortable silence. It seemed to Lindsey that while Kyle understood that Olive had been difficult, he still felt a loyalty to his first wife that kept him from acknowledging that she may have pushed someone too far.

Molly came back with cookies just as Lindsey and Robbie were getting ready to leave. The cookies were warm and chewy, and at Molly's insistence they each took a couple for the drive.

"Thanks for your time, Kyle," Lindsey said. "I'll keep you apprised of what happens with the memorial if you'd like."

"I would, thank you," he said.

"I'll see you out," Molly said. She closed the

office door behind them, leaving her husband behind as she took Lindsey and Robbie back through the house.

When they reached the front door, Molly glanced behind her as if to check that her husband was out of earshot. Then she opened the door and led them outside. Standing on the front porch, she met their gaze with a determined one of her own.

"Kyle might not like to talk negatively about that needy old cow, but I don't mind a bit," she said. "That woman made my life a misery when Kyle and I first got together, so much so that I almost dumped him. She followed me, hired a detective to dig around in my past, made up vicious lies and rumors about me, anything to discredit me with Kyle."

"Wow," Robbie said. "No wonder you don't seem overly sad at her passing."

"If I'd had anything in my past, she would have used it to break up Kyle and me, and I wouldn't have my children or my husband or the life I love," Molly said. "I'm sure of it. And the thought of never having to take another call from her at two in the morning when she's having a 'crisis'? Yeah, not really going to miss that."

"Was she like that the entire time you've been married?" Lindsey asked.

"No, she'd disappear every now and again, usually when she got a new boyfriend. That would keep her occupied for a year or two," Molly said. "But even after we had our son and daughter, if she suddenly became single, she would come back into our lives, playing the damsel in distress, but I knew what she was really doing."

"What was that?" Robbie asked.

"She was trying to get Kyle back," Molly said. "She thought all she had to do was crook her little finger and he'd come running. She really thought he was still hers."

"She didn't," Robbie said. He sounded like a fourteen-year-old girl, and Lindsey had to turn her face away to hide her smile.

"Oh yeah, she did," Molly said. "She'd call him constantly for help with this, advice about that—it was ridiculous. Thankfully, as soon as she found another boyfriend, she'd forget about us for a while."

"Can you think of anyone who would want Olive dead?" Lindsey asked. "Anyone in her life that she might have complained to Kyle about?"

Molly tapped her forefinger to her lower lip. "So many people, so many motives. Truly, to know Olive Boyle was to want to kill her."

Robbie cringed and Molly winced.

"Too harsh?"

"A smidgeon," he said.

"Sorry," she said. "My bitterness lingers. I suppose either one of her long-term boyfriends

241

might be looking to make their separation more permanent, assuming she was as clingy with them as she's been to my Kyle. Then there's her sister. There was a big old spat about their father's estate last year when their mother died, which was another time she kept calling Kyle for moral support, legal advice, a shoulder to cry on."

Lindsey tried to picture her life with Sully if he had an ex who kept cropping up. She wouldn't like it. As far as she could tell, Molly should be up for sainthood.

"We should ask the former boyfriends about the memorial, don't you think?" Robbie asked Lindsey and she nodded. He turned back to Molly. "What were the boyfriends' names?" He fished out his cell phone, and as Molly spelled the names, he typed them into his notes app. "And the sister, do you know where she lives?"

"She's in the next town over in Madison," Molly said. "She lives on the Davidson family estate—you can't miss it. But why do you want to talk to her?"

"Oh, same reason, to see if she approves of the memorial," Lindsey said. She could feel Robbie staring at her as she continued their whopper, but she didn't even blink.

Molly nodded as if this made perfect sense.

"Thank you, Molly, you've been very helpful, love," Robbie said.

Molly blushed a deep shade of scarlet and then

waved a hand at them. "Oh, it was nothing, really. If you have any more questions, stop by anytime, like Wednesday night at seven when my bunco group meets, and if you could just say you're an old friend, that'd be perfect."

Lindsey grinned. She couldn't help it. She liked Molly Boyle. With a wave she and Robbie headed for his car.

Once they were seated inside, Robbie glanced at his phone. "According to my GPS, we're five minutes away from the Davidson estate," he said. "What do you say?"

19

L et's do this," she said.

Robbie grinned and shot out of the driveway and back onto the main road.

Lindsey glanced at her phone. Evening was rapidly approaching, so she sent a quick text to Nancy and Sully, letting them know where she was and when she'd be home. She had learned over the past couple of years, the hard way, to always let people know where she was.

The GPS directed them to the road where the Davidson estate was located. Robbie flipped on his turn signal and headed down a gravel drive bordered by enormous, colorful maple trees with wide fields on both sides. The fields soon gave way to a large marsh, where a narrow stream cut through the tall grass. They drove over a wooden bridge, wide enough for only one car at a time, and continued until the marsh turned back into fields. Up ahead a large stone house loomed, looking like something out of another era.

The structure made Lindsey think of the library's pages, Heather and Perry. She couldn't help but picture them here, playing Elizabeth Bennet and Mr. Darcy. She almost expected to see Perry in an artistically tied cravat and waistcoat giving Heather his arm so they could take a turn in the garden as she strolled beside him in an empire-waist gown and a wide-brimmed bonnet.

"Posh, isn't it?" Robbie asked. "I thought Olive had a bit of toff about her."

"In American, please," Lindsey said.

"Oy, let me rephrase," Robbie said. "Pricey crib, don't you think? Olive was most def a one percenter. Word."

He parked the car in front of the house beside an older Volvo that looked to have seen better days but was covered in bumper stickers from Alaska to Florida and every state in between. Lindsey had the feeling that whoever owned the car kept it most likely because of sentimental attachment than functionality.

"Ah." Lindsey laughed. "I agree. Do you think the memorial excuse will work on the sister? Maybe it's too common for this sort of family."

"Only one way to find out."

They climbed out of the car and approached the door. Given what Molly had told them about the estrangement between the two sisters, Lindsey wasn't sure how to handle the conversation. Still, the sister had been at the service, so she must have felt something for Olive—obligation at the very least.

Robbie rang the bell, and they waited in silence. Seconds passed. There was no sound coming from inside the house. He glanced at Lindsey and she nodded. He rang the bell again. Still, there was no response.

Robbie stepped back and studied the windows above them. It was beginning to get dark, but no lights shone from inside.

"Maybe she's not home," Lindsey said. It was getting cold and she was feeling it in her toes. She stamped her feet as if that would kick-start the blood in her veins and heat up her shoes.

"Did you hear that?" Robbie asked.

They stood still, listening. Very quietly, just over the whispery sound of the wind in the trees that surrounded the house, was the methodical *snick, snick, snick* of something metal.

"Follow me," Robbie said. He stepped off the front stoop and began to follow the noise, with his head cocked to the side as if that helped him track the noise better.

Lindsey hurried behind him, hoping they didn't find something she wasn't prepared to explain to the police, like another dead body.

A middle-aged woman, wearing a wide-brimmed straw hat and overalls, was standing next to a wheelbarrow while snipping away at an overgrown rose bush as if trying to tame its long, leggy vines.

"Ms. Davidson?" Robbie asked.

The woman started with a small yelp and turned to face them. Lindsey recognized her from the church service for Olive. She had only seen her profile before, and now she was taken aback by how much this woman resembled her sister: the same arching brows and narrow nose over thin lips and a prominent chin. While Olive had been painfully thin, her sister was well rounded, and her medium brown hair had a touch of gray in it. Lindsey assumed that like her sister, she was somewhere in her fifties.

"Oh, you gave me a fright," she said.

"So sorry," Robbie said. "You are Ms. Davidson?"

"Yes, that's me. How may I help you?" Her gaze darted from Lindsey to Robbie as if trying to decide if she should know them or not.

"We're here about your sister, Olive," Lindsey said.

The woman slowly lowered the small curved clippers she'd been holding and took off her gardening gloves. Her expression was pensive rather than grief-stricken, and Lindsey was beginning to wonder if there was a person alive who was grieving for Olive Boyle.

"Deadheading the last of the blooms?" Robbie asked, and he reached out to cup a large, dried-up blossom in his hand.

"Yes. We've had our first frost," Ms. Davidson said. "It was time." She glanced back at Lindsey. "What did you want to talk to me about Olive for?"

Lindsey introduced herself and Robbie and

gave her the same speech about a proposed memorial that Lindsey had given the board and Kyle. Ms. Davidson nodded. A small smile turned up one corner of her mouth, although it did not light up her eyes.

"Olive would like that," she said. "If it's my approval you're looking for, you have it."

"Thank you," Lindsey said. "Is there anything else you think she might have preferred, Ms. Davidson? I am having a hard time getting a sense of Olive."

"Please call me Margaret." She glanced up at the sky. "It's getting dark. I should call it a day."

She left the wheelbarrow where it was and walked around the side of the house and back to the front. She didn't invite them inside but stood on the driveway near Robbie's car.

Robbie and Lindsey exchanged a desperate glance. This was all they were going to get out of Olive's sister? Really?

"Do you think she'd want the name Olive Davidson Boyle or just Olive Boyle?" Robbie asked. "We want to get it just right."

Margaret stared at both of them. Her gaze was thoughtful, as if she was trying to make up her mind about something.

"Olive wasn't really a Davidson," she said. "We found out just last year when our mother died. Among her papers was Olive's original birth certificate with no father listed. My father,

Henry Davidson, adopted her. We never learned who her real father was. We were so shocked. We had no idea we were really half sisters."

"That can't have been easy," Robbie said.

"No," Margaret agreed. From the pained expression on her face, it was clear that was an understatement. "Matters that were already strained between us became unbearable."

"I'm sorry," Lindsey said. She couldn't imagine finding out such a thing about her brother, Jack, but then again she couldn't imagine things being strained between them. He was her first best friend, and he always would be.

"Olive was furious with our mother for never telling her the truth. She was angry with me because I'd been away, living first in Alaska and then in several other states over the years. I have a bit of the gypsy in my soul. Anyway, Olive felt that she had been the one who took care of our parents in their declining years, and as the oldest, she felt she should have been told the truth."

"Can't really fault her there," Robbie said.

"No, I didn't," Margaret said. "My parents should have been honest with her. Still, she was so bitter. She tried to contest the will and have the estate go solely to her instead of the fifty-fifty split my parents had decided upon. Unfortunately, what she didn't understand was that the will had an in terrorem clause that stated if either of us contested the will, we would forfeit our inheritance in its entirety. Olive ended up losing everything. The estate is still in probate. I'd been holding off, trying to give her time to reconsider or to figure out how to change my parents' directives, but I didn't know how much longer I could stall. I don't suppose it matters much now."

"Oh wow." Robbie gave a low whistle.

A single tear slipped down Margaret's cheek. "I felt terrible. I tried to tell her that we'd ignore what the will said and still split it, but she was so angry. She rejected me completely. I had so hoped we would grow old here together, but no. It clearly wasn't meant to be."

"Did anyone else inherit?" Lindsey asked. "Was there anyone else that Olive might have been angry with?"

Margaret stared off into the distance and then shook her head. "No, just me. I already told your police chief all of this. She even asked me if I had an alibi."

Robbie raised his eyebrows as if he couldn't believe what he was hearing, ever the actor, and then he asked, "Oh dear, did you have one?"

"Yes, I was at the local gardening club that night." She waved her pruning shears at them. "That's where they instructed us to deadhead our flowers after the first frost but before winter sets in."

"Ah." Robbie nodded. "Sound advice, that.

Of course you don't want to prune back the bushes themselves or they'll be vulnerable to the freezing temperature of winter."

"Exactly," Margaret said. Her voice wavered, and her nose was turning red. Lindsey had the feeling a crying jag was pending. She suspected Margaret was the sort who would want to be alone for that.

"Thank you for your time, Margaret," Lindsey said. "We won't keep you."

"Oh, thank you," Margaret said. She sounded grateful for the understanding. "I'm sorry. I think I'm still in shock from Olive's death. I was so sure that in time we'd make it right . . . but now, we'll never have that time and it will never be right."

She looked positively broken. Lindsey resisted the urge to give her a hug, thinking it might be awkward, but when another tear slipped down Margaret's cheek, Lindsey stepped close and gave her a bracing squeeze. Margaret huffed out a breath of surprise but then hugged her back.

After a few moments, Lindsey pulled away. Margaret wiped her cheeks with the palms of her hands and said, "Thank you, and thank you for the memorial to my sister. I think it's a lovely idea."

As they drove away, Lindsey watched Margaret in her side mirror. As she made her way into the house, her shoulders were slumped as if the weight of her grief sat all on her shoulders. It had to be a heavy load to bear to lose a sibling while estranged. Lindsey didn't think Margaret was feigning her grief.

"What do you think of Ms. Davidson?" Robbie asked after several minutes of contemplative silence.

They were driving the road that ran along the shore back to Briar Creek. It was now fully dark, and Lindsey hunkered into her wool coat. Even though the car was toasty warm, she felt a chill shiver through her from the inside out.

"I don't know. She seemed sincere, but who knows. If she killed her sister, she's going to do everything she can to hide it, isn't she? Hey, I didn't know you knew so much about gardening," she said.

"I'm British. It's in our DNA like tea and biscuits."

"And Shakespeare."

"Big Ben."

"Paddington Bear."

"The changing of the guard."

"Tolkein."

"Have you noticed all of your British references are literary?"

"Librarian."

"Quite."

The traffic was light and Robbie turned onto the road that would take them through the center of town.

"How about that bomb she dropped?" he asked. "Finding out your dad wasn't really your dad when your mum passes? That can't have been pleasant."

"No, especially since it sounds as if Olive was the one who was here taking care of them while Margaret was off seeing the world. It sounds like she had some resentment."

"But why try to take the entire estate away from her sister?" Robbie asked. "That seems punitive."

"If what Kyle said was true and Olive did have a narcissistic personality disorder, then it makes sense. If I remember right from my college psych classes, narcissists are pretty big on revenge, whether the slight they feel is imagined or real."

"Scary," Robbie said. "But she only managed to hurt herself."

"Which might have fueled her desire for revenge even more," Lindsey said. "We need to talk to her friends again. They have to know something."

"Kim seems rather fond of me," he said. "I can try to work my magic on her and get some answers."

"Be careful," Lindsey said. "I don't trust any of them."

"Don't worry about me, pet," he said. "I've got this."

They were stopped at a light, and Lindsey gave him an uneasy look. She didn't want him to be overconfident, not with those women. Instead of nagging him, however, she tried to focus on the upside. The more people they found that Olive had clashed with, the more suspects in her murder there would be, making Paula a less likely suspect.

"Where do you want me to drop you off?" Robbie asked.

Lindsey glanced at her phone. Sully had sent her a text asking her to meet him for dinner. She realized she was starving and Robbie probably was, too.

"How about grabbing dinner at the Blue Anchor?" she asked.

"Best plan I've heard all day," he agreed and drove straight there.

The Anchor was the only restaurant and bar in all of Briar Creek, so even on a slow night it was packed to the rafters with residents of their small town eating dinner, watching a televised ball game or enjoying an end-of-the-day beverage with friends.

When Lindsey pulled the door open and strode in, the smell of the night's special, baked stuffed cod with boiled potatoes, coleslaw and fresh-baked bread, hit her right in the nostrils. Sully was seated at the bar with an empty seat beside him, and Lindsey made for it.

Sully caught sight of her and stood. He opened his arms, and she walked right into them. As always, it felt like coming home. She leaned back to look up at him, and he grinned down at her.

"How goes the investigation?" he asked.

"Slow," she said. "Any word on whether Paula has surfaced?"

Sully shook his head. "No."

"It looks bad for her to have bolted, doesn't it?"

"It doesn't look good," he said.

Lindsey turned around to tell Robbie the news, but he wasn't there. She scanned the room, looking for his familiar reddish blond hair. Finally, she spotted him all the way over in the corner booth, sitting with Amy, LeAnn and Kim.

"What is he doing?" Sully asked.

"Interrogating the suspects?" Lindsey answered, but her words curled up at the end as if she was asking a question.

"Ah, he might want to be careful with Kim MacInnes," Sully said.

Lindsey turned to look at him with eyebrows raised. "Why is that?"

Sully put a hand on the back of his neck and looked sheepish. "She has a reputation as being a bit of a cougar."

"Really?" she asked. "And how do you know that?"

"Because a few summers ago, she set her sights on your boyfriend, and in an effort to win him, she—" Ian joined their conversation from behind the bar, but Sully interrupted him.

"No, don't—"

Ian threw a bar rag at Sully's face, cutting him off, and he continued, "And she hid aboard his water taxi, buck naked, and when he set out to pick up a fare, she popped out of the bench where he stores his life vests."

Lindsey turned a wide-eyed gaze on Sully. "No, she didn't."

Sully ran a hand through his thick curls and pitched the bar rag back at Ian with a glare. "We swore we would never speak of this."

"Did we? Maybe you did. I'm quite sure I would never make any such vow," Ian said. He ducked down behind the bar and then sprang up, batting his eyelashes, and in a girlish voice he yelled, "Surprise!"

Lindsey belly laughed. She couldn't help it. It was so ridiculous. Sully turned a vivid shade of red and scowled at his friend. "Next time we're out on the sound, someone is going to be swimming for shore."

Ian guffawed. "Aw, don't be mad. I'll go naked like your stowaway."

"Gah," Sully gagged. "Now I'm off my food for the night."

He looked at Lindsey, who grinned and then hugged him tight.

"Don't you worry," she said. "I won't allow any more naked girls to jump out at you—unless it's me."

"Check, please!" Sully shouted at Ian, who laughed at them.

Then Ian's eyebrows rose and he leaned to the right and said, "Not to alarm anyone, but I think our friend Robbie might have gotten himself into a compromising position."

Lindsey spun around and glanced back at the booth. Sure enough, Kim had looped her arm about Robbie, and even as Lindsey watched, she was sliding into his lap a bit like a boa constrictor slithered around its prey before strangling it.

"Uh-oh," Sully muttered. He jerked his head in the direction of the door. "Incoming."

"Huh? What?" Lindsey asked. She turned, following the direction he indicated, and saw the familiar navy blue wool coat with the badge fastened to it. Emma!

20

I f she saw Robbie with Kim on his lap . . . Oh, no, no, no. This was bad—so bad. Lindsey whipped around and faced Ian.

"Start a fire!" she yelled.

"What? In my restaurant? Are you crazy?"

"Well, do something! Cause a distraction. This is a matter of life or death!"

Ian blinked at her. Then without hesitation, he vaulted up onto the bar and began to do a Riverdance routine. Well, his version of it at any rate. Sully looked from him to Lindsey and said, "I don't know which one of you is crazier."

Then he began to clap a rhythm, and Lindsey joined in, pausing only to wave frantically at Emma. Emma looked at them like they were all insane—not completely wrong—and then, as if some sixth sense called to her, she turned her head and stared right at Robbie, who was trapped under the full force of Kim in his lap.

She turned on her heel and marched over to the booth, looking like she was getting ready to kick some cougar booty. As they watched, Ian stumbled to a halt, mindless of the bills some of the bar patrons had tossed at him, and Lindsey and Sully stopped clapping.

"Do you think she'll shoot him?" Ian asked.

" 'Cause that would likely be bad for business."

Lindsey bit her knuckle while Sully took a step forward as if there was anything he could do to prevent the slaughter that was about to happen.

To their surprise, Emma strolled right past Kim and Robbie to the party of five seated next to them. She then opened her wallet and handed a man at the table some cash. He nodded at her, looking delighted. Then she hefted the pitcher of beer sitting in the center of their table and turned back to Robbie and Kim. Without hesitation or warning, she tipped the entire contents of the almost-full pitcher right over Robbie's head.

With a yelp, Kim jumped off Robbie's lap, avoiding the worst of the splash. She grabbed a fistful of napkins and dabbed at her tight sweater and skinny jeans, flapping her hands uselessly at her sides when the napkins stuck to her clothes.

Emma leaned close, and in a voice that carried to every corner of the restaurant, she said, "If you wanted my boyfriend so badly, all you had to do is ask. Seriously, he's free to a good home!"

"What? No!" Robbie cried. He jumped to his feet. "Emma, love, it's not how it looks."

"You had a woman draped across you like a beauty queen sash," Emma snapped. "How is it not how it looks?"

Robbie shook his head, and droplets of beer flew everywhere. People all around them cried out, but he was oblivious as he smiled down at Emma with a grin that Lindsey knew from personal experience was full of mischievous delight.

"I knew it!" he crowed.

Emma glared at him.

"You care about me," he said. "Admit it. You, Emma Plewicki, are sweet on me, Robbie Vine."

"Oh my God, shut up," Emma said. "I am merely trying to keep you from contaminating a possible person of interest in an ongoing murder investigation."

"Ha! That's a load of malarkey," Robbie said. "And I should know because I'm full of it. You like me."

Emma pressed her hand to her forehead as if she was warding off a headache. She turned on her heel and stomped toward Lindsey and Sully.

"Come on, admit it," he cajoled as he followed, heedless of the trail of beer he left in his wake. "You like me. You really like me. I bet you even love me."

He was dancing around her, and she was ignoring him, signaling to Ian that she needed a drink. Ian shook his head.

"No can do. You're on duty," he said.

"Son of a—" Emma began, but then she spun on Robbie who was still chanting and snapped, "All right, I love you—oh—"

That was as far as she got before Robbie kissed her. It was likely meant to be a quick one, but Emma's arms looped around his neck and held him in place while she kissed him back. A collective *"Aw"* sounded in the restaurant, and Lindsey leaned into Sully, who wrapped his arm around her and pulled her close.

Lindsey glanced past Robbie and Emma and saw the one table who didn't feel any warm fuzzies about this clinch. LeAnn and Amy were gone, and Kim was alone, shrugging on her coat, looking the picture of misery. With a distraught expression, she raced for the front door.

As happy as Lindsey was for Robbie and Emma, she couldn't help but feel for Kim. This was a public kick in the teeth, and having suffered her own in the past, she knew exactly how it felt.

Lindsey stepped away from Sully with an apologetic smile and said, "I'll be right back."

She pushed through the restaurant doors right behind Kim, calling, "Hey, wait! Kim, are you okay?"

Kim pressed her key fob, and her car unlocked with a double beep. She glanced at Lindsey over her shoulder and frowned.

"What do you want?"

"I just wanted to make sure you're all right," she said.

"What do you care?"

"I . . . well . . . I just . . ." Lindsey stammered. She hadn't really thought about it. She just felt sorry for the other woman.

"Yeah, you don't care," Kim snapped. She sniffed and ran the cuff of her sleeve under her nose. "Just like everyone else. You just want to use me and abuse me and then throw me away."

"Robbie didn't mean to lead you on," Lindsey said. "I'm sure he feels terrible."

"If he does, it's only because he's soaked in beer, not because he has any feelings for me. I'm just one of the 'mean girls.' "

Lindsey's eyes went wide before she thought to school her reaction.

"Yeah, we know what you call us," Kim said. She glanced around the parking lot as if wondering how she'd gotten there. "And to think I used to be a happily married, well-liked, upstanding member of my community, all of that. God, I hate this place."

A sob bubbled out of her, and Lindsey froze. She had no idea what to say or do. She suspected if she tried to hug Kim, she'd likely get punched in the face.

"Do you want me to call your friends?" she asked.

Kim wiped her eyes, yanked the door of her car open and tossed her handbag in. Then she rounded on Lindsey with a narrowed gaze. "Friends? What friends? I don't have any friends."

Lindsey stood staring after her as she zipped out of the parking lot without even pausing to check for traffic. The bottom of her car seemed to bounce off the asphalt as she hit the curb, but even that didn't slow her down. Lindsey turned and hurried back into the Anchor, fervently hoping she didn't hear the sound of a crash as she went.

That was telling. Kim didn't feel that LeAnn and Amy were her friends, but why did she feel that way? Was Olive the glue that held the group together, and with her gone, was it unraveling? So many questions. So many suspects. And Paula missing.

How long could Lindsey keep covering for her with human resources before it cost Paula her job? They had to figure out who had murdered Olive and soon.

When Lindsey and Sully arrived at her apartment, it was to find Nancy, Violet, Charlene and Beth waiting for them in Nancy's apartment. Lindsey had let Nancy know that morning that she was moving in with Sully. She had been worried that Nancy would take the news hard. She wasn't just losing Lindsey, after all. She was losing Heathcliff as her buddy as well.

To Lindsey's relief, Nancy had clapped her hands in delight and hugged her close. She was thrilled with the news. Leave it to Nancy to let the good in Lindsey's life outshine any sadness she felt about losing Lindsey as a tenant. That was friendship. Lindsey couldn't imagine any of the mean girls treating one another as supportively, and she felt sorry for them. They were missing out on one of life's greatest gifts.

"All right, I rallied the troops, and we have enough boxes to tackle your bookshelves," Nancy said. "So you can get this move started."

She led the way upstairs, leaving the others to follow. They all grabbed some of the flattened boxes and climbed up after her.

"You do have room in your house for all of her books, don't you?" Violet asked Sully. They paused on the second-floor landing.

"Yes," he said. "I have a whole room that can be turned into her very own library if she chooses."

"Aw, that's so sweet," Beth said. "Aidan is converting my spare bedroom into a studio. He thinks I should continue writing my children's books. Man, I love him."

Lindsey grinned. "He's right. You should. You're going to get published one day. I know it."

Beth hugged her with one arm while clutching her flattened boxes with the other. "Best friend, maid of honor and boss all rolled into one awesome package." She looked at Sully with a beady eye. "Take care of my girl."

"Always," Sully said.

"And now I'm going to get all weepy," Charlene said.

Lindsey glanced over her shoulder to see Charlene fan her eyes. "It seems like just yesterday, Martin and I were moving in together. Now we've got three kids and a mortgage. Savor every second—it goes by so fast."

Lindsey looked at Sully in alarm. *Kids?* She'd never really thought about that before. They'd never even talked about that or marriage or any of that adult stuff. She felt panic begin to thump hard in her chest.

Sully's eyebrows rose as he looked at her face. He took her elbow and held her back, allowing the others to go ahead.

"All right if I use my key to go in?" Nancy called from above.

"Yeah, go ahead," Lindsey said. "I'll be right there."

By unspoken agreement, they waited until everyone was out of earshot.

"Darlin', are you going sideways on me?" Sully asked.

"Huh?" she panted. "Sideways or maybe upside down. We have to talk."

"No, we don't," he said.

"But we've never . . . I don't know . . . What if . . ." Lindsey dropped her boxes and sat down hard on the steps.

Sully kneeled right in front of her. "Hey, we

266

don't have to make any big decisions right now."

"Some might argue that moving in together is a big decision," she said.

"We're not some," he said. He studied her face. "What freaked you out?"

"The *k* word," she said.

He nodded. She couldn't tell if that meant he understood because he felt the same, or if he was now reconsidering their whole situation because she was undecided about procreating.

He leaned close, until they were nose to nose and eyeball to eyeball. "The *k* word freaks me out, too."

"It does?" she asked. "But you were so happy about Mary and Ian having a baby."

"Of course," he said. "A, because they've both always wanted kids. B, because uncle is the greatest job ever, as in you get to spoil them rotten and then give them back. And, C, Ian deserves to be tortured with a child just like him."

Lindsey felt her heart rate slow. Were they actually on the same page here?

"Hey, slackers!" Beth shouted from above. "This apartment isn't going to pack itself."

"Be right there," Lindsey cried. She turned back to Sully and said, "So, if we decided we want kids, that's okay?"

"Yup."

"And if we decide we don't want kids, that's okay, too?"

"Yup," he said again. "The key, darling, is that *we* decide together." He studied her face. "Are you okay now?"

"Yeah," she said. She was pleased to discover that she even meant it. "But clearly there are things we need to talk about."

"And here I thought we'd covered it with the 'seat being left up' and the 'floor is a hamper' things," he said. He handed back her boxes as they began to climb the last flight of steps. "I'm open to discussing anything."

"Good, because I'm going to make a list," she said. When he gave her a funny look, she pointed to herself and added, "Librarian."

Sully laughed. "I wouldn't have you any other way."

Paula did not show up for work again the next day. Her original text message saying she was taking some personal time was the only communication Lindsey had from her missing clerk. She knew Paula was avoiding being taken in for questioning, and given that the evidence really wasn't in her favor, Lindsey couldn't blame her. Lindsey called Paula's partner Hannah, but if Hannah knew where Paula was, she wasn't saying and Lindsey didn't press the issue. That was a job for the police.

In an effort to help, Lindsey found the paper-work that human resources demanded for an official leave of absence and filled it out on Paula's behalf. She didn't need to submit it yet, but in a couple of days, it would be the only thing that would keep Paula from losing her job permanently.

Given that Paula's absence put them a person down at the circulation desk, Lindsey left her office to go assist Ms. Cole out front. Just like it was the library director's job to plunge a toilet in case of an emergency, it was also her responsibility to step in wherever she was needed. Ah, the glamour.

The lemon was, ironically, in shades of all yellow today, from a pale butter-colored top to a retina-searing Day-Glo skirt that Lindsey couldn't look at directly because it made her see spots when she looked away.

"Paula won't be in today," Lindsey said. "I'll help you catch up with the backlog."

Ms. Cole looked at her over the reading glasses perched on her nose. "So, no luck finding the killer then?"

"Not yet," Lindsey said.

Ms. Cole looked as if she was about to chastise her, and Lindsey braced herself for the terse rebuke. Just in time, a woman approached the desk, interrupting whatever the lemon was about to say. Lindsey welcomed the distraction until she recognized the buxom blonde in front of her.

"Hello, Kili," Lindsey said. Although she

greeted the reporter, her tone was far from welcoming.

"I'm looking for Paula Turner," Kili said. She tossed her blond hair and leaned on the counter as if she planned to adhere herself to the furniture until she got what she wanted.

"Paula isn't here."

"Then where is she? I checked her apartment and talked to her landlord. No one seems to know where she's gone. To me that screams of a murderer on the run."

"Oh, for Pete's sake," Lindsey snapped. "Could you be any more of a hack?"

Kili gasped and reared back as if Lindsey had slapped her.

"I'll have you know I have won awards—"

Ms. Cole snorted, interrupting her tirade.

"I have!" Kili insisted.

"Not really the point," Lindsey said. "Listen, I am sorry I called you a hack, that was rude, but you're going for the easy suspect by tracking down Paula, and you know it."

"I happen to know about her past," Kili said. "I haven't gone on air with it yet because I wanted to give her the opportunity to explain."

"Very big of you," Lindsey said. "I imagine it is also due to the fact that it's based on rumors and innuendo."

"Maybe," Kili said, admitting nothing.

"You could do that," Lindsey said. "You could

deliver half the story with lots of speculation, but wouldn't it be better to be a real investigative reporter and get the whole story?"

Kili stared at her for a moment. "I'm listening."

"Paula didn't murder Olive Boyle."

"Says you."

"I happen to be right," Lindsey said.

"And, yet, you can't prove it, can you?"

"I will." Lindsey made her voice sound firm. It was the voice she used when going into battle at budget meetings.

"All right," Kili said. "I'll hold off on the story on one condition."

"Name it."

"We investigate together, and if we don't find a more viable suspect than Paula, you give me an exclusive interview as the employer of the murderer."

"Done."

Ms. Cole drew in a breath, as if she didn't approve of this maneuver, but what choice did Lindsey have? A deal with the devil was about the only thing she hadn't tried.

"So, if not Paula, emphasis on the *if,* then who do you think killed Olive Boyle?"

"Her ex-husband, his wife, her half sister, one of her friends, one of the people in town she tangled with," Lindsey said. "It's a long list."

"No, it isn't," Kili said. "Her husband had no reason to kill her, and neither did his wife—"

271

"That we know of," Lindsey interrupted.

"Yes, Olive was difficult to several townspeople, but does that warrant killing her?" Kili asked. "I read the police report from that night. The only reason you found Olive at all was because her friends came back to the library looking for her when she didn't show up near their car. How could one of them have murdered her if they were all together?"

"The last time anyone saw Olive Boyle was just before the auction closed," Lindsey said. "That was a half hour before the event ended. Any of her friends could have killed her and met up with their group without arousing suspicion."

Kili stared at her. Lindsey could see she was mulling over this news, turning it around in her mind as if to study it from every angle.

"What were the women wearing?" Kili asked.

"Relevance?"

"Bloodstains," Ms. Cole said. "Did any of the friends have bloodstains on their clothes?" Both Kili and Lindsey looked at Ms. Cole in surprise. She shrugged. "It's not brain surgery."

Lindsey turned to Kili. She frowned in concentration, trying to remember what the other women had been wearing. The only one she could picture clearly was Olive in her beaded black dress. The others were fuzzy at best.

"I've got nothing," she said.

"Really?"

"Sorry," Lindsey said. "Kind of had my mind on other things."

"All right, say I agree that the friends warrant looking at. How do you suggest we go about that?"

"Divide and conquer," Lindsey said. "I'll dig into Kim MacInnes's background and see what I can come up with, and you can start with LeAnn Barnett. Whoever finishes first can then look at Amy Ellers."

"What are we looking for?" Kili asked.

"A reason to murder Olive Boyle," Lindsey said.

"Duh, I was looking for something a little more specific."

Lindsey blew out a breath and wondered if she was crazy, trusting Kili at all.

"None of those women shed a tear when Olive was found dead," Lindsey said. "If the friendship was genuine, wouldn't they have been more upset? I suspect they were friends with Olive out of necessity, not affection. If that's true, then what was Olive holding over them to keep them in line?"

"Interesting angle," Kili conceded.

"Report back in later today," Lindsey said. When Kili didn't move, Lindsey bugged her eyes at her and made a shooing motion with her hands.

"Fine, I'm going," Kili snapped. "But I'm telling you right now: if we don't find anything suspicious on the friends, I am going after Paula Turner with everything I have."

She stepped back from the counter, jutting her chin up in the air like she was some sort of tough guy. Then she walked out of the library with a swagger that was completely unwarranted.

"Do you really trust her?" Ms. Cole asked.

"Not even a little," Lindsey said. "But what choice do I have? Emma is going to lose patience with Paula's disappearing act. I'm afraid she may put out a warrant for her arrest if she doesn't surface soon."

"Let's hope Kili's a better investigative journalist than she is a person," Ms. Cole said. "Otherwise, it will be easy for her to pin the murder on Paula and spin the story so that it sounds like Paula is a guilty fugitive, and you'll be forced to give an interview to support that theory."

Lindsey felt her heart clutch in her chest. Poor Paula. She did not deserve this. It was a risk pulling Kili into the investigation, but Lindsey couldn't do it alone, and it was pretty clear that Robbie was now going to be of little or no use to her when it came to the mean girls.

She finished checking in all of the books in the drop. Then she did a scan of the library to make certain that everything was as it should be. The ficus in the reading corner looked a little droopy, so she wandered over to it to stick her finger in the pot and see if it was dry. Honestly, she had no idea when she'd watered it last. Plant care was yet another thing they hadn't really prepped her for in library school.

The soil felt desert dry. Lindsey went to fetch a pitcher of water, and while she was tending the plant, she glanced out the window to enjoy the view of the islands out in the bay before going back to her office. It was a clear, crisp autumn day, and the sunlight sparkled on the ocean while the seagulls rode the breeze, ducking and diving into the water as they foraged for a meal.

Lindsey saw a crowd gathering in the gazebo that stood at the edge of the narrow park across the street from the library. It only took her a moment or two to recognize the motley crew as the hat-shop-owning Londoners who were visiting Briar Creek.

She watched as the handsome Andre Eisel crouched on one knee. His smile was a slash of white teeth against his bronze skin as he smiled at Scarlett, the redhead, while holding an expensive-looking camera up to his face. She was wearing a confection of powder blue on her head, and she strutted, striking ridiculous poses as he snapped off pictures.

The other two women, Fee and Viv, also took turns posing while the remaining men, Nick, Harrison and Alistair, stood nearby, sometimes jumping into the photos with the girls or just patiently holding on to the ladies' fabulous hats while they took in the beauty of the islands. She watched as they pointed out the boats docked all along the pier. Briar Creek and the Thumb Islands really were a boater's paradise.

She wondered if they were using the natural backdrop to shoot advertisements for their hat shop. Maybe it would go on their webpage or in a print catalog. The thought made her smile. They had said at the dinner that Andre was a professional photographer. How fortunate for them . . . or perhaps for Paula.

It hit Lindsey then. Andre had been taking pictures the night of the dinner. He had covered the event, the speeches, the dancing and the auction.

Lindsey left the ficus and hurried into the back room. She left the watering can on her desk and grabbed her coat. She had to go talk to him. She had to see if he'd kept his pictures from that night. If he had, it was highly possible that he'd gotten a shot of the killer.

21

Lindsey yanked on her jacket as she dashed across the street. Luckily, today had been a boots, slacks and sweater sort of day, so her mobility wasn't hampered by a skirt and heels.

"Hi!" she cried with a wave. The group had left the gazebo and was walking toward the docks, probably to take more pictures.

Andre, who was checking out the last pictures he'd shot, had fallen behind the group. He glanced up when he saw her and smiled.

"Hello, Lindsey the librarian," he said. "What brings you to the park?"

"You, actually," she said.

He tipped his head to the side, and the diamond stud in his earlobe caught the sunlight and glinted at her.

"Me?" he asked. He sounded intrigued, then he winked at her. "I don't know what the Notting Hill Library told you, but I returned those books. I swear."

Lindsey laughed. She liked his humor. Nick Carroll dropped back from the others and joined them.

"Are you in trouble, love?" he asked Andre.

"It does have a way of finding me, doesn't it?"

"Andre, did you get that last shot?" Scarlett

asked as she hurried over with one hand holding the hat onto her head against the gusts of cool air coming from the water. "I think I want to use it for the website. Oh, hello, Lindsey."

"Hi." Lindsey pulled her jacket closer about her, as she'd rushed out of the building without closing it and the breeze was brisk.

Scarlett's pale blue hat, a wide-brimmed velvet cap with matching plumes of feathers and some intricate ribbon work left Lindsey dazzled. Why, oh why, couldn't Americans get on board with the hat thing?

Andre held up his camera and showed Scarlett the display. She made a soft *squee* noise and then squeezed his arm.

"You're the best," she said. "These are going to look fantastic. Viv and Fee have really outdone themselves with these hats."

"Ginger, look lively," Harrison said as he moved to stand beside Scarlett. He looped his arm about her waist and pulled her close. "We only have a half hour until the Man U game is on."

"We're almost done," she said. "You won't miss your precious soccer match." She rolled her eyes, and Lindsey tried not to laugh.

"It's football," he said. Harrison glanced at Lindsey and smiled. "Good to see you again, Lindsey. Sorry to hear about that unfortunate occurrence at the library."

Lindsey raised her eyebrows and Scarlett shook her head. "Brits are the masters of understatement. Truly, it's an art form. Is everything all right? Can we help you?"

"No!" Harrison, Andre and Nick said at the same time.

Lindsey glanced at the men and then back to Scarlett.

"Ignore them," Scarlett insisted. "If there is anything we can do . . ."

"Actually, there is one thing—" Lindsey began.

"Oh no," Andre said. He glared at Scarlett. "How is it this sort of thing follows you wherever you go?"

"Stop!" she said. "You haven't even heard what she has to say yet."

"I don't need to," he said. "It's going to have to do with the murder, and you know how I feel about dead bodies."

"You're not a fan," Nick said.

"No, I'm not," Andre said. "And yet, they just keep popping up, don't they?"

"You do have the devil's own luck with that," Harrison agreed.

"No, not me," Andre said. He pointed at Scarlett. "Her!"

Lindsey looked at Scarlett, who shrugged. "There have been a few episodes. Not my fault."

"Wrong place, wrong time?" Lindsey asked.

"Exactly," Scarlett said.

"I feel you," Lindsey said. She turned back to Andre. "Which is why I was hoping to talk to you. I noticed that you had your camera the night of the dinner and was wondering if you'd be willing to share any pictures you took from the party with me."

"That's it?" he asked. "That's all you want from me?"

"Yes. Why?"

"No reason," he said. "Just making sure there wasn't more to it. You know, nothing that might get me beat up or killed. I can email the file to you. Would that work?"

"That would be fantastic," Lindsey said. "Thank you."

"Oy, were we going to be taking pictures today or Thursday?" Fee called from the pier.

Lindsey pulled her cell phone out of her pocket and held it to Andre's. Once they connected, she said, "Message me and I'll text you my email."

"All right," he said. "I'll be sure to send the file as soon as we're done here."

"Hat-a-boy," Nick joked.

Andre rolled his eyes. "That was beanie-th you."

Scarlett groaned and Lindsey laughed.

"You know what they say: hatters gonna hat," Harrison said.

"You really got a-head of that one," Scarlett

280

said. No one laughed except for Lindsey, which only made her laugh harder.

"I like you," Scarlett said. "Clearly, you're my people."

"Because I bowler you over?" Lindsey teased, and Scarlett let out a whoop.

"You are brimming with good puns," Scarlett said. Again, no one laughed except Lindsey. "Oh, come on. That was a good one. Lindsey liked it."

"Because she is cap-tivated by your lack of word skill," Nick said. Then he raised his arms in the air and shouted, "For the win!"

"He's going to be unbearable now," Scarlett said with a shake of her head. "We'll see you again, Lindsey?"

"Definitely." Lindsey grinned as the group crossed the park to meet their friends and finish their photo shoot. She knew it was a long shot, but maybe Andre's photographs would help piece together the events of the evening. Feeling a surge of optimism, she strode back to the library to see what she could find out about Kim MacInnes and the other mean girls.

Lindsey's search online for information about Kim didn't turn up much. She was divorced, as she had said. She'd gone to college in Tennessee but had returned home to Connecticut to marry her high school sweetheart. They were married for fifteen years but had no children. When Lindsey searched for Kim's ex-husband, Bill, she discovered he was living in Mystic, Connecticut, and had remarried. He had two small children, and judging by the pictures his new wife put on social media, he was very happy.

She used the online telephone directory to find the number for his house and was relieved when a woman answered. Like with Molly's oversharing, Lindsey had a feeling she'd get more information out of the second wife than she would the husband.

"Hi, my name is Lindsey," she said. "I'm calling from the Briar Creek Library to speak with Bill MacInnes."

"Briar Creek?" The woman's voice was immediately wary. "Why do you want to talk to Bill?"

"It's about a mem—" Before Lindsey could go into her spiel about a memorial being set up for Bill's old neighbor, the woman cut her off.

"Listen, Bill hasn't lived in Briar Creek for years," she said. "Any debts his crazy ex-wife racked up are completely her own problem. He is not liable for her money issues anymore."

"Ah, okay, I was just hoping—"

"Listen, I'm sorry if Kim's gambling is out of control again and if she's shirking on paying her bills, but I really must ask that you bill collectors stop calling here," the woman said. "My husband cannot help you."

The woman ended the call with a click, and

Lindsey stared at the phone in her hand in some surprise. So, Kim had a gambling problem. From the sound of it, it was rather serious. Had Olive been holding that over Kim's head? Was Kim trapped because of the debt she had accrued? And now that Olive was dead, what did that mean for her?

By the time Kili returned to compare notes, Lindsey had received the photographs from Andre and was going through them one at a time, hoping to see something.

Kili knocked on her office door and strode in, closing it behind her.

"What did you find out?" Kili asked.

"Kim's a gambler, big-time, which is probably why her husband left her," she said. "I suspect that Olive helped her out by paying her bills for her. Basically, she owned Kim."

"Nice," Kili said. She sat across from Lindsey, looking at her as if perhaps she had under-estimated her before. "Anything else?"

"Not much," Lindsey said. "But I did confirm that LeAnn is still married—at least there's no record of a divorce—but no one has seen her husband in ages."

"That's because he's living with the mother of his two children down in Florida," Kili said.

Lindsey gave her an appreciative glance, and Kili buffed her red nails on the lapel of her blazer.

"Do you think Olive knew?" Lindsey asked.

"Oh yeah," Kili said. "I called Mr. Barnett in the guise of a Realtor who was interested in buying his house here in Briar Creek. He told me straightaway that he had nothing to do with it or the woman who lives there, who claims to be his wife."

"Claims? So, they're not married?"

"Oh no, they are, but only because LeAnn won't grant him a divorce. And it's not about money. LeAnn is loaded. He's not paying alimony. They didn't have kids. It's merely that she doesn't want to be divorced. He said that she thinks it's some sort of personal failure."

"But he has children with someone else," Lindsey said. She was trying to wrap her brain around it. "He's got a whole other life and family."

"Yep, but LeAnn won't let him go," Kili said. "I asked him if he knew Olive Boyle, and he confirmed that he did. In fact, he thinks she's the reason why LeAnn wouldn't grant him a divorce."

"Why would Olive care?"

"He thought LeAnn kept him dangling, saying he was away on business instead of off living with his new family, just to torture Olive with the fact that LeAnn was still married when Olive wasn't." Kili made air quotes around the word *married,* making it clear that any marriage between LeAnn and her husband was bogus.

"He also said that Olive tracked him down a few months ago and was ecstatic to discover that he was with someone else. He was sure she planned to taunt LeAnn with the information. He thinks they were more frenemies and than friends."

"So, Kim was in debt to Olive financially. That had to chafe," Lindsey said. "And LeAnn was hanging on to her husband just to appear to be in a better relationship situation than Olive, which Olive recently discovered was false. That had to have been an ugly scene. While not exactly motives for murder, they arc consistent with Olive's other toxic relationships."

"It's almost as if the only way Olive could have someone in her life was if she had complete control over them," Kili said. "What about Amy?"

"I've got nothing. My online search turned up so many matches that I need to find a way to whittle it down with a place of birth or school attended or some such thing."

"It was the same for me," Kili said. "It's like there isn't a specific cyber footprint out there for her, which is very weird."

"She's younger than the others, too," Lindsey said.

"Meaning?"

"Just an observation but you'd think she'd be hip to the whole sharing every moment of her life online thing, so we could find something."

Lindsey saw Kili examine her reflection in the window glass. She wondered if younger reporters were already chomping at Kili's heels. While male newscasters got more distinguished and smarter with age, females just got put out to pasture.

Lindsey wondered if Kili felt like she was on borrowed time. Maybe that was why she was so aggressive. Lindsey couldn't really fault her. She would hate it if keeping her job was dependent upon her youth.

"So, what are you working on there?" Kili asked. She nodded toward Lindsey's computer screen.

"Nothing, just some work stuff."

"Uh-huh, looks like dinner party pictures," Kili said. "I thought we were working together. Why are you shutting me out?"

"I'm not." Lindsey had to clasp her hands together to keep from covering her monitor from Kili's prying eyes.

"Please, you're studying the photos, trying to see if you can spot the killer," Kili said. She raised one eyebrow at Lindsey as if daring her to disagree.

"Okay, fine. I am, but I got them from a British photographer, and I don't know that he'd be all right with me sharing them with anyone else. It was just a hunch that they might give us some information on who was where and at what time."

"Let me see," Kili said. She didn't wait for an invitation but stood and pulled her chair around the desk to sit beside Lindsey.

Forced to scoot over, Lindsey adjusted her seat and turned the monitor so that Kili could see the photos, too. Lindsey had been halfway through examining them, but Kili took over the mouse and moved the file back to the beginning.

"I already checked those," Lindsey protested.

"Two pairs of eyes, blah, blah, blah," Kili said. She was studying each photograph, looking for who knew what.

Lindsey let her have a few minutes to catch up and studied the notepad on her desk where she'd jotted down some observations.

"To answer your question from earlier, Olive's friends were wearing all dark colors with the exception of Amy, who was in a pale blue dress," Lindsey said.

"What about at the end of the party?" Kili asked. "Any shots of them?"

"I hadn't gotten that far," Lindsey said. She gestured to her notepad. "I was focusing on keeping track of where everyone was during the party."

"You mean on where your employee Paula Turner was, don't you?"

Lindsey didn't dignify the question with an answer. They continued flipping through the pictures. Sadly, there were none of a person pocketing their steak knife for later use, nor were there any of a person sneaking out of the party covered in blood. Equally, there were no shots of Paula after the dinner to determine her exact whereabouts, just a couple of shots of her at the table and out dancing, and that was it.

"Good pictures," Kili said. "Just not very useful."

"Oy, what's this?" Robbie entered Lindsey's office without knocking. He stood in the doorway with his hands on his hips, looking outraged. "Have you replaced me with *her?*"

22

Yes, I'm working on the Olive Boyle murder with Lindsey," Kili said. "If that's what you're asking."

"Oh no, don't—" Lindsey began but Robbie interrupted.

"What? You're working with her?" he asked. His eyes went wide as if he couldn't believe what he was hearing.

"She uncovered some good stuff on LeAnn," Lindsey said.

"Let me get this straight," Robbie said. He raised one finger in the air as if to emphasize his point. "She's your new partner."

"No," Lindsey said at the same time Kili said, "Yes."

"Ah!" Robbie gasped and clutched at his chest. "You're heartless."

"No, I'm not," Lindsey said. "What I am is desperate to prove that my clerk is innocent so that she can come back to work."

"Has your girlfriend told you anything about the case?" Kili asked him.

Robbie looked sulky when he answered. "No. She won't discuss it. It's making me mental."

"If you want to help, we need intel on Amy Ellers," Kili said.

"She's right. I wasn't able to find much," Lindsey admitted. "I know from asking about that she moved into her house a few months ago, but not much is known about her before she appeared in Briar Creek. She's apparently not super social and spent most of her time with Olive."

"She did not seem terribly susceptible to my charm," Robbie said. "She called me a sourdough."

"Don't be a quitter," Lindsey teased. Then she frowned. Sourdough was a weird thing to call someone. She opened up the urban dictionary on her computer and searched the term.

"Yeah, Lindsey's right. You've still got it, you know, for an older guy," Kili said.

"I don't like you," Robbie retorted.

"Just stating the facts." Kili shrugged.

"There has to be a reason she's so private. Maybe she's in the witness protection program," Robbie said. "And Olive figured out who she was so the CIA or the FBI or whoever is in charge of that had to kill her. That's why we can't figure it out. It was a professional hit."

"Wouldn't Amy just have been relocated?" Kili asked.

"Spoilsport," he snapped.

"Reality much?" Kili returned.

"Enough you two," Lindsey said. "Listen, the term she called you—*sourdough*—that's an Alaskan term, meaning someone who has lived in the north country their whole life. But when she called you that, it was clearly a comparison insult as if she had nothing but contempt for the type of person who was tenacious enough to survive in the wild. I think she has to be from Alaska. We need to find out more about her. Any ideas on where to start?"

"I'm going to ask her for an interview," Kili said. "Everyone loves to be interviewed. If she declines, then we know she's hiding something."

"That's shaky reasoning," Lindsey said. "And it won't give us any more information, especially if she declines, which she will if she's as private as she seems."

"Do we really need to know her backstory, or do we just need her to think we do?" Robbie asked.

Kili squinted at him. "Continue."

"You've been using the 'memorial for Olive' reason to talk to everyone. Why not use it on her friends, and then when they're here, we can let them know that we know their secrets," Robbie said.

"And the killer will be revealed when they panic," Kili said. "Brilliant."

Robbie inclined his head in thanks as he sat in the vacant seat.

"I don't know," Lindsey said. "This sounds like it might become dangerous if one of them is the killer, and I promised that I would not do anything dangerous."

"It's a meeting of a bunch of bitter women. How can it be dangerous?" Kili scoffed.

"One of which might be a murderer," Lindsey argued. "If they had no issue stabbing a friend, I really don't see them hesitating to shank one of us."

"You're being dramatic," Kili said. She glanced at Robbie. "Come on, back me up."

"I think having a meeting in a public place, here at the library, for instance, would keep us all safe," he said. "If we want to have a cover, we could invite the ex-husband and the sister and the library board as well."

"The police really have nothing on this yet?" Lindsey asked.

"Emma's playing it close, while waiting for the forensics. It's only been a few days," he said. "The medical examiner hasn't given his full report yet."

With both Robbie and Kili staring at her, Lindsey felt the pressure building. She really didn't want to do anything dumb. She never wanted to feel like she did the last time she faced off with a killer. But then again, she felt an obligation to Olive to figure out who did this, to Paula to help clear her name and to herself because she was pretty good at figuring these sorts of things out, and she didn't want to quit doing what she knew was right just because she'd had a bad scare.

"All right," she said. "I'll call everyone together to discuss the final plan for Olive's memorial. All manipulation aside, I really do think a small garden with a bench will be a lovely way to remember her."

"Even if she was a miserable old cow," Robbie said. Both women looked at him. "What? Just because she was murdered doesn't mean she wasn't an awful person. One could argue she wouldn't have been murdered if she wasn't so lousy."

"He has a point," Kili said.

"In any event, I'll arrange the meeting and let you two know when it is. I'm hoping for tomorrow. Will that work for you both?"

"I'll make it work," Kili said.

"Same," Robbie agreed.

Lindsey turned back to her computer. She inserted a flash drive and downloaded the file of pictures onto it. She handed it to Robbie and said, "Give this to Emma. It's pictures from the dinner. We didn't see anything in them, but maybe she will."

"That should get you out of hot water with her," he said. "At least a little bit."

"She doesn't believe that I don't know where Paula is, does she?"

"Well . . . no," he said.

"I really don't," Lindsey said. "In fact, I'm pretty sure she didn't tell me specifically to keep me from having to lie for her."

"That occurred to Emma, too, after a rather heated exchange between us over bagels this morning."

"I'm sorry, Robbie. I don't want this situation to cause issues between you and Emma."

"Don't you worry," he said. "We like our relationship with a little fire in it. It keeps things hot."

"And, ew, on that note, I'm leaving," Kili said.

"What? Did I overshare?" he asked.

"A touch," she said. She jotted down a number on a sticky note on Lindsey's desk. She tapped it with one red fingernail and said, "Text me."

Lindsey nodded. As the door shut behind her, Robbie looked at Lindsey and said, "I hope you know what you're doing, trusting that viper."

She blew out a breath and said, "Me, too."

The meeting to finalize the plans for Olive's memorial was set for midafternoon the next day. Lindsey had pulled together some light refreshments from the local bakery and had the coffee maker going. As if it wasn't enough to have the friends and the ex and the sister, she'd also invited the library board. She wanted this meeting to appear as legit as possible.

Because she couldn't find any reason for

Robbie and Kili to be present at the meeting, she reserved the glassed-in conference room right next to the one where she was holding her meeting, knowing that it was easy to listen through the glass walls. Floor-to-ceiling shades covered the glass wall between the two rooms and would keep them from seeing or being seen. It was the best she could do.

Robbie and Kili took their spots fifteen minutes before the meeting was to start. Lindsey tried not to be nervous, but as the library board filed in, she found that her palms were sweating even as her fingers were icy cold. That wasn't normal, and she could only assume that it was panic, making her heart race and her throat dry.

She poured herself a cup of hot coffee and took her seat at the head of the table with a blank pad and a ballpoint pen sitting in front of her. She forced herself not to doodle, even though she knew it would calm her down.

Olive's friends arrived next. LeAnn looked pinched and miserable, Amy looked mean and Kim defeated. It was as if they found comfort in their misery and were unable to shake it off. Lindsey had always thought it was Olive's temperament that ruled the group, but now she wondered. With Olive gone, shouldn't a new personality emerge?

Then again, perhaps it was their grief over losing Olive that made them so miserable.

Lindsey tried to picture that, she did, but it just wasn't clicking. Not one of them had cried at Olive's service. She believed her suspicions about Olive being manipulative were correct and that these women weren't her friends so much as her hostages.

When Kyle arrived, Lindsey saw LeAnn stiffen, but she didn't say anything, for which Lindsey was relieved. Judging by the way Kyle chose to sit as far away from her as possible, Lindsey suspected he was hoping to avoid another scene like the one after Olive's funeral as well.

At the top of the hour, everyone was in attendance except for Olive's half sister, Margaret. Although she had said she'd come, Lindsey wondered if she'd had a change of heart. The sisters had been estranged, after all, so maybe she didn't feel right coming to the meeting.

While the group talked in low murmurs amongst themselves, she glanced out the window toward the parking lot to see if Margaret had arrived. She saw several people come and go but not Margaret.

"Are we ready to start?" LeAnn asked. "I do have other things to do today."

Longtime board member Lydia Wilcox glanced at her over the tops of her glasses. The look was frosty to say the least, and LeAnn squirmed in her chair.

"Of course," Lindsey said. "I was waiting on one more person, but—"

The door banged open, and on a gust of air, Margaret Davidson hurried into the room. "Sorry I'm late. Traffic . . ."

Everyone turned to look at her, and she ran a hand through her hair as if she could minimize the staring if she just straightened her part and tamed her wild curls.

"It's fine," Lindsey said. "Please come in."

Margaret took one step into the room, and Amy erupted from her seat. Her fists were clenched at her sides, her mouth was clamped in a thin tight line and a deep furrow formed in between her brows. She was the picture of fury.

"What are you doing here?" she snapped.

Margaret recoiled. She waved at Lindsey and said, "I was asked to come."

"I did invite her," Lindsey said. She noticed Amy was shaking. "I thought as Olive's sister, she should have approval over what we finally decided."

"Approval?" Amy spat. "That's a laugh. What? You didn't steal enough from your sister before and now you want your sticky fingers all over her memorial, too?"

Margaret put her hand to her throat and her eyes went wide. She blinked at Amy as if she had no idea what to make of her.

"I don't think this is the time—" Lindsey began and then paused.

She glanced past Margaret and saw four

eyeballs peering at her between the shades of the next room. Robbie and Kili. She waved her hand at them to tell them to go away, and when Amy glared at her, she swung her arm uselessly in the air in a tra-la-la sort of way that was totally unfitting the present moment of tense hostility.

"Are you kidding? This is the perfect time." Amy took a step toward Margaret until she was looming over her. "Olive told us all about what you did, how you stole the family estate out from under her, after being away for years and letting her do all of the caregiving. You're nothing more than a thief!"

"That's not true," Margaret said. "I would have been happy to split everything with her, but she was so angry. She refused."

"Split it? Why should she have had to split it with you? You weren't there to take care of anyone. You didn't earn it, and then you just waltzed back to Connecticut to take your share and hers, too," Amy cried. "You took the only thing that ever mattered to her. Then you abandoned her. You stuck her here with all the responsibility and just took off on your merry way. Do you have any idea how much you hurt her?"

Margaret blinked rapidly as if trying to keep back the tears. Lindsey knew she needed to step in between the two women, but it was such a raw moment that she didn't know what to say. This was the most emotion she'd seen out of Amy or any of Olive's friends.

"Amy, I don't know that this is the appropriate time to get into personal family stuff," Lindsey said. "I know you've lost a friend, but Margaret lost her sister."

"Ha!" Amy scoffed. Then she turned on Lindsey. "You're just as bad as she is. You're shielding Olive's killer just because she works for you."

"There is no proof that Paula Turner—"

"Blah, blah, blah, yes, she did, and everyone knows it," Amy cut her off.

She turned around and grabbed her purse from the floor.

"None of you cared about Olive Boyle," Amy continued. "Not one. This whole thing is a ridiculous farce to alleviate your guilt for not caring that she's dead. If you want to go ahead and plan your memorial, be my guest, but you can count me out. I'll buy my own memorial to her when I inherit my share."

She shoved past Margaret and stomped to the door. Then she spun around and stared Margaret down. "Despite what Olive did to the rest of us, what you did to her was even worse. You're even more despicable than she was, and that's saying something."

The door slammed shut behind her, and Lindsey glanced at the assembled group. "Um . . . perhaps . . . meeting adjourned."

23

Everyone ignored her. They broke out into hushed whispers in their little groupings as they tried to decipher what Amy had meant when she said she would inherit. Inherit what?

"Do you think she knows something that we don't?" Kim asked LeAnn. "Maybc Olive left everything to us, her friends. I mean, who else does she have?"

"Shush," LeAnn said and jerked her head at Margaret.

"Oh, right." Kim lowered her voice but Lindsey was close enough to hear her. "But why would Amy think she was inheriting anything? She must know something. We should ask her."

"And say what?" LeAnn asked. "Hey, you sound likc you're expecting a big payout. Care to share what you know?"

"Wait, if she knew she was going to inherit, wouldn't that give Amy a reason to murder Olive?" Kim asked.

"She couldn't have; she was with us at the time Olive was murdered," LeAnn said. "Remember?"

"No, actually, I don't," Kim said. Her voice grew louder as she tried to puzzle it out. "I mean, I know I said she was with us, but can you really remember what happened that night? It was so chaotic. How long does it take to stab a person anyway? Seconds? She totally could have left us, stabbed Olive and gotten back to us before we even noticed she was gone."

"Ah," Margaret gasped. Her cheeks were flushed, and she looked horrified. "How can you speak so casually about murder? The murder of my sister."

"Oh, puleeeze," Kim said. Her voice was thick with mocking disdain. "Olive hated you, and it seems like it was mutual. Don't pretend you care."

"I do—" Margaret began, but Kim turned her back on her.

"Knowing how Olive had it in for the librarian and her lackey, anyone who was intent on murdering Olive only had to be at the library dinner to realize they could kill her and then pin it on them," LeAnn said. "Genius."

When Lindsey looked at her as if she couldn't be serious, LeAnn looked away and said, "In a totally psychopathic sort of way, of course."

There was a knock on the door, and Robbie and Kili came in.

"Lindsey, we have a library emergency," he said.

Lindsey blinked.

"Yeah, there's, like, a book problem, a problem with a book, you know, something like that," Kili said.

"Sure," Lindsey said. She glanced at the others in the room, "Excuse me."

Lindsey pushed the two of them into the corner of the room, where she could still hear what was happening.

"Wow, just wow," Robbie whispered. "That was a heck of a tirade, but it begs the bigger question of what could Amy possibly be inheriting from Olive and why?"

Lindsey shrugged. She glanced over her shoulder at the board members who had yet to leave. They were sitting at the table as if entranced by the entire spectacle.

"I need to know—were they very close, Olive and Amy?" Margaret asked LeAnn and Kim. Everyone turned to stare at her. "Sorry, I don't suppose it's my business, but that woman seemed very attached to my sister, so I was just wondering how close they were?"

Kim and LeAnn regarded her suspiciously, and Kim said, "If Olive left anything to Amy or us, you can't interfere with that."

"I would never," Margaret protested.

"Sure, you wouldn't," LeAnn sneered. "Just like you didn't bilk Olive out of her inheritance."

Margaret pulled her coat around her more tightly as if it could ward off the ugly feelings she was receiving from LeAnn and Kim.

"I didn't steal her inheritance. There were legalities that I couldn't work around. I tried to talk to Olive," she insisted. Lindsey couldn't help but notice that her voice lacked conviction. She wondered if the others heard it, too.

"Amy was closer to Olive than we were," Kim said. LeAnn gave her a look and she shrugged. "What? It's true. They had a codependent, mother-daughter, let's-pretend-we're-the-Gilmore Girls vibe happening. Amy looked up to Olive, and Olive basked in the glow even though Amy could be pretty snarky when she felt like it."

"How long did they know each other?" Robbie asked, joining the conversation.

"A few months, maybe half a year," LeAnn said.

"And Amy thinks Olive has left her an inheritance? Huh. Weird." Kili snapped her fingers. "Unless they were lovers?"

Kim and LeAnn exchanged a considering look, then LeAnn shook her head.

"No," Kim said. "Olive liked men. In fact, she had a big scheme to get her ex back."

"What?" Kyle choked on his coffee, and Lydia slapped him on the back so hard that he almost fell out of his seat.

"Olive told us that she planned to get Kyle back and she would do whatever it took," Kim continued. "She said that Molly didn't stand a chance of keeping her man. She called her pathetic."

Lindsey thought of the lone picture of Kyle and Olive on their wedding day in her study.

"That would certainly give someone a motive for murder, wouldn't it?" LeAnn studied Kyle as if intrigued by him. "Say, maybe a wife who was intent on hanging on to her hubby?"

"No, whatever you're thinking, the answer is no," Kyle said. "Molly would *never* harm Olive."

"You sure about that?" Kim asked.

Lindsey thought about Molly's delight in meeting Robbie. Yeah, she just couldn't see her as the sort to crash a library fund-raiser and stab her husband's ex-wife from twenty years before in the back. Then again, she had admitted to disliking Olive pretty intensely.

"If they've only known each other a few months, where did Olive and Amy meet?" Lindsey asked, trying to keep the dialogue on track.

"I'm glad you asked that," Kili said. She had been flipping through her phone as if reviewing her notes from the case. "I made a timeline for everyone involved. Now none of us could find much backstory on Amy before she arrived in Briar Creek a few months ago—which is weird, but whatever—so she had to have met Olive here in town unless . . ."

Robbie looked at her as if she couldn't possibly mean to end her sentence there.

"What? Don't leave us in suspense! Out with it," he insisted.

"Well, the only time Olive left Connecticut recently was to go on an extended trip to Alaska about six months ago, right before Amy appeared in town," Kili said.

"Alaska?" Kim asked. "They met in Alaska? They never told us that."

"No, in fact, they never told us how they met at all," LeAnn agreed. "I just assumed that they became friends when Amy moved to our street."

Kim and LeAnn exchanged a glance as if they were reconsidering everything they had ever known about Olive and Amy.

"Did Amy ever talk about her past?" Lindsey asked. "Who her people were? Where she came from? Anything like that?"

"No, she said she was leaving her painful past behind her," LeAnn said. "She made it sound as if she was leaving an abusive situation behind. Honestly, I thought she was hiding out. I mean, her hair is clearly an over-the-top boring dye job, and her glasses are fake. I assumed she was trying not to be recognized."

"That's right," Robbie said. "I looked through her glasses once, they were worthless."

"She was very clear that she was starting over here," Kim agreed. "She always sounded very optimistic about it."

"About the house," Kili said. "I looked up the properties on the street—"

"Thorough of you," Lindsey said. "I'm impressed."

"Thank you, I try," Kili said with a dash of sarcasm. "Olive owned the house Amy lived in."

"She bought a house for a woman she'd just met? Okay, that's unusual," Lindsey said.

"Unless they really were lovers. It could be Olive liked boys and girls," Robbie said. "Margaret . . ."

He paused to address Olive's sister in the crowded room. Lindsey scanned the room, too. Margaret was gone.

"Huh, she just left?" Lindsey asked. "That was . . ."

"Abrupt," Kyle said. He looked agitated.

Kili frowned. "Too abrupt."

"What are you thinking?" Robbie asked.

"That we may have just given a killer a new target," Lindsey said.

"What? Who?" Robbie asked.

Lindsey ignored him and turned to Olive's ex-husband. "Kyle, was there any family scandal concerning Olive?"

"You mean other than finding out her father wasn't her father?" he asked.

"Yes, was there anything else?" Lindsey asked. "Did she have anything in her past that she was hiding?"

"I'm sorry, you're going to have to speak plainly," he said. "I'm not sure what you're getting at."

"Did either Olive or Margaret have a child?"

Kyle's eyes went wide. "No! God, no, at least not that I'm aware of . . . but honestly, Margaret was away at school when I came into the picture, and then she took off to Alaska. I don't really know anything about her except that she's Olive's younger sister, half sister, and that Olive always seemed to resent her, which reached a boiling point when Olive discovered that their father really wasn't her biological father."

"But he adopted Olive, so he would have been the grandfather to any child born to either Margaret or Olive," Lindsey said.

"Are you saying you think Amy is the daughter of Margaret or Olive?" Robbie asked.

"Margaret did take off to Alaska in her youth, and Olive and Amy did meet there just a few months ago," Kili said.

"The question is whether their meeting was happenstance, or did Olive go there looking for Amy?" Lindsey asked.

"If it was six months ago, then it was a few months after Olive found out her father wasn't her real father and she lost her portion of the estate by fighting the terms of the will," Robbie said. "But if it's still in probate, could she have gotten it back by providing another heir?"

Robbie and Lindsey looked at each other and together said, "Amy."

"We need to go over there right now," he said.

"Agreed."

"Go where?" Kili asked. "I'm not following."

"No, you're not," Lindsey said. "I need you to stay here and find out everything you can about Amy Ellers. I'm betting Ellers is her adoptive name. See what you can find out about the Ellers family in Alaska, specifically if they adopted a baby girl around thirty years ago."

"Why?"

"Because I think Margaret went to Alaska to have a baby and give it up for adoption," Lindsey said. "I think Amy is her daughter and as such would rightfully inherit some of the Davidson estate, especially since it's still in probate. If Margaret did kill Olive to make sure the estate remained hers, then she'll go after Amy next."

"Oh, wow, okay. But where are you going?" Kili asked.

"To make sure another murder doesn't happen," Lindsey said.

She turned and ran for the door, slamming into a big, burly chest on the way.

Sully caught her by the upper arms before she landed on her butt.

"What's going on?" he asked. He set her back on her feet, looking at her with concern.

"We'll explain on the way, merman," Robbie said. "Right now we have to stop a killer."

Sully looked at Lindsey, and she shrugged.

"Maybe," she said.

He nodded as if this made perfect sense. "All right. Let's go."

Lindsey stopped at her office to grab her handbag so that she had her phone and her hooded sweatshirt, since the temperature had dropped and it would be even colder by the water. They took Sully's truck, which was parked out front, and while he drove, Lindsey called Emma on her cell phone.

"She's not answering," Lindsey said. "Why isn't she answering?"

"I don't know," Robbie said. "Maybe her phone is off."

"Chief Plewicki, how can I help you?" Emma answered just before Lindsey ended the call.

"Emma, it's Lindsey," she said. "Listen Sully, Robbie and I are on our way to Amy Ellers's house. I'm not sure, but I think she might be in danger. Crazy speculation, but I think she's related to Olive Boyle and stands to inherit all of Olive's estate plus a portion of the Davidson estate."

"What?" Emma squawked. "How did this come about?"

"There was a meeting at the library . . ." Lindsey began but then stopped. "That's not really the point. The point is I think Olive's killer is her sister, Margaret, and I believe she's going to strike again and Amy is the target."

"Do not go into the house," Emma said. Lindsey could hear her breathing become rapid, and she knew Emma was running for her car. "I repeat, do not go inside."

Sully parked the truck right in front of the house. Lindsey was wedged between the two men and looked past Robbie at the large stone and glass building very much like Olive's. Nothing seemed to be amiss.

"We won't go in," Lindsey promised. "We'll stay parked right in front—"

Robbie opened his door and climbed out.

"Hey, understudy, get back in here," Sully said.

"Oh no, is Robbie out of the car?" Emma asked.

"Possibly standing in front of it," Lindsey hedged.

"Don't let him go near the house. I mean it," Emma said. "I'm on the other side of town. In fact, I have Paula with me."

"Paula? Is she all right?" Lindsey asked.

"Yes, she's fine. She's been staying with her girlfriend Hannah's aunt Claire on her farm," Emma said.

"Oh," Lindsey said. The news that Paula was safe made her sag a little bit with relief. "Tell her things are going to be okay, please, and sound like you mean it."

"Fine. We'll be there in fifteen minutes. I'll see if I can get another officer out there faster. Do not go near the house. Repeat, do not go near the house and don't hang up."

"All right, got it," Lindsey agreed. She noted a familiar dark blue Volvo covered in bumper stickers parked in front of the house. She'd seen this car before. But where?

Robbie walked over to the old car and glanced inside the back window. Then he spun around and looked at Lindsey.

"Pruning shears," he said. "There are pruning shears in the back."

"Margaret," she said.

That was it! This was the same car they'd seen at Margaret's house. A cold chill rippled through her, and in a flash she remembered that she'd seen this car one other time. The day of the library dinner she'd seen Olive arguing with someone in a blue Volvo outside the library.

"We have to go in," Robbie said.

He started up the walkway. A scream ripped through the quiet and made the hair on the back of Lindsey's neck stand on end. Robbie started to jog toward the house, and Sully moved past Lindsey to go with him.

"What the hell was that?" Emma asked.

"It came from the house," Lindsey said. "We're going in."

"No!"

"Emma, we have to," Lindsey said. "Send backup if you can."

She dropped the phone into her pocket before Emma could protest, and she ran after the boys.

"Who are we looking for?" Sully asked.

"Margaret Davidson or Amy Ellers. The car belongs to Margaret, and we think she's here to kill Amy to make sure her inheritance stays intact, because we suspect that Amy is actually Margaret's daughter, whom she gave up for adoption almost thirty years ago, unknowingly giving Amy a heck of a stake in the inheritance. But Olive knew and we think that's why Olive brought Amy here."

"Oh boy," Sully said. He took Lindsey by the elbow and moved her to the side of the house out of sight of any of the windows. "You wait for Emma right here."

"But—"

"No."

"I agree," Robbie said. "Sully's military. He's our best bet."

Sully turned to look at him with his eyebrows raised in surprise. Robbie shrugged at the concession.

"I'm going around back to look for a point of entry," Sully said. "Robbie, you watch the front and make sure no one leaves."

"Got it."

A crash sounded from the house, and Sully kissed Lindsey quickly on the head and dashed around the side of the house, hunched over, staying below the windows. Robbie crept to the corner and peered around it, keeping watch on the front.

Another scream sounded, and Lindsey felt her heart clutch in her chest. Sully was going in there. He was entering a house with a suspected murderer. She couldn't stand it. She began to ease backward until she was at the corner, giving her a view of the back door.

There was no sign of Sully. There was, however, a sliding glass door on the patio that had been left open, leading into the lower level of the house. It would be so easy to peek from there. Without overthinking it, she crept across the lawn and then over the small wall that enclosed the patio. She pressed herself up against the back of the house as if she could make herself as slim as a shadow and then waited, listening for any noise from inside.

She couldn't hear anything over the pounding of her own heart. Her hands were sweating, and she clenched them into fists, trying to calm her breathing before she took a look inside. She pulled the hood on her sweatshirt up over her head, hoping it would camouflage her light hair.

She slid down the wall, figuring it was better to watch from down below. She eased her head around the door and looked inside. It was dark, and she could only make out shapes of what looked to be a family room with squashy furniture and a big TV. It was empty. She leaned in closer and listened to hear if anyone was moving. She had no idea if this was where Sully had entered the house, as there was no sign of him.

Another crash sounded, and Lindsey lost her balance and fell to her knees just inside the door. Since no one was in the room, she couldn't make herself leave, not knowing where Sully was and whether he was all right.

She didn't bother to rise but scuttled on her hands and knees into the house. She hid behind a big fluffy couch and then a chair. She moved so that she was in the shadows of the perimeter of the room. A shallow flight of stairs leading up to the first floor was on the far side of the room, and she knew she'd have to take them upstairs to find out what was happening. She also knew that they would leave her visible to anyone from above.

The sound of footsteps running above her, light ones and then heavy ones, convinced her that she needed to be up there to help. She made for the stairs. She had just reached the top when an arm clotheslined her across the chest, knocking her down the stairs to sprawl on the floor.

When she glanced up, it was to see Margaret staring down at her with wide eyes and a large kitchen knife clutched in her fist. In full panic, Lindsey scuttled away from her in an uncoordinated crab walk that was awkward and slow, as her feet gave out beneath her, giving her no traction.

Oh, man, Margaret was going to stab her just like she had Olive. Why hadn't she listened to Sully and stayed outside? Why?

24

O h my God!" Margaret cried.

She lunged toward Lindsey, who dropped onto her back and raised her legs, getting ready to kick Margaret into next week if she tried to stab her.

"Back off!" Lindsey yelled.

"I'm so sorry. I didn't know it was you. I thought you were her," Margaret babbled.

"Who? Amy?" Lindsey asked. She tried to keep her voice even as she scurried to put the squashy chair in between them.

"No, Molly Boyle," Margaret said. "She's here. She wants to kill Amy, my niece."

"Niece?" Lindsey shook her head. "I thought Amy was your daughter?"

"No, she's Olive's daughter," Margaret said. "I'm the one who took her to Alaska as an infant to find a family for her."

"Why would Molly want to kill her?" Lindsey asked. "That makes no sense."

"Because she thinks that Amy is Kyle's daughter, too," Margaret said. "Molly killed Olive because she was going to use Amy to take Kyle away from her, and now she wants to kill his child, too."

"Why should I believe you?" Lindsey asked.

"Because I'm telling the truth. In the meeting this afternoon, the second I heard that Amy was from Alaska, it all started to fall into place. Olive went to Alaska six months ago to find her daughter so that she could use her to gain back the inheritance she'd forfeited by contesting the will and to try and win her ex-husband back. LeAnn said Olive had a big plan to get her ex back; this had to be it. Molly must have figured out what she was doing and decided to stop her."

"How do I know Molly is really here?"

"Didn't you see her car?" Margaret asked. "It's the mom mobile out front."

Lindsey blinked. There had been a high-end minivan in front of this house, just like the one she'd seen in the Boyles' driveway the day she went to visit them about Olive's memorial. She'd been so distracted by the Volvo she hadn't recognized it.

The fear pouring off of Margaret was hitting Lindsey in waves. She wondered if her phone was still connected to Emma's and if Emma could hear this conversation and know what she was walking into.

She and Robbie had been wrong. It wasn't Margaret but Molly who had stabbed Olive. She remembered Molly's dislike of her husband's ex. She could only imagine how Molly would have reacted if she found out that Olive had a child with Kyle and she was going to use that child to win him back. Margaret was right. LeAnn had admitted that Olive had a big scheme to win him back.

"Does Kyle know that he has a daughter?" Lindsey asked. He seemed devoted to his two children, and she couldn't imagine he'd have let a child of his be adopted by a family across the country unless he didn't know.

"No, no one knew," Margaret said. "I don't know how Molly figured it out, but she must have been tipped off. Maybe Olive told Amy and Amy went to meet her father?"

"Where's Amy now?" she asked. "We have to get her out of here and away from Molly."

"I don't know," Margaret said. She looked like she was about ready to cry. "When we were talking at the meeting, and I realized that Amy was my niece, I raced over here. Molly was here already. No one answered the front door, so I came around the back. When I peeked in, she came at me with this knife, but I kicked her and she dropped it and ran back up into the house. I was checking the house when I caught sight of you. Sorry I knocked you back."

"It's okay."

The tread of footsteps sounded above again, and Margaret tensed. "We have to find Amy before Molly finds us. If she discovers us, she'll kill us all."

"You go and wait for the police," Lindsey said. "I'll make sure Amy is okay."

"I can't leave her. I'm her aunt," Margaret protested.

"It could be that Amy isn't even here," Lindsey said. "Go."

"No, we leave together," Margaret insisted.

She nodded at Margaret, pretending to agree with her. She did not have time for this. Sully was here, and Lindsey couldn't leave him alone with a killer. If she could, she'd get Amy out of harm's way, too, but she couldn't do it with Margaret underfoot.

"Let's go," Margaret said. She turned and led the way to the door. Once Margaret went through it, Lindsey slid the door shut and latched it.

Margaret's eyes went wide. She banged on the glass. "What are you doing? She'll kill you!"

"Go call for help!" Lindsey hissed. When Margaret didn't move, she mouthed the word *Now!*

Margaret turned and ran away from the house. Lindsey heaved a sigh of relief. Okay, one person safe. Now she just had to find Sully and Amy and get the hell out of here.

She pulled her phone out of her pocket to see if she was still connected to Emma. The call had ended, probably with her fall. She couldn't risk making any more noise by calling again, so she pocketed her phone and crept up the stairs.

She paused at the top step. She didn't hear anyone moving. Where would Molly be? If Margaret had taken her knife from her, would she have gone for another?

Lindsey felt terrible for suspecting Margaret of Olive's murder. It had seemed that Margaret had the most to gain given the vastness of the Davidson estate, but if Olive had been making a play for Kyle by using their child as emotional leverage, then that gave Molly a powerful motive to eliminate her competition. Kyle had admitted that he was forever stepping in to help Olive. How would finding out he had a daughter with her have impacted their relationship? Lindsey couldn't even imagine it but understood why Molly must have felt as if her whole world was collapsing. Maybe after all of these years of Olive causing trouble for her, she'd finally snapped.

The downstairs of the house was very much like Olive's, which seemed appropriate since Olive had owned it. Sparsely decorated, very modern, it had no personal touches to signify what sort of person lived here. Lindsey didn't see anyone in the wide hallway at the top of the staircase. She walked very swiftly and very quietly in the direction of the kitchen.

It was empty. She tilted her head to listen to the house. She didn't hear anyone walking around. She desperately wanted to call out to Sully, but if Molly was still in the house, she didn't want to let her know that they were both here, too.

She hunkered down behind the granite counter, peering up and over it as she made her way through the room. There was a doorway on the opposite side of the kitchen, and she headed in that direction, thinking she would work her way through the house room by room until she found Sully and Amy. She could only hope she wasn't too late.

Sully was a big guy with military-style fighting skills. Surely he wouldn't have been taken out by a mild-mannered housewife. Of course, the fact that she was crazy and had already killed someone was not exactly in his favor, but still, he was a big boy, or so she kept telling herself as she tried to beat down the panic that wanted to render her catatonic.

The dining room opened up in front of her, and she slid into the room, scanning as she went. There was no movement, no sound in the house. It was making her nervous, and she had to force herself to slow down and not hurry.

Where the hell was Emma, or any of the Briar Creek police for that matter? The town wasn't that big. How long could it really take for them to get here?

The dining room led into a living room. The white leather furniture indicated that there were no pets or children in this house. No one who had kids or pets would have chosen white leather.

Lindsey crouched as she hurried into the room. It, too, appeared to be empty, so she figured everyone had to be upstairs. She was just passing the double doors that were open to the front foyer when she heard a noise behind her.

Instinct had her ducking low and spinning just as a heavy glass vase sailed right by her head. A flash of long blond hair much like her own identified Molly Boyle, who shrieked and reached for another glass objet d'art. Lindsey didn't wait to see if her aim was any better the second time around. Instead, she bolted for the stairs across the foyer and pounded up the steps to the floor above.

It occurred to her when she was halfway up that she would be trapped on the second floor with a lunatic on the first, but if she could find Sully, then they could overpower Molly. At least, she hoped they could. With no sign of him, she was beginning to worry that Molly had already—No! Lindsey cut off that thought. She couldn't go there.

With Molly having spotted her, Lindsey figured she had nothing to lose. She reached the hallway and began to run down it, glancing into rooms as she passed by, yelling, "Sully! Amy! Anyone!"

The phone in her pocket began to buzz, and she pulled it out and glanced at the display.

"What's going on in there?" Robbie asked. "I heard a crash."

"It's Molly," Lindsey said. "She's the killer. Is Margaret out there? She'll tell you."

"Margaret? I thought she was the killer," he said.

"So did I, but she said that Molly killed Olive to keep her from stealing Kyle back," Lindsey said. "Molly just tried to bash my head in, so I'm thinking she's right. Ask Margaret. She should have reached you by now."

"I'll look for her."

"Any sign of Emma?"

"She called and said she's five minutes out," he said. "Lindsey, I don't like this. Get out of the house. Now."

"But Sully—"

"Is a strapping lad and can get his own self out," Robbie said. "Do this for him. Do it now."

"I'm on my way," Lindsey said. "I'll leave my phone on."

"Be careful, pet," he said.

"Always."

Lindsey was going to get out of the house. Just as soon as she checked the last two bedrooms. She had no idea where Molly was, and her sense of panic was making her hands shake. She just wanted to find Sully and get the hell out of this crazy house.

She kept her back to the wall as she moved down the hallway. She was returning past another empty bedroom when an arm shot out and a hand clamped over her mouth and she was yanked into the room.

She started to buck and fight, but Sully spoke into her ear, "It's me, Sully. It's okay."

She immediately went limp in relief. When he released her, she spun around and hugged him close.

"Thank goodness you're all right," she said. "I was terrified."

"Molly is—"

"Margaret is—"

"The killer," they said together. "No, she's—" They did it again.

"You first," Sully said. "Molly?"

"She was downstairs," Lindsey said. She pushed her hood off of her hair and glanced up at him. "She threw a vase at me. I'm pretty sure she thought I was Amy."

"Yeah, well, Margaret tried to filet me with a big old knife," he said.

"What?"

"Yeah," he said. "I came in, and she came out swinging. She barely missed me."

He held up his arm, and Lindsey felt all of the blood drain from her face when she saw the slash in the fabric of his own sweatshirt. She wobbled a little on her feet.

"It's okay," he said. "I'm okay. I shouted in surprise, and she ran off."

"One of them is a murderer," she said. "I sent

Margaret out of the house, but Robbie said he hasn't seen her. Oh God, what if I was wrong? What if Margaret is the killer? But if she is then what is Molly doing here?"

"We need to find Amy and get out of here," he said.

"I haven't seen her," Lindsey said. "You?"

"No, but Margaret was fighting with someone when I came in," he said. "I assumed it was Amy but maybe it was Molly."

"Maybe she got out already," Lindsey said. "This whole thing is a nightmare. I mean, is the killer Margaret or Molly? They both have reasons to kill Olive and to go after her daughter."

"Two suspects, and both of them are here," Sully said. He looked at Lindsey, his bright blue eyes narrowed in thought. "*Why* are they both here?"

Lindsey felt the bottom drop out of her stomach. She had a sudden chilling thought. Perhaps Amy's scene at the library meeting hadn't been the passionate speech of a distraught friend or reunited daughter. Maybe it had been the final lure in a trap.

"Perhaps Amy was never here," she said.

"What do you mean?" he asked.

"I mean I think I know who Olive's killer is, and her name does not begin with an *M*."

Sully stared at her. "Amy?"

Lindsey nodded. "There was so much misdirection. Paula and me as suspects because Olive was going after our jobs. We were the first targets, but I was visible for the entire party and had an alibi and Paula went underground. So then the suspicion fell on Margaret, since she inherited everything from Olive and it was clear there was no love lost between the sisters, at least on Olive's part.

"But that didn't stick because Margaret proved she was willing to split the estate despite Olive contesting the will. So then there was Molly, seemingly trying to hang on to her husband against Olive's bid to win him back by using their daughter—a daughter I'm betting Kyle doesn't even know he has—but there's one problem there."

Sully studied her for a moment and said, "Amy's not his daughter."

"That's my hunch," she said.

"Mine, too," he agreed. "Otherwise, why wouldn't Amy have sought her father out before? What was she waiting for?"

"Maybe she and Olive were trying to figure out a way to fake Amy's records so it appeared that Kyle was the father," Lindsey said.

"It disturbs me that I can see Olive doing something like that."

"Me, too. But when you remove all the smoke and mirrors, there's only one person with a real motive to kill Olive, and that's Amy. Olive abandoned her as a baby and then found her only to use her. Amy must have hated her for that, especially if Olive promised her money and then didn't come through. Maybe trying to prove Amy was Kyle's daughter was too difficult, and Amy was tired of waiting."

"And on that horrifying realization, you and I are leaving," he said.

The reality that Amy was most likely Olive's killer had Lindsey freaked out enough that she didn't argue. "How? We don't know where she is, if she's even here, or when she might strike."

"We're going right out the front door," he said. "Text Robbie so we don't scare him stupid."

Lindsey fired off the text and then tucked away her phone and took Sully's hand. He gave her fingers a quick squeeze before leading her out of the bedroom and back into the hallway. It was clear, and they moved toward the stairs as fast as they could, while trying to make no noise. They had just reached the top step when an ominous clicking sounded behind them.

Sully pushed Lindsey up against the wall and stood in front of her before turning to face the sound. It was Amy Ellers, standing with her feet apart and both hands holding a gun, which was pointed directly at them.

25

A terrified feeling of déjà vu swept over Lindsey, making her breath choppy and her body shake. Panic was making her vision tunnel into a little pinpoint that circled around the muzzle of the gun. She closed her eyes for a moment to chase it back.

"Drop the gun," Sully said. He didn't sound afraid at all, and Lindsey let his courage steady her.

"No," Amy said. She tipped up her chin, looking like a teenager defying curfew.

"It's over, Amy," Lindsey said. "Both Molly and Margaret are gone. You can't use them to cover up Olive's murder anymore."

She hoped she sounded sincere. She had no idea where Molly was or why Molly had attacked her. She could only think that Molly must have been so freaked out that with Lindsey's hood up she had thought Lindsey was Amy, trying to kill her, and it had been pure instinct that made her attack.

"Well, that's a pity. They were supposed to kill each other. I used the meeting to clue Margaret in to the fact that I was her long-lost niece—my God, she's a dense one, isn't she? And Molly was even easier. I placed one tear-filled call this morning, about how I was Kyle's daughter but my crazy aunt Margaret was trying to kill me over her inheritance. What a sap. Pro tip: don't try to save your husband's estranged daughter by his first wife. It will get you killed. It's especially stupid, given that I'm not even his."

"You're not?" Lindsey feigned surprise, hoping to keep Amy talking.

"Please, do I look like the progeny of some stuffy doctor?" Amy scoffed. "Olive told me I was the product of a torrid affair she had with some artist guy. Apparently, I have his eyes. No matter. For my purposes, pretending to be the doctor's kid was working for me."

"You're mental," Sully said.

"Am I? Or am I just really good at getting people to do what I want? I guess I'll just have to frame Olive's murder on you two then, won't I?" Amy let go of the gun with one hand and tapped her chin with her index finger. The happy pink of her nail polish caught Lindsey's gaze.

With her amber eyes and dark hair, she looked so innocent, not the type to stab her birth mother in cold blood or hold a gun on people while threatening their lives. When she smiled at them, it was the first time Lindsey had ever seen the smile reach her eyes. It was chilling.

"Oh, I've got it!" Amy said. "Lindsey the librarian killed Olive Boyle because Olive was going to fire her. When I figured it out, Lindsey came after me, but her big, burly boyfriend arrived and tried to stop her from killing poor little me, the innocent victim of Lindsey's psychotic rage. Unfortunately, he had to kill her to stop her, and then, distraught over killing his love, he shot himself."

She put the back of her wrist to her forehead in a feigned look of despair.

"Such drama," she said. "The newspapers will eat it up."

"No, they won't," Lindsey snapped. "That story will never fly. Too many people know we're here. Too many people know you're the real killer. You'll never get away with it."

"Sure I will. I will convince Molly and Margaret that they got played by you two, and I will cry the big tears and make everyone feel sorry for me," Amy said. Her voice was so confident, it actually made Lindsey nervous. "And then I'll do what I do best: I'll disappear. Now where should we set the stage?"

She glanced around the stairs as if considering the placement of furniture as opposed to dead bodies. The sound of tires squealing interrupted her, and she glanced out the window.

"Oh dear, the police are here," she said. "Sorry, kids, but your time is up."

She put her free hand back on the gun and took aim. Sully yanked Lindsey to the floor and covered her body with his at the same time that someone erupted out of one of the bedroom doors with a yell.

Robbie took Amy down in a flying tackle. Molly and Margaret were right behind him. Molly was holding a glass vase, looking ready to bring it down on Amy's head, while Margaret snatched the gun out of Amy's hands and held it out with two fingers, off to one side and pointing down as if it might go off all by itself.

"Get off me," Amy thrashed. She started kicking Robbie, so Molly sat down on her legs while Robbie grabbed her arms and pinned them behind her back.

"Sorry, pet, but you're not going anywhere but jail," he said.

The front door crashed open, and Emma dashed up the stairs with Kili right behind her.

"Exclusive," Kili cried. "I demand an exclusive."

"Calm down or I'll toss you out on your backside," Emma said.

"Are you threatening me?" Kili countered. "When I just interviewed the Elkerson family in Alaska and learned all sorts of interesting facts about our little Amy Ellers, really Elkerson, here?"

"All right, you can stay, but no questions until I say."

Kili nodded. Emma took in the scene in front of her and blew out a breath. In one long sentence, she read Amy her rights while she took the cuffs off her belt and clipped them onto Amy's wrists. Before Robbie could stand up, she grabbed his face and kissed him hard on the mouth.

"When I say wait outside, I mean wait outside," she said.

"Don't be mad at him," Sully said. He shifted off of Lindsey and helped her into a seated position. "Robbie saved our lives."

Robbie raised his eyebrows at Sully's use of his first name, and Sully shrugged.

Emma looked at Lindsey. "I think our men are becoming friends."

" 'Bout time," she said.

"You can't arrest me," Amy sputtered. "I'm not the killer. They are!"

Officer Kirkland, a big, redheaded hunk of a guy, bounded up the stairs. He took the scene in at a glance. "Aw, man, I always miss all of the action." Emma glanced at him with one eyebrow raised, and he said, "Sorry."

"It's fine. Take Ms. Ellers out to the car, and do not let her out of your sight," Emma said. "I'll be right out."

Kirkland lifted Amy up by the elbow and guided her down the stairs. She started protesting immediately.

"Ow, you're hurting me! Ow, oh, I think you broke my arm. Police brutality! You're my witnesses. He's beating me!" she hollered all the way out the door and into the yard.

"You're my witness that she's lying," Emma said to Kili.

"Yep," Kili agreed. "And I'm going to keep being a witness." She hurried down the stairs after them.

"Are you all okay?" Emma asked the group.

Both Margaret and Molly nodded, Robbie grunted and Sully and Lindsey reached for each other's hands, twining their fingers together as if to reassure themselves, once again, that they'd made it out alive.

Emma took the gun from Margaret, and Molly put the vase she'd been clutching down on the floor. She was pasty pale and shaking, and Margaret didn't look much better.

"How did the three of you get up here?" Lindsey asked.

"After I threw that vase at you—sorry, I thought you were Margaret," Molly said, "I ran out the front door right into Robbie."

"And I felt horrible for leaving you," Margaret said. "I was climbing back in an open side window when these two showed up and tried to pull me out, thinking I was the killer."

"We had a brief scuffle," Robbie said. It was then that Lindsey noticed he had scratches on his forearms and what appeared to be a bruise on his cheekbone. "Whilst these two accused each other of murdering Olive. Upon further discussion, we realized they both had alibis, and it occurred to us that the situation was being manipulated. That's when we figured out that Amy was actually orchestrating the whole thing."

"So we all climbed in the window and came up the back staircase, hoping to reach you before she did," Molly said.

"Your timing was epic," Sully said. He ran his free hand over his face and then squeezed Lindscy's shoulder as if to reassure himself that she was fine.

"All right, let's get out of here," Emma said. "I think you could all use some fresh air and sunshine before we head down to the station."

They arrived outside to find Kyle, Molly's husband, waiting for her. He raced forward and grabbed her and held her close.

"I'm sorry, I'm so sorry, I didn't know," he said. "Olive never told me that we had a child."

Lindsey paused beside them. "You didn't."

"What?" He pulled back.

"Amy told us she isn't your daughter," she said. "Olive had an affair, and Amy was the result."

"It's true," Sully seconded her.

Molly sagged against Kyle. "I know it's stupid, but I'm really glad I'm the only woman you've had children with. I always felt like it was the only thing I had to offer you that Olive didn't."

"Oh no, Molls, you have given me so much more than she ever could, unconditional love being up there at the top with our kids," he said. "You've never been second to her, ever. It was my guilt over loving you so much more than I could ever love her that made me try to help her when she called. I never loved her like I love you. My God, if I lost you . . . ."

Kyle's voice broke, and he hugged her close. They moved away from the group, and Margaret fell into step beside Lindsey and Sully.

"Are you all right?" Lindsey asked her. "It has to be rough discovering that your niece killed your sister."

Margaret sighed. "It is. The family we found to adopt her, the Elkersons, is a nice family. Funny, I should have caught the tweak in the last name there: Elkerson is a lot like Ellers. You know, I was the one who took her to Alaska and handed her over. I thought I'd keep in touch and watch her grow up, but I didn't. It was too hard, plus I was young and selfish. I wanted to travel and see the world. Looking back, I realize it was my first time away from all of Olive's eternal drama, and I was so tired. Four thousand plus miles seemed a solid buffer."

"Will you go back to traveling?"

"No." Margaret shook her head. "My life is here now." She glanced at Sully and Lindsey, who were still holding hands. "I'm sorry you were dragged into this. My sister, her daughter, what a mess."

"Not your fault," Sully said. "I'm just really glad you and Molly helped Robbie sneak back in. You're very brave."

"While hiking in Canada, I once took on a bear with a broom," she said. "It gives a gal an overinflated sense of badassery."

Lindsey laughed and then hugged her. "Come see me at the library sometime."

"I will," Margaret said. She walked over to the police car where Officer Kirkland was keeping watch over Amy.

A crowd had gathered. The crafternoon ladies were at the front of it all, hovering around Paula, who, upon seeing Lindsey, began to cry. Lindsey noted that the spectators ran pretty deep with residents and tourists. She even spotted both the cupcake bakers and the London-hat-shop people. Probably, they hadn't expected this much excitement on their leaf-peeping trip to New England.

A black-haired fur ball busted out of the crowd and charged Lindsey. She crouched down, and Heathcliff launched himself at her. Hugging his wriggling body against her, Lindsey felt for the first time as if everything was okay.

"Did you hear the news?" Violet LaRue asked as she set up the food table for crafternoon the following Thursday afternoon.

"About?" Charlene asked, looking mildly exasperated that her mother hadn't offered more information than that.

"The hat-shop people. You know, the group visiting from London," Violet said.

"I thought they left this morning," Nancy said.

"They did, but last night, they took a final cruise around the islands on Sully's boat, and that hottie Harrison proposed to Scarlett, the redheaded girl, and she said yes."

"Sully told me it was very romantic," Lindsey said. "He said even he watered up."

"Oh, my brother, the big, strong marshmallow," Mary said. "That's what the love of a good woman will do for you." She maneuvered herself in front of the couch and grabbed the back of it while lowering herself and her ever-growing pregnant belly onto the seat. "Speaking of which, how is the cohabiting going?"

"Really well," Paula and Lindsey said together, and then they laughed. They were filling up their plates, and Lindsey was pleased to see that Paula was looking rosy cheeked and happy again.

Lindsey liked to think that the people of Briar Creek, particularly the library folks, had proven to Paula that they believed in her. They hadn't turned on her. They stood by her even when she was a suspect. She was one of them, and she never had to worry about not belonging ever again.

Mary glanced between them. "That's right.

You and Hannah took Lindsey's old apartment in Nancy's house."

"Best tenants ever," Nancy said.

"Hey!" Lindsey protested.

"Sorry, my dear, but Hannah is very handy," she said. "She's already fixed my dryer and a squeaky door, and she put in all the storm windows over the weekend."

"I shared Heathcliff with you," Lindsey said.

Nancy smiled at her. "That's true. How does my boy like his new home?"

"He loves it," she said. "We're thinking of getting him a buddy."

"Oh, so the family is getting bigger," Beth said with a grin. She tucked her thumbs into the straps of her green corduroy overalls, the ones missing a button that she always wore when she read *Corduroy* to her kiddos. "Do I hear wedding bells in the offing?"

"Only your own," Lindsey teased. "Or maybe it's the cupcake bakers'. Didn't they leave a few days ago because Angie and Tate are getting married in a few weeks?"

"They did, but I heard they're going ahead with the plan to open a franchise here with Willow, so it looks like we'll be seeing more of them," Violet said.

"Good," Nancy chimed in. "I like that guy Marty. He's got spunk, plus he likes my cookies."

"Ha! Cookies? Is that what the kids are calling

it these days?" Mary joked, and Nancy blushed a hot shade of pink.

"Hush you," Nancy said, but it lacked heat. "So, what did you all think of Poirot's last case in *Curtain*?"

"Oh, now look who's changing the subject to our book to avoid chatting about her love life," Lindsey said.

Nancy gave her a chastising look and then said, "Did you know that in nineteen forty-nine a reporter discovered that a romance novelist named Mary Westmacott was actually Dame Agatha Christie?"

"No way," Charlene said. "How did I not know that?"

"Most people don't," Lindsey said. "But she was actually quite good. In fact, one of her romances, *Absent in the Spring*, was written in three days and is considered a tour de force."

"She was fifty-four when that one was published. It just goes to show you never know what a gal might have up her sleeve," Nancy said.

Lindsey exchanged a look with Violet. Could Nancy, after all these years, finally find a new love? The thought made Lindsey grin.

Today's spread was inspired by their book of the week. Given that Christie was a British author, Violet had consulted Robbie, and in addition to tea and biscuits for dessert, they were enjoying Cornish pasties; kedgeree, a buttery dish consisting of flaked fish, rice, curry powder, hard-boiled eggs and parsley; and Yorkshire pudding. Since the day outside was gray and wet, this was the perfect comfort food.

"I have to say, I liked the way she wrote this case. It was clever and tricky like all her stories are but also had Poirot's usual funny matchmaking," Violet said. "I always preferred him to Miss Marple."

"What?" Charlene looked shocked at her mother. "How can you say that? Miss Marple is such a multilayered female sleuth, unlike Poirot, who was already an investigator, so it's not like his character grows much at all."

"He drinks hot chocolate," Violet said.

"So?"

"I find that charming."

Charlene rolled her eyes then hugged her mother with one arm while balancing her plate of food with the other. As the group settled into their seats, Lindsey glanced around the room. Thursdays really were her most favorite day at the library. She loved her crafternoon buddies.

"Ahem." Ms. Cole stood in the doorway to the room. She was holding a copy of *Curtain* in her hands.

"Ms. Cole, did you need me?"

"No," she said. "That is . . . I was wondering . . . I read this week's book."

Lindsey glanced at Beth, who raised her eyebrows in surprise. The lemon had been vocally opposed to the crafternoon group from the day Lindsey had implemented it. Did her presence here mean what Lindsey thought it meant?

"Would you care to join us, Ms. Cole?" she asked.

"Please call me Eugenia," she said. "Or Ginny for short."

The room was silent for three solid beats while the group processed the appearance of the lemon, who apparently wanted to join them. A stunning turn of events.

"Well, all right, Ginny." Paula jumped to her feet, grinning broadly at her coworker. "Come on, let's get you a plate. We're knitting this week. Do you know how to knit?"

The lemon, er, Ginny held up a canvas bag with knitting needles and yarn stuffed inside. "I don't, but I'm willing to learn."

"That's the spirit," Paula said. "We'll make a crafternooner out of you yet."

"Did you know that Dame Christie wrote Poirot's last case thirty years before it was published?" Ginny asked the group. "She waited until she was ill before she released it."

"How did I not know that either?" Charlene cried.

The group settled in for their discussion, and Lindsey pulled her cell phone out of her pocket.

She thumbed through her contacts until she found Sully. Then she sent him a text.

Just wait until you hear what happened today.

His reply was immediate.

No dead bodies?

Lindsey smiled.

None. I promise. But I have to say, the library is never dull. Never.

The Briar Creek Library
Guide to Crafternoons

A crafternoon is simply a book club that does a craft while enjoying some good food and discussing the latest book of their choosing. To give you a starting point for your own crafternoon, here is a readers guide to Patricia Highsmith's *The Talented Mr. Ripley*, instructions for knitting a simple beanie and recipes for cheese and spinach strata, Yorkshire pudding and Mr. Chesterton's apple pie.

Readers Guide for
The Talented Mr. Ripley
by Patricia Highsmith

1. What are the characteristics found in a likable character? Would you say Tom Ripley is likable?

2. How does being an outsider, someone who does not fit into society, work for Tom Ripley? How does it determine his choices?

3. What is the most suspenseful moment in the book? How did you feel when you were reading it? What outcome were you hoping for?

4. Is there any justification for Tom's actions in the novel? If so, what is it?

5. Were you hoping that Tom would be successful in the end? If so, how did the author, Highsmith, make you feel that way?

Craft:
Knitted Beanie

100 yds of bright-colored bulky or super
   bulky yarn
Size 13 knitting needles
Yarn needle

Cast on 40 stitches.

Work knit 1, purl 1 ribbing for six rows.

Work in stockinette stitch (knit one row, purl one row) until piece measures 9 inches, ending with a purl row.

Next row, knit 2 together across until twenty stitches remain.

Purl 1 row.

Knit 2 together across until ten stitches remain.

Cut a 12-inch length of yarn and thread onto yarn needle.

Knit the last row from the knitting needle to the threaded yarn needle. Pull the stitches tight then whip stitch the two sides together, creating the hat. Tie off the yarn and weave the end back into the hat.

Recipes

CHEESE AND SPINACH STRATA

1 10-ounce package frozen spinach,
  thawed
1½ cups finely chopped onion
3 tablespoons unsalted butter
1 teaspoon salt
½ teaspoon black pepper
¼ teaspoon nutmeg
8 cups cubed French bread
6 ounces grated Gruyère cheese
2 ounces finely grated Parmesan cheese
2¾ cups milk
9 large eggs
2 tablespoons Dijon mustard

Dry spinach with a paper towel, then finely chop. Cook onion in melted butter in a large skillet over medium heat, stirring frequently, until soft. Stir in ½ teaspoon salt, ¼ teaspoon pepper and nutmeg and cook for 1 minute. Add spinach, then remove from heat. Spread one-third of bread cubes in a buttered 3-quart casserole dish and top with one-third of spinach mixture. Sprinkle with one-third of each cheese. Repeat layering twice, ending with cheeses. Whisk together milk, eggs, mustard and remaining ½ teaspoon salt and ¼ teaspoon pepper in a large mixing bowl and pour evenly over strata. Chill, covered with plastic wrap, for 8 hours to allow the bread to absorb custard.

Preheat the oven to 350°F. Let the strata sit at room temperature 30 minutes before baking. Bake the strata, uncovered, in the middle of the oven until golden brown and puffed, about 45 to 55 minutes. Let stand 5 minutes before serving.

YORKSHIRE PUDDING

3 large eggs
¾ cup whole milk
¾ cup all-purpose flour
¾ teaspoon kosher salt
¼ cup bacon drippings

Preheat the oven to 450°F. In a medium mixing bowl, whisk together eggs, milk, flour and salt until smooth but not over-mixed. Let the batter sit for 30 minutes at room temperature.

Pour the bacon drippings into a square baking dish. Put the dish in the oven and get the bacon grease smoking hot, which takes about 10 minutes. Carefully take the dish out of the oven and pour the batter into it. Put the pan back in the oven and cook until puffed and dry, 15 to 20 minutes. Serve immediately.

MR. CHESTERTON'S APPLE PIE

4–6 Granny Smith green apples
¾ cup granulated sugar
1 tablespoon flour
1 teaspoon cinnamon
9-inch frozen pie crust

Peel and slice apples. Mix with sugar, flour and cinnamon.

Pour into pie shell, spreading them out. They'll shrink as they cook. Sprinkle with topping.

TOPPING:

½ cup brown sugar
¼ cup butter
⅓ cup flour
¼ teaspoon cinnamon

Mix the above with a pastry cutter or fork until it is dry enough to sprinkle on top of apples. Completely cover pie with topping.

Preheat the oven to 425°F. Put the pie on a cookie sheet and bake for 10 minutes. Reduce heat to 350°F and bake at least 45 minutes longer until the apples can be pierced easily with a fork. If the topping gets too brown, cover it with foil. Remove from the oven and allow to cool before serving.

Books are produced in the United States using U.S.-based materials

Books are printed using a revolutionary new process called THINKtech™ that lowers energy usage by 70% and increases overall quality

Books are durable and flexible because of smythe-sewing

Paper is sourced using environmentally responsible foresting methods and the paper is acid-free

Center Point Large Print
600 Brooks Road / PO Box 1
Thorndike, ME 04986-0001 USA

(207) 568-3717

US & Canada:
1 800 929-9108
www.centerpointlargeprint.com